dolce

dolce

rachel blaufeld

Dolce
Copyright © 2015 Rachel Blaufeld

Paperback ISBN: 978-0-9970707-1-2

Edited by
Pam Berehulke
www.bulletproofediting.com

Cover design by
© Sarah Hansen, Okay Creations, LLC
www.okaycreations.com

Photo credit
© Hill Creek Studios

Formatted by

www.emtippettsbookdesigns.com

Warning:
Content contains explicit sexual content and crude language, and is intended for
mature audiences. Parental/reader discretion advised.

Not too long ago, I wanted to quit all of this. My words weren't coming, my head hurt, and my fingers ached.
A fellow author told me not to do it, and shared a little of her own story to encourage me to move forward. She didn't know me well, nor did she have any vested interest in telling me to continue. Despite that, she gave her ear willingly and her advice graciously.
This is for you, Sarina Bowen.

author's note

The following story is a spinoff of *Vérité*, but it's not necessary for you to read it first. There are a few glimpses into characters from *Vérité* in this book, but this is a complete standalone story.
Dolce is a separate angst-riddled romantic comedy set a few years in the future, after Tiberius from *Vérité* graduated.
In order to make this sports story work, I had to exert some artistic license in terms of athletic seasons, as well as dates and times of college events. I also made up a college town (Hafton, Ohio), a college (Hafton State University), and team (the Fighting Green), so fans could go on cheering for their own universities and not be hindered by my story.
Much like, *Vérité*, for me *Dolce* was about thinking, debunking stereotypes, and love.
Thank you in advance for reading and falling in love with my ballers.

about this book

"Who just stole my thunder across the Hafton airwaves, you ask? Right now, right this very second, listeners, I have Hafton's one-and-only, the main man with the ball in hand, Blane Steele is in the studio. Mark my words—he'll not only steal the ball, but your lady's heart too. Watch out, gentlemen, the Stealer is in the house!"
— *Sonny Be Knocking Boots, Hafton Radio 96.9*

Coed antics.

Chaos.

Angst-ridden twists in fate.

Caterina is an intern. Sonny is her shock-jock boss. And Blane is a good-hearted baller . . . except when he steps on the court. Between on-air dares, an evil feminist professor, a straight-shooter of a coach, and rumors from the league surrounding Steele, these three are destined to screw it all up.

Rather than a love triangle, this is a friends-to-lovers story where the disc jockey acts as the catalyst, and a basketball player finds his life transformed when center court intersects with love.

chapter one

Blane
October

Sonny hit the On Air button and words began spewing from his mouth faster than basketballs from the automatic gun. The guy barely came up for air, and he was damn good—even though he was an obnoxious prick.

I leaned back in my chair, waiting for my interview to start. My hair was still wet from my post-workout shower, a flimsy dark gray Hafton T-shirt stuck to my chest, and skinny sweats hung low on my waist. I flung my feet up on the table, letting the shock jock roll with it. After all, it was his show. At least, that's what I thought.

"Wassup, Hafton? Sonny Boots here on the radio, working for all of you around the clock, rocking some old school Beastie Boys this Thursday. Don't you worry your pretty little heads; I'll be mixing it up later for you barflies. I know you all will be itching to go out and get loaded. I'm pulling some funky tracks as I speak, but if you have a request, e-mail the station or tweet me at Sonny B underscore KnocknBoots. You got all that?"

Rolling my eyes for no one to see, I grabbed the mic. "They got it, dude. And if not, it's plastered on the big sign above the station."

My voice sounded a little more gravelly than usual. I must have shouted more than I thought in pickup today. *Clearly, I'm not meant to be a radio announcer.*

Sonny jumped back in. "Who, you ask, just stole my thunder across the Hafton airwaves? Right now, right this very second, listeners, I have Hafton's one-and-only, the main man with the ball in hand, Blane Steele in the studio. Mark my words, he'll not only steal your ball, but your lady's heart too. Watch out, gentlemen, the Stealer is in the house!"

This got a laugh from me. *Sports Illustrated* had dubbed me "the Stealer" last year after my sophomore season, and the moniker stuck.

"Steele's a well-known predator," he continued, "on the court and off. He's getting ready to start his third year of eligibility, and NBA gossip has been swirling around him since the end of last year. Oh, and every lady in the house is swooning for him, especially after that breakout sophomore season. Forgive me, but why the heck didn't you go to the big guys last year? Why are you still here in the middle of Ohio, gracing us with your glory?"

"Yeah, I know, but credit wise I was going into my senior year. I redshirted my first year, so I wanted to finish my degree, be the first person in my family to graduate," I mumbled into the mic. Quickly realizing I was tarnishing my bad-as-hell rep, I added, "And I like you too much, Sonny. Why would I give up another year of listening to you and your stupid antics?"

"I'm not here to talk about your nice-boy tendencies or to flatter myself, although the compliment is welcome. Today, I have one thing on my mind, and it's what the ladies all want too. *Bad boys of ball,*" he growled, lowering his voice for effect before continuing.

"Not since Jamel Lincoln and Trey Dawson graduated has there been a basketball player with as bad a rep as Steele's. That's right, Haftees, right here in the flesh across from me, I got your six-foot-four, blond, always-tan-and-beautiful stud muffin."

A deep laugh rumbled through my chest at his introduction. Okay, so I was a bit of a ladies' man, but why not? The girls were there for the taking, and I wasn't about to question my luck. Although lately it was getting old, but I wasn't about to share that little nugget with Sonny Boots.

Leaning into the mic again, I said, "And how is that y'all would know? Didn't Trey and Jamel graduate four years ago, *Sebastian*?" I spent time drawing out Sonny's real name, my Southern drawl making an appearance.

"Hey now, Steele, it's Sonny to you. Sebastian's for the ladies only. And for the record, I'm a fifth-year senior. You know that because I was working at this very station when your lanky, bony butt walked in here as a freshman, requesting some 'good' music. What was it you wanted to hear? The theme song from *Grease*?"

"I hear you making fun of me, Sebastian," I said with a grin.

Truth was, Sonny had been a semi-decent friend to me since I landed in the middle of Ohio, plucked from the good life in sunny Florida. With only a smidge of a tan remaining and earbuds stuck in my ears, I'd wandered into the radio station when I first arrived, looking for someone to complain to about the shit music being played. Sonny was the intern back then, and now he was hanging on to every last vestige of college life, afraid of the real world.

A small piece of me got it. After all, I'd decided to wait to go pro until I finished my degree. *Who the fuck does that?*

"Bottom line, people, I like it here so much, I don't want to leave." Sonny shoved his hand through his signature unruly blond hair and playfully twirled his chair in a full circle for my benefit.

"That's what they all say to me," I said, then raised my voice to a falsetto. "I like it here so much." Returning my voice to normal, I added, ". . . when they're in my apartment."

Sonny returned to the mic. "Listeners, I can see my good friend is going to torture me this evening, so let's ask him about the upcoming season before I kick his behind out of here. He must have been with so many women, he's starting to think like one."

I rolled my eyes again, even though no one could see me but Sonny.

"So, Blane, what do you say? Are we looking at a 'ship this year?"

A nervous chuckle spilled from my mouth. The college sports analysts were predicting it, the magazines were printing it, and my coach was demanding it. Regardless, the thought of winning the national championship made my head throb and my stomach churn.

"Well, it's a long road to the 'ship, but if any squad can do it, I think this year's is the one. Trey Dawson's brother, Mo, is starting at power forward, and we got Ashton Denube and myself in the back court along with the D-man, Demetri, at center, and Alex White at small forward. It's a formidable lineup. We have to stay focused, healthy, and on target."

"I forgot about my boy, Mo, also known as Moby Dick. I can say that . . . it's like the book. So, did the coach rule out parties and girls?"

"No, he most certainly did not," I lied. "We're grown men. We make our own choices, and Conley trusts our shit."

"You can't say that on the air, Steele."

"What? The coach knows we're not giving anything up." I wasn't saying anything he didn't already know. He was the head coach of a squad full of hooligans and womanizers.

"I meant s-h-i-t. You need to say crap or something else, my man.

As for the coach, I'm sure babysitting all of you gets old after a while."

"We're all very good boys," I said with a wink.

Just then, the door to the studio flung open and a short, curvy young thing with a headful of black curls swore like a sailor when she toppled over a tower of CDs and a lamp.

"Fuck me. Sorry about that," she muttered through clenched teeth as she righted the lamp.

Sonny ran his hand like a knife across his neck, motioning for her to shut up.

Apparently, he was used to thinking quickly on the air. Without missing a beat, he swung the mic in a full circle, grabbed the head, and announced, "How about we take a quick break? You know what I got for you all? *The* song, the one! The actual song the team is going to jam out to this year in the locker room. Turn your radios up, Hafton, because you heard it here first at WHSU 96.9, the new theme song for this year's basketball squad."

He flicked his finger over a switch, and "Greased Lightning" poured out from the speakers.

"I'm sorry, Mr. Boots," Little Miss Curves whispered.

"What did she just call you?"

I stared down my friend, my mind filling with a bunch of ugly scenarios. Freaking Sonny had a bad rep as it was, and here he was asking his intern to call him by some pet name? He might be my friend, but I knew his faults.

What now? Was the sucker going to get slapped with some kind of sexual harassment charge? Could they do that in college?

Christ, I may be a bit of a man-whore, but I don't get off on making women jump through stupid hoops, or get hard from high-and-mighty power trips. If there's one thing my good-for-nothing dad taught me, it's women rule the world. The power of pussy, he called it.

"What the heck did you just say?" Sonny asked with a wicked grin on his face, his voice dangerously low.

"I didn't say anything."

"Yes, you did," the girl said in a hushed voice from near the door. "The power of pussy."

"Did I just say that out loud?"

The chick with big brown eyes and a mass of curly black hair nodded.

"Fuck," I muttered.

I knew it all the way down to my size thirteen basketball shoes—Sonny wasn't going to let me forget what I'd just said.

The song ended and he was back on the airwaves. "Sonny B. back here, and you're not going to believe what I learned while we took a break. Blane Steele has gone soft; he's become a champion of women's rights. Are you a women's studies major, my man? Let me guess, you're doing some sort of community service at the . . . what do you call it? Wow, I'm never at a loss for words." He snapped his fingers, searching for the zinger he wanted.

"Got it!" Sonny crowed as he slammed his palm onto the table in front of him, rattling the mic. "Planned Parenthood."

I shook my head and leaned to the mic. "Nah, I'm more of a numbers guy. You know, logistics. And of course, putting points up on the scoreboard is my calling."

I tried to divert Sonny with my boring major, but no such luck.

His eyes sparkled with glee. "All right, Hafton, we want a win this year. We want to see the Stealer here and his gang holding up the trophy. We need to see them dump cold Gatorade on Coach Conley, or whatever you barbarians do, and to do that, I think Steele here needs to stay focused. And since he's become such a champion of women's rights, let's see if he can go all season without any *liaisons*, for lack of a better word. He shouldn't be wasting time taking advantage of innocent women."

"You double-dog daring me, Boots?" I spat out at the mic.

"You know it!"

"You're on, Sonny B., and now I'm out of here to my monastic existence. Are we allowed to say that on the air?"

I stood, flipped off the asshole who'd just destroyed my social life, and strode toward the door. The curvy chick opened it wide for me before I even remembered she was still standing there.

"Thanks," I mumbled. "After you."

I leaned into the door frame as I propped the door open with my elbow and gestured for her to walk ahead. Avoiding my eyes, she slipped past me with a muttered thank-you.

As the door clicked shut behind us, I said to her, "Yeah, well, a hand job may be nice, but I guess that's out after what I promised inside there." I tilted my head back toward the studio and laughed at my own joke.

She turned and shot me a hard glare, her oversized sweatshirt sagging off one shoulder.

Most other girls I knew would have been fine if I dropped trou right there and whipped my dick right the fuck out. Their hands would have been just itching to grab me. *But not this one.*

"Kidding. I was kidding." I lifted my hands in the air in surrender.

All of a sudden, I felt ashamed of my behavior. I wasn't that guy. *Was I?*

She raised an eyebrow, making me question my character some more.

"I'm serious. Kidding. Listen, don't let him boss you around. Once upon a time, Sonny was an intern too. A lowly, pimply one."

"I'll keep that in mind." Her words were thick with an East Coast accent and heavy with doubt. "See you around," she said, dismissing me at the supply closet.

I started walking toward the exit when I stopped and shouted, "What's your name, my fair maiden?"

She turned, bracing the door with her shoulder. Planting her hands on her hips, she cocked one to the side.

"Do I look like a fair maiden at the top of the tower?"

Stunned, I shook my head. I'd never been challenged like that—ever.

"It's Caterina." She turned on her heel and started to enter the closet.

"It's Blane. Nice to meet you, Caterina," I hollered over my shoulder.

"Actually, everyone calls me Catie," she yelled back.

Without looking back, I shook my head. *Semi-sweet, foul-mouthed Catie and Mr. Sonny Fucking Boots.*

What an odd pair.

I didn't have time to get involved in whatever situation they had going. I had a basketball season to get ready for, and apparently, a libido to keep in check.

Loud laughter echoed down the hall as I exited the elevator and walked toward my apartment. Coach allowed me to live off campus with two of the other starters as long as we avoided any bad press. We were typically discreet, although I suspected I'd hear about today sooner rather than later.

"Wassup, Priest Steele?" Ashton yelled the moment I opened

the door. "Looks like Demetri and me are going to be the only two getting any pussy this season!" He doubled over in fits of laughter before bolting upright and shouting, "Shit! You made me mess up my season."

"I can win your *NBA 2K* season while you're busy with all the pussy, Denube," I tossed back, and slumped down into the leather chair opposite the couch where he and our teammate from down the hall, Alex, sat.

"Where's D?" I asked.

"He had to go to the tutoring center. Coach laid into him this morning because he hasn't shown up to his stats class all trimester."

"Fuck, what the hell is wrong with him?"

"Same thing that's wrong with you. He's a cocky son-of-a-bitch," Alex shot back, dreads flying as his long fingers worked the game controller.

"Slam dunk!" Ashton called out, his fist punching the air in celebration of his video game win. "Oh, I'm sorry to mention that . . . since you won't be getting any slam dunks, my man."

I flipped him the bird. I was doing a lot of that today.

"Shit, I don't know why I even agreed to do the stupid show. I'm an idiot. Big-time," I muttered as I made my way back to my room. I slammed the door and fell onto my bed, snatching my phone out of my pocket.

Ninety-five notifications waited for me. Texts and tweets about my dare, and an e-mail from Coach Conley.

Superb.

I scrolled through Twitter.

@HaftonFan101:
Move along girls, @BallerSteele has sworn off s$x while

on the air with @SonnyB_KnocknBoots #findanewman #Steeleisoffmarket

@CollegeBBallFan:
Just in: Across my feed, @BallerSteele confirms Hafton gunning for the 'ship & says no nooky allowed #Steeleisoffmarket

@HaftonSweetiePie:
Hey, @HaftonFan101 Hearts breaking around campus, especially mine - I thought you were mine @BallerSteele? I don't want to #findanewman

I switched to my text messages, and they were about the same. Then I e-mailed Coach.

I was to report to his office first thing in the morning. *Duh.*

chapter two

Catie

It was late, after midnight, but I felt grimy so I went to shower.

The bathroom was deserted, which came as no surprise considering it was a Thursday night. Most of the women on my floor had showered and gone on the prowl. I guess I could call them girls and not women, but being a women's studies major, it had been drilled into me to refer to the female of our species as women.

At the end of the day, we were still girls with a lot to learn. Look at how I'd been sucked into calling my boss, who was nothing more than another student, Mr. Boots.

I undressed, peed, flushed, and flip-flopped toward the shower with my extra-large towel tucked tight around my body. Since I was apparently the only one home on the quiet dorm floor, I placed my phone on the shelf outside the shower and set it to play Tori Amos.

No big surprise there, right?

Tori's rich voice singing melancholy tunes filled the silence while warm water sluiced over my hair and back. I didn't bother to rush since there was no one to save warm water for, and I needed time to deal with my embarrassment and outrage.

Of course, it was all my own doing. The absurd fiasco was entirely my fault. I was the one who insisted the fifth-year senior shock jock vouch for me.

All I wanted was to have my own radio call-in show, one where women could pick up the phone and anonymously put out in the open what happened behind closed doors. A place where they could rage against the glass ceiling, or the ridiculousness of the government trying to decide what they could or couldn't do with their bodies. Basically, an on-air support group.

Maybe they were being demoralized at work?

Like me.

Or they didn't feel loved by anyone.

Sort of like me, but that isn't essential for happiness. Or is it?

I fantasized about SiriusXM picking up my show and broadcasting it nationwide. I did have a warm and inviting voice, or so I'd been told. That's about the only compliment I ever received.

I poured some cheap mango-infused shampoo—seduction in a bottle—into my palm and scrunched it through my thick curls, my only decent feature.

"You have great hair," my sisters would tell me. They had dainty features and long, lithe bodies, and spent their days perfecting themselves.

"Good thing you don't want to do TV," Clara had told me. She'd always towered over me, and now had eight inches on my five foot three. She was my older sister and the nicer of the two, but she could be a bitch when she wanted.

"No, I don't want to be on TV, Clara, because that would mean the women voicing their concerns wouldn't be anonymous. And yes, no one wants to look at fat little me for an hour," I'd told her one day in the room we shared back home.

She'd been posing in the mirror, turning and twisting and looking at herself in every which way, her dark hair sleek and straight, thanks to one of those crazy-expensive treatments. I'd been stretched out across my bed in lounge pants, my hair tied on top of my head, reading a romance novel stuck inside a biography. The heroines of my secret steamy novels were to be admired; they found men to love them and support them.

I hadn't even asked Clara's damn opinion. I always wished I could have been the one to have my own room. Cedes, the baby, got it. She was the perfect one, Mom's favorite, a size four even at five foot nine. She was smart too, but not "too smart." Whatever that meant.

Rinsing my hair, I inhaled and took stock of my situation. Why the hell was I using something advertised as *seduction in a bottle*?

But more importantly, how did I get stuck working for a prick? A guy who made me so nervous, I capitulated to his ludicrous demands. I needed to drop that shit.

Even worse, I had Clara to partially blame for my wishy-washy behavior. She'd instructed me to act more demure, like a damsel in distress. Based on her work experience, she'd said, "a little giving in" went a long way.

Why the hell did I listen to her? For one thing, she hated me, and more importantly, I wasn't a natural capitulator.

Sebastian Jones might be a legend, a Twitter phenomenon as Sonny Be Knocking Boots, and my only ticket to getting my own show here at Hafton. But that didn't mean I had to bow to him. Like Blane said, Sonny had been an intern once too. When that ass-wipe was finally gone, I planned to clean up the station. We could bring on a legitimate sports person and do some fun bits, ones not reminiscent of Howard Stern.

Except now Blane was involved, and he was privy to what hoops Sonny was making me jump through. If any of the women in my major found out, they'd banish me. I'd be exiled from the program, the women's studies community, and would be the laughingstock of campus—and my family—for that alone.

If they knew I'd flirted with a jock? *Ugh.*

But everyone calls me Catie?

It had been the most flirtatious line of my life. I laughed out loud in the shower at that. I was so lame when it came to men, and that was normal men, not perfect guys like Blane who were also campus legends.

I'd seen him play, and now I'd breathed the same air as him. Both his athleticism and sheer presence made my heart race. I knew one thing for sure—no matter how handsome I thought Blane Steele was, I wasn't the kind of girl for him.

Although he did seem sort of kind, the way he stopped to chat with me and asked me my name.

Oh God. *But everyone calls me Catie?*

I could just hear my sisters now. Clara and Mercedes would roll their eyes, batting their fake eyelashes and howling with laughter over what a mess I managed to make before I even finished my sophomore year. My outspoken Cuban mom, Glory, would pretend to reprimand them, but would then turn and laugh behind my back. As usual, I'd land on the doorstep of my dad, looking for warm affection and homemade Italian comfort food.

The water began to run cold, so I turned it off and grabbed my towel before shutting down my music.

As I walked back to my lonely single dorm room, I decided to find Blane Steele and offer him whatever he wanted—especially since he'd gone celibate—to keep the humiliating details of my internship to himself.

I couldn't bear the thought of this all falling apart. I had big plans, and I couldn't fail. Plus, I needed this internship. It was part of my financial aid package.

I could always be a coffee girl.

Maybe Blane would take pity on this desperate shrimp, and I wouldn't have to beg him—or bribe him—to keep his mouth shut.

My alarm shrilled, forcing me to get up and turn it off on my dresser. I hurried to use the bathroom, washed my face, and rushed back to my closet. After pulling on a thong and leggings, motorcycle boots, and tossing a bulky, tattered, off-the-shoulder gray sweatshirt over my camisole and bra, I was ready for class.

After all, I was the one who chased after Professor Cora Stanwick all of last year to let me into her senior lecture, An In-Depth Look at Pornography and Its Ill Effects on Women of Every Age.

Frantic, I ran through the dining hall and grabbed a sub-par cup of coffee before racing across campus to Stanwick's class. It was chillier this morning than I expected for this early in October, but I didn't have time to run back for a coat.

The witch was standing at the classroom door, waiting for the last few stragglers, when I breezed through the outside door.

"Morning, Ms. Presto. Glad to see your begging to sit in my class isn't a burden to you."

"Good morning, Professor Stanwick. I'm here, ready to go!" I replied, my half-assed attempt at being chipper, while her blue eyes narrowed at me as she used my surname.

I'd always wondered why she wasn't a model instead of focusing on the struggles of regular women. She was pretty enough, despite the severity of the way she dressed, but I supposed she was a bit too patrician for that. And about twenty years too old, from the looks of her.

I breezed through the door and she pulled it shut after me, the lock clicking into place. There were no latecomers to an In-Depth Look at Porn, nor were there curiosity seekers who might want to tweet they watched porn in class. No, my classmates were women's studies majors who took the issues seriously.

"Hello, class. Today will be the last lecture before the midterm, and then I plan to move forward whether you understand the material or not. Can someone summarize last week's reading?"

No one ever volunteered. It was like serving yourself up to be a sacrificial lamb at a sorority roast.

"How about you, Caterina?"

I knew she was going there. It wasn't a Friday without Professor Stanwick testing my intelligence and patience.

Fuck. I stood and cleared my throat, careful not to knock over my coffee as I tugged my sweatshirt down over my butt.

"Last week, we finished our unit on using pornography to rise to stardom. We looked at the lives of Jenna Jameson and Kim Kardashian, focusing on the differences between the two women. Jenna, a full-blown adult-movie star, changed the perception of pornography for many, making them feel it's a legitimate career. But we know it to be what it's always been, a misogynistic attempt to keep women down."

Warming to the subject, I spoke with a little more confidence. "Pornography sexualizes women and does nothing to promote their inner growth. Kardashian played into reality by pretending a sex tape had been released of her, one that we speculate she made especially for that purpose and released herself. They're two very different women, both noted for their sexuality, and cashing in on it daily."

Stanwick nodded and motioned for me to sit. It wasn't in her to say "thanks" or "good job."

Addressing the class, she said, "If you were to pick a pornographic path—not that any of you would—would you take the Jameson route or the Kardashian one, and why? Twenty minutes. Open your composition books and start writing."

The sounds of paper shuffling and pens falling to the floor filled the air.

The lone guy in the lecture piped up. "You could pretend to claim abstinence and then quietly continue to bang every chick in sight. Isn't that what Blane Steele copped to last night on the radio?"

I slid a little further down in my chair, silently wishing he would opt out of the course.

"I heard that yesterday," one of the women said. "I thought I was hearing things, but he's a guy. He can make hollow claims or promises and get away with it."

"That's enough," Stanwick said, standing by the lectern. "I didn't say we were discussing the patronizing ways of our student athletes or school shock jocks." She threw her shoulders back in indignation, straightening her pants suit jacket.

Stanwick's following this? Interesting. I better get my work scenario straightened out.

Finally, the room quieted as everyone hunched over their papers and wrote away.

chapter three

Blane

I decided to skip the rest of my Friday classes. Even with my head tucked into a hooded sweatshirt, trying to stay incognito, I was still getting all kinds of attention. Unwanted attention, thanks to Sonny. *The asshole.*

"Hey, Steele, whatcha doing this weekend? Crocheting?" some young wannabe jock yelled at me before howling with laughter.

What the fuck? What the hell happened to dudes respecting me? *Oh, right. I gave up pussy.*

Trekking across campus toward College Avenue and the serenity of my apartment, I felt Coach's words weighing me down. Like a thousand-pound elephant, they sat on my spine, bouncing up and down, each syllable worming its way through my nervous system. Although we'd talked behind closed doors earlier that morning, I knew rumors would circulate about our conversation later in the locker room.

"I get you were having fun with your buddy, *Sonny Boots*," Coach

Conley had said, pushing out Sonny's name on an angry growl. Apparently the shock jock didn't have as many fans as he thought.

"But if you made a promise on the air, son, you better follow through. I don't care how silly it is. You're in your last year, and may I remind you—we *do* want to win a championship. So, there's no room for error. I agree, I can't babysit you punks when you're hanging out and partying, but I will punish you if things get out of hand and negatively impact this program."

"I didn't know Sonny was going to do what he did, sir," I'd stupidly answered.

"Well, he did, and you did something to lead him there., so now you're one hundred percent committed, and one hundred percent focused. Think of it that way. Now, get out and go work out or something. I'm counting on you, Blane. You were my go-to man all last season, and now I've got to let you move up to the big dogs after this year. Give me something to remember you by. And close the door on your way out."

That's all he'd said, but he was right. I owed the school a championship, and I did agree to an on-air interview with Sonny, so this was all on me.

Shit.

In my head, I could see it. National champions. The NBA. Parties, girls, basketball every day/all day—that would be my life for as long as I was healthy. It was floating in front of my face, and I wanted to reach out and grab it like a three-dimensional movie.

Deep in thought, I almost didn't hear Ashton yelling, "Dude! Where you going?"

He was leaning out the door of the coffee shop on the edge of campus, wearing a Hafton Ball T-shirt and sweats hanging low on his hips, and AF-1's on his feet. Pretty sure he didn't drink coffee or tea, so I knew he must have ulterior motives for being there.

I splowed him up—slapping his hand, then morphing into a handshake—and asked, "What the eff? You becoming an intellectual now? Hanging out in coffeehouses?"

"Can you shut the door?" a smooth voice called out from behind the counter, and when I looked up, I knew why Ash was hanging out there. A tall, blue-eyed, blond drink of water was working the espresso machine. She was model-worthy, and just his type.

"Oh yeah." He smirked back toward the girl.

Bells tinkled overhead as the door closed behind me, and I found myself being dragged toward a table.

"Sit down, take a load off, brother. Tell me your troubles," Ashton said.

"Who are you? Oprah? Dr. Phil?" I slapped his shoulder. "What's her name?" I asked him as he lifted a disposable cup of coffee.

"Who?"

"The blonde who has you drinking coffee all of a sudden." I cocked my head back toward the counter and tugged off my hood.

"Cappuccino, my good friend, made by Ava herself."

"Crap, could you have a bigger smile across your ugly mug?" I slapped the table this time, stifling a laugh.

"I love when you talk ghetto, white boy, but let me tell you about this grill." He swiped his hand in front of his pearly whites, nearly as shiny as his shaved head, and laughed loudly. "This is the money maker, my man."

Turning serious, he tossed his arm over my shoulders and leaned in. "You're not letting this Sonny thing get to you, are you? We were kidding last night, you know."

"Nah, I know you were kidding, and it's fine. Coach said I have to behave now."

He laughed again, his coffee long forgotten.

I know he's not a coffee drinker. Or cappuccino.

"You'll be discreet, that's all. You got us to cover for you. We're not going to let your dick shrivel up and die an early death."

This time I laughed, hanging my head, my whole chest rumbling. My guffaws traveled the length of the shop, disturbing everyone trying to have a quiet moment.

"Anyway what do you think of Ava?" he asked. "For me, not you, you monk. Apparently, she's a transfer and a hoops fan. Endless possibilities, my friend. Just like our season."

He rolled his eyes toward the counter, looking to see if the blonde was watching, and took another sip of his cappuccino.

"God, this is shit," he whispered to me, and winced as he took another swallow.

This time I slammed my fist into the table. "Knew you weren't going soft."

The little bells over the door rang again, and I looked over to find Caterina from the radio station walking in.

"Oh shit!" I yanked my hood back up and stared at our pale purple table as if it were the most fascinating piece of shit I'd ever seen.

Ashton's gaze zeroed in on Caterina as she made her way toward Ava.

"Damn," he said, "she's curvy in all the right places. Wish I liked that type. I like 'em lithe and long like a tiger all stretched out, but that little girl is stacked with curves. Moby would love her. He likes 'em a little bigger; likes to grab and roll."

"Dude, shut the fuck up," I barked at him.

Some strange surge of protectiveness came over me. Yeah, I barely knew the chick, but she was all kinds of cool and spunky. I liked the way she swore and wasn't ashamed to be her clumsy self. Fuck Sonny for backing me into a corner and making me go cold turkey on the ladies. This one was soft and supple, and had a mouth on her. Not in the way most men like to think about a mouth, but still good and sassy.

What's up with her acting all helpless with Sonny? I knew he was a cocksucker, but to make her call him some stupid name? And she went along with it? I couldn't get behind that shit.

Then there was also the tiny fact that she'd witnessed Sonny's bullshit dare with me.

"What?" Ashton interrupted my private rant, whipping his head around so fast I was concerned he might have whiplash. "You calling that? That's not your type. I thought you'd be wanting to meet Ava's roomies."

Calling that? As if.

The way Caterina had challenged me at the studio proved she wasn't the woman for me. I did kind of like it, though. No one but my mom had ever done that before. Not even my cousin Gigi, until recently when she started to harp on me about my future.

"No fucking dibs," I said. "What are we? A bunch of lame chicks sitting in a coffee shop?"

I tried to distract Ashton, but knew it was a lost cause. We were seconds away from him calling attention to the oblivious woman, and then we would relive the entire throw-down with Sonny.

Just what I wanted . . . to be mortified. Again.

"Uh-huh, who's the girl?" Narrowing his dark eyes, he leaned close and whispered, "Did you go and bang someone already? Not even twenty-four hours after your deal with Sonny?"

"No. Stay out of it, Ashton. She works for Sonny and saw the whole thing."

"No shit!"

This time he slapped the table. His cappuccino went flying in the air, causing everyone—including Caterina—to turn our way.

chapter
four

Catie

After Intro to Porn, I'd spent an hour in the computer lab writing an essay for English Composition. My stomach growled the whole time, and I quickly realized I needed something to eat and some major caffeine before I finished it and went in to work.

As I headed toward Mean Beans, my favorite coffee place, I decided not to chase down Blane Steele. The night before, I'd been firm in my resolve to make him swear to secrecy, hyped up on Tori Amos and sensually scented shower gel.

Today was a different story. If it got out, it got out. At least I'd be doing a favor to all women who would work with Sebastian later in life. He'd be forced to treat them like legitimate human beings. That was my first step in regaining my confidence and self-control with the class-A asshole.

After I placed my order for a full-fat cappuccino with an extra shot and a cranberry orange scone, there was a huge commotion. The whole place erupted into laughter, and I scanned the cozy interior for the culprits. Seated in the corner were none other than Blane Steele and one of his teammates. Ashton Denube, I was pretty sure.

Yes, I was a fan, but I'd deny it if asked. Women's studies majors typically weren't sports fans, but I was. My classmates liked documentaries on saving women and children from HIV in third-world countries, and my sisters watched reality TV and shopped.

Me? I sneaked into sporting events on the weekends, grabbed popcorn, and enjoyed the action. It reminded me of my dad, of his warm hugs and soft eyes. We'd enjoyed many a game together.

Standing a few feet from me was the man who'd dominated my thoughts for the last twenty-four hours. I'd been ready to beg him not to say anything about *Mr. Boots*; then I'd decided to flat-out ignore him.

Now, my pulse twitched in my wrist and my nerves twisted up my spine at the sight of him. Embarrassment flooded my cheeks. Not only because of what he'd witnessed, but because of the way I'd allowed myself to think of him the night before.

Accessible. Even if it were only for a matter of seconds, I'd allowed myself to dream for a moment—in the shower, no less—about what he would be like. To kiss. To date. To sleep with.

A deep voice came from behind me. "Damn, Ava, my girl. I spilled."

I turned and found myself eye level with Denube's chest. When I lifted my chin, my eyes met his dark brown ones, and his smile widened.

"Hey there, little lady," he said with a wink.

"Um, hi."

"One sec, Ash baby, let me help her," the barista purred, "and then I'll get you a new drink."

Ava, I presumed. *Oh God.*

Then I heard, "Why don't you let me buy you all a round of coffee, and I'll take a bottled water?"

Ava turned and her eyes went wide, but clearly not because of me. "You're Blane Steele!" She clapped her hands. "My roommate, Vicki with an *i*, loves you. She was so depressed this morning after your radio show last night. Oh. My. God. Wait until she hears you were here!"

Oh. My. God. I'm in a reality show. Forget watching one.

Ava apparently forgot all about helping me first, because she grabbed a cold bottle of water and steamed a fresh cappuccino for Denube while rambling on and on about *Vicki with an i*. Apparently Vicki had moved away in middle school, but now the girls had been reunited in college.

"Here you go, Blane, and this one is special for you, Ash." She continued to preen, radiating sexual energy while I tapped my hand on the counter.

Blane stepped up behind me and dropped a hand on my shoulder. "I think you forgot Caterina's order."

We still hadn't even acknowledged each other, yet he was advocating for my beverage and setting my shirt on fire? I glanced at my shoulder, checking for smoke.

Ava frowned. "Sorry. I didn't realize you knew her, or were together."

"When I said I wanted to buy everyone a round of coffee, I meant Caterina here too."

Still no face-to-face acknowledgment, and I wasn't going to be the one to turn around. *No fucking way.* The stubborn Italian and Cuban in me would not be the first one to say hello.

Ava grabbed the lever on the espresso machine and put in the grinds, then pumped her arm with gusto. She didn't take her time pouring in my shots or frothing my milk artistically. Basically, she tossed everything in the cup and shoved it across the counter to me without even making eye contact.

Noting the *K* she'd used when she scribbled my name, I couldn't resist giving her a jab. "By the way, it's Caterina with a *C* the next time you need to write my name on my cup."

As I reached for my beverage, a large hand came around me and picked up the cup.

"Here you go, Caterina with a *C*. Good to see you. Again."

I turned and looked up at him, since my gaze was even with his chest. "Thank you, Steele."

He tossed some money on the counter after Ava mumbled the amount. Then she resumed kissing Ashton's ass.

I picked up my cappuccino and the scone I'd ordered, and felt warm fingers on my lower back.

"Why don't you sit with us?"

My spine zinged where Blane touched me, a huge red flag. I was entering a no-go zone. I liked the way his large paw felt, and not only was that forbidden for a woman like me, but he was off-limits too. Not my type.

I leaned to the side, slipping away from his hand as I whispered, "As I recall, you're not supposed to be touching women right now."

It was my second poor attempt at flirting in as many days. I yearned for him to say he'd rather do nothing other than touch me, or maybe that he'd been thinking about it all night. Like me.

Blane shook his head. "It was just a brotherly touch; friendly, you know? My cousin Gigi would probably call it 'gentlemanly.'"

"That's nice to hear, but I have to finish an English essay before work, so I can't chat. Hope you're not suffering too much after yesterday," I added before scurrying away to the other side of the coffee shop.

I wanted to be nice to this guy, to smile and stare at his gorgeous face. After all, he seemed like an ally yesterday when he mentioned Sonny being an intern once. But he had to go with the *brotherly* thing, which was a harsh reminder I would never be who he really wanted to touch on her lower back.

"Listen," Steele called out as he hustled after me. He slipped into the seat next to me at my table. "I don't know what I said wrong, but I thought we could be civil. You saw Sonny take me down, and the whole atmosphere at the studio."

"And by that, you mean the way he demoralizes me on the job?"

I was seething mad he knew, but titillated that he was across from me. I was embarrassed he knew, but turned on with him this close.

All in all, I was confused as all get-out.

This man was doing weird things to me. I'd admired him from afar on the court all last year. His prowess with a basketball made my heart stutter.

I was familiar with several sides of him. The determined look he got when he drove the ball up the court. His boyish grin after making a basket. His freshly showered look when he left the field house—I'd caught it once or twice.

Yet in his presence, I didn't know who I was or what I wanted. In twenty-four hours, he'd played with my mind in so many ways, I couldn't even count. The night before in the studio, I'd desperately wanted to tell him I was a fan or whatever groupies do, but I let the opportunity pass. Didn't they carry permanent markers and ask for their boobs to be signed?

Now Blane was seated across from me and wanted to have a serious chat. Who was this guy?

And who am I? I barely recognize myself since yesterday.

"I was referring to the dare. But seriously, why do you call him Mr. Boots?" he asked, interrupting my inner dialogue and setting his water down on the table.

Shrugging, I said, "We don't really even know each other, so it's not something I feel like going into. It's just that I need that internship, and Sonny has a lot of pull."

The truth was, I needed to set a boundary with this guy, establish control, do something proactive for my mental state. Determined not to care that there was a sexy-as-fuck male across the table from me anymore, I pinched off a corner of my scone and popped it into my mouth.

"We could get to know each other. Apparently I now have a lot of time on my hands." Blane shrugged, giving me the boyish grin I'd seen so many times from afar.

Up close, it was so much better. Brighter. Blinding. Lethal.

"As friends. Brotherly, right?" I said, tossing his words back at him.

He cleared his throat. "Uh, yeah. Is that okay? I don't know if you heard, but I've sworn off everything and everyone else."

I wanted to be mean in a vicious women's-lib way, to let him know that I wasn't going to be some chubby replacement for his usual female conquests while he served his celibate sentence.

Instead, I replied, "It's okay, but I really have to finish this paper. Maybe another time?"

"Cool. I'll be seeing you, Cate," Blane said, shortening my name in his own way, sexing it up. He winked at me as he stood up and walked away.

He probably didn't even realize he'd added that wink. Flirting came that naturally to him.

chapter
five

Blane

It was eight o'clock Sunday morning and I was on the gun, my body covered in sweat, my arms aching from shooting jumpers. The balls flew at me in a continuous loop, one after the other, and I stroked them into the net.

"Impressive," a deep voice shouted over the gun. "I haven't seen you miss one yet. Looks like that vow's doing you wonders."

I couldn't stop and look because I would get hit in the head with a ball, so I shouted back, "Nah, I'm just this good."

My teammate Maurice Dawson crossed in front of me and flicked the switch, shutting the machine down. "How 'bout a little one-on-one?"

I crossed over to the bench and toweled off, grabbed my water, and took a swig while nodding. If he wanted to go toe-to-toe, that was his choice. He was going to lose this morning.

I tightened my laces while I waited for Mo to lace up his shoes. We'd been at Hafton together for three years. I'd come straight out of a pieced-together scholarship at a four-year Catholic high school, paid for using a little money from the diocese, some from the YMCA, and a bit more from my own parish.

He'd come from a year at prep school after four years at Saint Something-or-other, following in his brother's footsteps. Now his brother coached for Brooklyn, and it was pretty much a given Mo would do something for that organization when he was done here. He was in no rush; he loved the athlete status even more than his brother had. Although Trey had been known at Hafton as a notorious womanizer and a lover of Crown Royal, he was apparently tame compared to his little bro.

Mo stood and stretched his wingspan, twisting his torso back and forth, and then bent to touch his toes. His dark skin, darker even than his reputation, wasn't slicked with sweat yet like mine, but we'd soon take care of that.

I raised an eyebrow his way. "What are you doing in here early on a Sunday?"

"Couldn't sleep."

"Not enough sex last night?"

I grabbed a ball and started gunning him chest passes. He shot the ball back to me with enough power to knock out a city.

"Nah. I got a situation."

"Want to talk about it?"

A few passes later, he said, "Got a girl knocked up."

I palmed the ball, stilling its movement, and looked up.

"Yep, I'm gonna be a dad. None of the other guys know, and I want to keep it on the DL during the season. I thought I'd come in here and get a little work done in the quiet. Wasn't expecting to find you here."

"Well, I got my own issues and couldn't sleep either."

"Not enough sex?" he asked with a grin, flipping my own question back at me.

"Well, there's that, but my shot is on point, so maybe Sonny's on to something."

Mo snorted. "I don't know, don't care. That's enough girl talk. Let's play."

And that's what we did. We played for an hour, no talk, nothing. It was exactly what we both needed. Peace and quiet. Of course, Mo thought I only wanted respite from the bet with Sonny, but I knew better.

I'd been bored with the pussy parade for a while, and wasn't sure why. Now I knew. Apparently, I enjoyed a side of brain with my women. At least, a half portion of wit and an appetizer of snark. Of course, I hadn't sampled the lady goods that went along with my latest interest, but I imagined them to be tasty.

With growing responsibility on my shoulders, a need to look for something more meaningful felt appropriate. But Sonny had effectively clipped my balls and hung them on his studio wall, stalling any attempts at starting a relationship. At least, for the rest of the season.

Against my better judgment, I'd partied pretty hard last night, holding up the bar and crushing one drink after another. Yet when I got home, I'd spent the better part of the night unable to crash, my brain on overdrive thinking about Caterina—Cate—and what it was about her that gave me pause.

"Let's get some breakfast," Mo shouted from the bleachers. "Wanna go to the diner?"

I nodded, tossed a hoodie over my drenched chest, lifted the hood over my damp hair, and shoved my feet into slides. We slipped out of the field house and made our way toward College Avenue. The fall air was damp and the campus still quiet; mostly everyone who was anyone was sleeping off a hangover.

Once we were seated in our usual corner of the diner, Cassie came over to take our order.

"You're early?" Her statement came out as a question.

I gave her a chin bump and a wink. "What's up, Cass?"

"Not much. Working a double like always, paying the bills." She rested her hands on the table, leaning forward the slightest bit to give us a full view of her double-Ds.

Yeah, we'd had a few rounds together during my freshman year. Cassie was a ball baby, and made no secret she'd like a way out of her blue-collar life . . . and she'd like the easy way to get there.

But we weren't a fit. She was too domineering for me; I liked to be in charge in the bedroom. She was also pretty demanding out of the bedroom, and I definitely wasn't ready for that back then.

"No doubt you look good doing it." Mo winked at her. "I'll have chicken and waffles, a large milk and big water, and a fruit bowl," he rattled off, cutting short the small talk.

"Steele?" She lifted her eyebrow when addressing me, rolling her pencil along her bottom lip.

"I'll have the hangover special, eggs over easy, turkey bacon, and home fries. Milk and water too."

"Okay. Be right back with your drinks."

As soon as she'd walked away, Mo leaned forward and said, "Christ, you could bend her over this booth and do her from behind, and she wouldn't give a good goddamn."

"I'm not going to, so don't get in a panic. You'll still get your waffles." I snagged a straw from the dispenser and pulled off the wrapper, ready for my drink. "My throat's dry as fuck," I muttered.

"What'd you do last night?"

"I went three rounds too many with a vodka gimlet, some fancy combination Missy was mixing at the bar. The place was lit up with smoke, someone brought a hookah—you know, I didn't hit that. Not my thing. Got the NBA whispering to me that I got to stay clean. Fuck that, they're haunting me in my dreams."

"I hear you."

Cassie brought our milk and water, then our food, and Mo and I ate in relative silence, breaking for a little hoop talk before heading back to our places.

Back in my apartment, I tried to get into a video game, but eventually passed out in my chair. I awoke sometime later to the radio blaring. Wiz Khalifa faded out, and Sonny's voice boomed throughout my pad.

"Sonny here with your Sunday jam, helping you all get over your partied-out selves and get ready for the week. Who's studying? Tweet me, tell me where you're at; we'll play you something special for being a good boy or girl! On a much more serious vibe, I'm about done with my tenure in this neck of the woods, the vast wasteland known as Ohio. I've got to say, I'm going to be sad to leave. That's why I need to do two things before I go—see another NCAA title in ball, and find a replacement."

"Fuck, this guy has got a hard-on for you," Ashton mumbled over Sonny's monologue.

The shock jock ramped up the drama. "Last time Sonny B. saw a 'ship was with my main man, Jamel, four years ago. But my new main guy, Blane Steele, is going to give us the gold this year. How do I know?

Right here on this station, he promised his undivided attention was going to ball. No more girls, no more escapades. If you're listening, Steele, call in and let me know how that's going! In the meantime, I finally got an intern, listeners. A regular badass on the mic, Catie P. is here in all her throaty splendor to give you our next song."

Ashton turned big eyes my way. "Shee-it," he drawled out. "Sonny B. is handing his mic over to a lady?"

"Shhh. No one asked you, Denube." I waved a hand to hush my roommate and moved to the edge of my seat.

And there she was, Cate coming over the airwaves.

"Thank you, *Sonny*." She drew out his name, the *n*'s rolling off her tongue like it was the first time she'd said his first name, and it probably was. "Pleasure's all mine to be here at Hafton News 96.9, but I have to say, I have some pretty big shoes to fill. Or maybe not, now that I look at them."

Low-pitched feminine laughter came through the speakers, filling my head as she got her dig in with Sonny.

"Oh, you're a funny girl?" Sonny shot back. "Introduce the song."

"She's good. Ribbing Sonny," Ashton said with a laugh, and I shushed him again.

His face brightened as realization hit. "Damn! Is this the girl from the coffee place?"

"Will you shut up, Ashton?"

"Ha! She is." He started doing some awful running-man imitation through the apartment.

"Oh no," Cate cooed into the microphone. "I insulted the god of Hafton radio, and now I'm being told to switch to music. That's my cue, listeners. Let's slow things down a bit tonight and take it back a decade or so with Sheryl Crow's 'Leaving Las Vegas' for all of you nursing a headache."

Her voice faded into the soulful tune, and I wanted to rush to the station and demand Sonny put her back on for the night. Just so I could listen.

I was allowed to do that, right? It was just listening.

chapter
six

Catie

Behind closed doors, Mr. Boots might have had me cowed, but put me on the air and I found my backbone.

I was getting over his crap as fast as I could. I was born to talk, and talk was what I would do on the airwaves. Plus, Sonny couldn't exactly put his obnoxious ways on display in front of his audience. So when he gave me a chance to introduce a song, I took my opportunity, making sure to get a dig in.

"Catie, get back in here," he called out over Sheryl's crooning. Sounded like my small-shoe comment didn't go over so well behind the scenes.

"Yes, Mr. Boots?" I asked, injecting whatever I imagined Southern hospitality to sound like.

Sonny was kicked back in the control room with his motorcycle boots propped up on the table. His headphones were slightly crooked, allowing him to free an ear, and his strawberry-blond hair was a mess.

"The bitchiness thing," he said, "I don't know if I would have gone that direction the first time, but you were okay. More fire, babe. I'm giving you a real chance." He focused his blue eyes on me, lasering in on every one of my imperfections, targeting my insecurities. "You want to be on the radio, right?"

I nodded.

"Then I would suggest you don't diss me on my own show. You got me? Channel that heat elsewhere." He half smiled.

"Okay. I was only trying to let some of my East Coast humor show. You gave me thirty seconds to win an audience, and I really wanted to. I'm sorry."

As soon as the words were out of my mouth, I mentally kicked myself. Glass-ceiling lesson number one: Never apologize on the job. How many times a day did I do that with Sonny?

He shook his head, and I had no idea what to do with that.

What kind of modern woman apologizes or grovels to their chauvinistic boss? *One who's going to die a nasty death, that's who.* I crossed my fingers in an effort to ward off lightning striking me down, or falling dead of a heart attack.

Sonny waved a hand, dismissing me. "You're done on the air for the night. Go stack those CDs in the back for next week. They're prizes for the concert out on College Avenue. In fact, you can be in charge of handing them out."

Despite my Cuban and Italian genes roaring at me from deep in my cells, I swallowed my Jersey attitude and attempted to be polite to a man who didn't deserve it.

"I'm happy to do it, but honestly, I don't know how you're ever going to find a replacement if you don't let them get to know the audience. And I say that in the most respectful way."

Sonny narrowed his eyes, studying me. He knew he had me by the lady balls. There was nowhere else to do an internship in this crappy small town during the school year. When I'd told him my aspirations like a fool during our initial job interview, I could see the realization hit him. He could make me do whatever he wanted. Or at least, he thought so.

"Maybe I'll fail a class and be short a few credits." He gave me a mean smirk. "Then I won't need a replacement."

They're right. Apologizing gets you nowhere.

Stuck in the closet stacking CDs, I cursed to myself as sweat trickled down my back. *Jesus C.,* why did the heating vent have to be in the closet? It was about a thousand degrees in the tiny box, and the door refused to stay open and allow fresh air inside.

I tore off my sweatshirt. Left to my own devices in a tank top and leggings, I tossed the stupid plastic cases into piles organized by local artists.

Maybe I would get strep or chicken pox, or a million lice crawling around my massive head of hair, and not be able to go to the Hafton Music Fest. I'd been looking forward to it, but now thanks to my stupidity and inability to follow rules, I'd be stuck behind a table and not onstage spinning tunes.

This was the exact kind of thing Clara had warned me about. Of course, she'd hidden behind good intentions. No doubt, she'd meant to ruin my plans. *"Catie, if you act all aggressive and barracuda, they're going to stick you in the corner. Act demure and appreciative."*

Bitch. She'd set me up for failure, and now I was clawing my way out like a cat in heat stuck in the gutter. I stomped my foot just thinking about it, and a pile of CDs came toppling down on my arm.

I stomped again.

A knock sounded on the door, followed by a muffled, "You okay in there?"

I yelled back, "Yeah," and went back to stacking and organizing.

There was another knock.

I was in no mood for more Sonny Boots and his dictatorship. "What?"

"Can I come in?"

I grabbed the handle and flung the door open, nearly knocking myself over. Standing tall above me was a mirage—one that resembled Blane Steele holding a bakery bag.

Stunned, I blinked hard, trying to be sure I was awake, but had no idea what to say.

He smirked down at me. "Hey."

"Um, hi. What are you doing here?"

A bead of sweat trickled down my spine. I tamped down the urge to sniff my pits and quickly wrapped my arms around myself, remembering I was practically naked.

"I heard your big moment," he said. "You were good. Funny, I mean. I would have liked to hear more."

His blond hair flopped over his eyebrows, skimming his eyelashes, and I wondered how he saw clearly when he played ball. Then I remembered he always wore a dark green sweatband. In fact, there were rumors he didn't wash it as long as the team was winning, one of those sports superstition things. All of a sudden, I wanted one to keep.

Oh God! Gross.

Wait a minute . . . Blane Steele thought I was funny. He heard me on the air tonight!

"Um, thank you?"

Blane stood there wedged sideways between the door and me as the bright lights from the hallway flooded the dark space, highlighting all of his perfections.

And my imperfections.

I snatched my sweatshirt and pulled it over my head, tugging it down hard to cover my butt.

"I don't know. You sounded like you were having fun, and I wanted to congratulate you." He held the bag up in the air and waved it from side to side. "Ashton went back to Mean Beans, so I tagged along to grab you a scone like you had the other day. A celebratory scone, I guess you could say."

"That was thoughtful," I said, wary. "Is that what you usually deliver to all the ladies?"

I didn't know what the hell to say. Standing before me was one of Hafton's most notorious man-whores, fumbling over his words and bringing me scones. Clearly, he could see I didn't need any more scones. My mom would insist I say I wasn't hungry, pretend to be stuffed even if I hadn't eaten all afternoon.

"It wasn't really thoughtful, more selfish. I wanted to see you, since we're friends and all, and I didn't know how to reach you. So the scone is more like a bribe or an incentive."

He flashed me a smirk, sly and full of raw sex, drawing my attention to his lips. They were perfect, very masculine, and not really pink or red but somewhere in between. Stubble lined his jaw, all blond and scruffy, framing his mouth.

He wanted to see me?

My eyes traveled his face until they met his. Crisp and clear green pools of cocky speculation stared back at me, and I was pretty sure my panties disintegrated. I quickly stared at the floor, expecting to see a pool at my feet, gushing from my girlie parts—which were most certainly not into all my women's lib and what-not.

"Well, it was good you had your best interests in mind."

"And yours. When's Sonny putting you back on the radio? Do you have time for a quick break?"

I cleared my throat and turned to resume slapping the CDs back into a neat pile. "I don't know, definitely not tonight. But I have to finish this, so I think a break is out." I waved my hand over the disorganized mess next to me, and tried not to pout like a lovesick sorority girl.

"What's this you're doing? Seems a bit below your pay grade." He leaned one arm against the doorjamb, flexing his bicep against the sleeve of his T-shirt. His eyes crinkled in what appeared to be sincerity.

"This is part of what I'm supposed to do. I'm getting these ready for the music fest, where I'll be grounded." The last part came out on a mumbled whisper, more for me than my present company.

"What did you say? Grounded?"

I'd never felt smaller, and it wasn't just because of his six-foot plus frame looming over my five feet three inches. "I shouldn't have made that joke insulting Sonny. He gave me a chance and I fucked it up—messed it up. Excuse my language."

"You were being funny. I ate it up, as I'm sure everyone else listening did. He's being a prick. You need to go talk with him. And for the record, I've heard the word *fuck* before."

This time he smiled big, showing his dimples, and the combination made my traitorous nipples harden.

Lock it down, Catie.

"You want me to say something to him, Cate?"

Cate. His nickname for me was sophisticated and sexy. I'd always been cute Catie or cuddly Caterina.

"No, don't," I blurted. "It will just make it worse."

"Okay, but you should."

I felt myself biting down on my lip, trying to keep from smiling. Someone wanted to stick up for me, wanted me to stick up for myself. It was a heady feeling, and one I'd never experienced before.

Hoping I wasn't glowing at his attention, I said, "I have to get back to this shit."

Blane laughed. "I love the way you swear. You may be tiny, but your mouth is mighty."

He tossed the bag in the air, and I caught it.

"Don't forget to give that mouth some sustenance," he called out as he moved his foot from the door and walked away.

"Thanks," I called back, hoping my voice carried out the closing door.

I sank to the floor, holding a hand to my chest as I blew out a long breath.

"What was that all about?" I whispered to myself.

Lord if I know.

chapter seven

Blane

I wasn't sure what compelled me to pop in and visit Cate at work—or why I gave her a nickname. Her name was Caterina, not Cate.

As I ran the track around the football stadium, my hair flopped into my eyes again. I cursed as I ran my hand through it, shoving it back before wiping the sweat from my forehead. Where the heck was my sweatband?

It was Tuesday, and it was a miracle I'd made it all of five whole days of celibacy without pulling my dick straight off my body from all the jacking off.

As I pumped my arms and my feet slapped a rhythm around the track, my mind kept wandering to Cate. Something about that chick challenged me, and I liked it. Maybe it was the whole not-getting-laid mandate. Forbidden fruit and all that.

At least, that's what I kept telling myself.

I slowed my pace as I rounded the track so I could bring my shirt up to wipe my face, and spotted one of my football buddies coming from the tunnel.

"If it isn't the Stealer!" Toots hollered. "What are you doing? Working off some sexual tension?" He headed my way as I stopped to cool down.

Toots was a senior and was Hafton's second-string quarterback. His arm wasn't good enough to get him into the NFL, but it didn't seem to bother him. He loved football and the benefits that came with it, especially since he wasn't all that good-looking. But football wasn't his life. He was majoring in accounting and enjoying having a beautiful woman, despite his pockmarked face.

"Is my sex life all anyone can talk about?" I leaned over my knees and tried to breathe through my nose.

"Nah. That's mine. The ladies can't seem to stop talking about me and my shlong."

"Shut the fuck up, Toots. We all know you're a one-woman guy. Berit would have your balls on a skewer if she knew you talked like that."

Toots laughed and brushed back his shaggy brown hair. "Seriously, what's up? What're you doing in my neck of the woods?"

I stood up straight, breathing deeply. "Got a lot on my mind. Whole place is talking about the 'ship. I know we're a team, but I'm feeling a lot of pressure to carry the load. Plus, I got the added bullshit of whether to enter the draft."

"I hear you, man. But you've got what a lot of us will never see. A future doing what you love."

I nodded. "Maybe. I don't know. One week, you feel like you're an invincible college dude, and the next, you're an adult. And fucking Sonny took away my one stress reliever, the little shit." I laughed out the last part, trying to lighten up the conversation.

Toots shook his head. "You're the one who's dumb enough to be friends with him. You know he always pushes the limits. He's a cock-blocking shock jock."

"Cock-blocking shock jock. Try saying that three times fast!" My laughter ripped through the empty stadium, echoing off the bleachers. "Think he can he put that on his résumé?"

Toots laughed with me, his large frame shaking.

I slapped him on the back and said, "I'm outta here. Catch you soon."

Toots headed in the other direction to start his run as I jogged out the side entrance and down the hill to the field house. Coach would tear me a new one if I was late to work out.

I left the field house a couple of hours later, my hair still damp from the shower, dripping a little on my Hafton sweatshirt. My phone buzzed, and I slid my hand into my back pocket to pull out my phone, curious as to who the hell was bothering me.

"Hi, Mom," I said. "How you doing?"

"I'm good, baby. How are you?" A rustling came over the line, and her voice muffled a little as if she was speaking away from the phone. "Slow down, Rocky!"

"What are you doing, Mom?"

"I'm walking the dogs, and Rocky is chasing after some pretty piece of Rottweiler. Rocky!" My mom kept shouting the dog's name, and I was forced to hold the phone away from my ear.

"Mom? You should call me later and free up your hands."

"Nah, don't be silly. I got one of those earpiece thingies, and I'm hands-free. I just turned to walk in the other direction, and Rocky's not distracted anymore. The little guys are easy, doing their thing, so I'm all yours."

My mom was a bit of a kook. Dad walked out on us years ago, and since then she'd spent her time writing romance novels and adopting dogs. She was definitely not your typical stay-at-home mom with milk and cookies on the table, but I loved her.

She'd put her life on hold when she found she was pregnant with me, married my dad, who she never really loved, and tried to make a life in a trailer park. When that failed, she picked up the pieces and raised me as a single mom, making ends meet with her writing and a full-time job in a coffee joint.

"You doing okay, Mom?"

"I'm good. I took in this cat until he gets adopted. He's a diabetic so it's tricky, but the Yorkies like him, and Rocky is managing. Oh! I forgot to tell you, my last book went to the top of Amazon's charts. Not bad for a high school graduate."

"That's great, Mom. But do you really need a diabetic cat? Don't you think you have enough on your plate?"

"It's one little kitty. The animal league gives me his medicine, so hush up, Blane. Are you ready for your season?"

"Yeah. I'm ready."

"I'm proud of you, son. You didn't have to stay in school, could've left for the major leagues early, but you're sticking it out."

"Mom, it's the NBA, and I'm going pro after this season. I'll be good and employable when my professional career ends. I'm a few credits shy of graduating, and I'm wrapping them all up."

"Blane, honey, I don't care if you drive trucks like your asshole father. I just want to know you're happy. I don't like your future being unknown. Gigi says those agents really take advantage of some guys, so you need to get someone good when you're ready. I want to make sure your father isn't advising you, honey." Her breathing puffed into the phone, and I could hear the dogs yapping in the background.

"Don't start with Dad. He did the best he could too. And what the heck does Gigi know? She's a waitress."

I wasn't just saying that; my dad did do the best he could. Yes, he was a commercial trucker and spent most of his nights in the cab of his rig after fucking some cheap broad, but he loved me.

"I know; I'm not getting into it about your dad. And Gigi is a waitress down by U of Jacksonville, so she hears things. By the way, is your dad coming up to see you play?"

The way we were bouncing from subject to subject, family member to family member, was giving me a headache. I would rather have gone back to discussing the diabetic cat.

"Yeah, he took some routes up this way so he could stop and see a few home games. And you know he'll be at the Xavier game, up here before the holidays? The same one you'll be at, so keep the peace."

Those two could go at it when given the chance. Unfortunately, it usually ended up in post-divorce make-up sex and another round of bickering, so I tried to keep them separate when I could.

"I know. I wouldn't miss it . . . seeing my boy play on the hardwood. Never, sweetie. Hey, Rocky!"

"Listen, Mom, go walk the dogs. I'll talk to you soon."

"All right, sweetie. Love you."

"Love you too."

By the time I ended the call, I was at the bottom of the hill on College Avenue, heading toward Mean Beans. Out of nowhere, I wanted a coffee—except I wasn't a coffee drinker.

The bells chimed over the door as I stepped into the lavender-hued java mecca.

"Dude!" Ashton yelled from the corner.

Christ, I didn't need to deal with him again.

"Look at us! A bunch of real coffee drinkers," he joked.

"And pussies," I added. "My dad would yank my man card so fast if he knew I was hanging out in gourmet coffee places. The golden arches is for real men."

"I'll make sure to let him know you drink lattes now the next time he's in town."

I punched Ashton in the shoulder, ignoring his fake wince as I scanned the place and locked in on who I was looking for. Cate sat hunched over a textbook with her long, curly hair hanging around her face, a scone to her left and a steaming cup of something on her right.

Ashton followed my gaze and scowled. "Dude, now's not the time to get involved."

"Shut the fuck up, Ash. You're in a coffee shop too, ogling some blonde."

"I'm not in line to go pro, and I certainly didn't make a bet with Sonny." He poked his finger into my chest and stared me down hard. "And I'm definitely just looking to get laid. You have the eyes of someone wanting to get involved."

"How the hell would you know?" I muttered while walking to the counter.

Ava brightened when she saw me. As she opened her mouth to greet me, I brought my fingers up to my lips, motioning for her to be quiet.

"Hey, Blane," she whispered, her brows pinched in a *V* of confusion.

"Hi, Ava," I said quietly.

"My roommate said to give you this."

She pulled out a heart-shaped sticky note with *Vicki* and a number written in red lipstick, but I gave her an apologetic smile and waved it away.

"Um, thanks, but it's not a good time. I don't want her to be disappointed." I pushed back my hood, thinking, *I must be losing my mind.* Keeping my voice low, I said, "I was wondering what the girl in the corner is drinking, and I'd like you to make another."

"Who? The plain girl from the other day? Catie with a C?" Returning to her regular voice, Ava said, "She's wearing earbuds."

"Oh. Do you know what she's drinking?"

"Yeah, a full-fat latte. Can you believe that? Who drinks that? No one I know."

"I didn't ask that. How 'bout you make me another?" I shoved a few bucks in the tip jar and slapped a ten on the counter.

"What about you, Blane? Want something?"

"You know what? I'll have a hot cocoa. Full-fat and whipped."

I watched Ava turn toward her expensive coffee machine and frown at my lack of appreciation of her charms. Steam filled her face, and yeah, she was hot—but a bitch. That used to do it for me, but not anymore.

With the latte and cocoa in my hands, I made my way toward the corner. I set the drinks down on the table next to Cate before tapping her on the shoulder.

"Holy shit!" She jumped in her seat, nearly toppling the pile of work in front of her. "You scared the hell out of me."

God, I love her foul mouth.

She pulled out her earbuds, letting them dangle above her cleavage. My eyes automatically shifted down, appreciating the view, and I quickly raised them to her face. When she cocked her head and raised an eyebrow, I felt a smile tug at my lips but schooled it.

"I brought you a refill." I grabbed the paper cups and swung them over to her table.

"Really? Let me get you some money." She reached around her back and snatched her bag.

"It's on me."

"Why?" She turned her dark eyes on me, her brow furrowing. Indignation practically seeped from her pores.

"Just being nice, Cate. That's it. No ulterior motive."

She raised an eyebrow again.

"May I sit?"

"Go right ahead."

"So, what're you doing?" I asked, taking a sip of my dessert in a cup. God, that shit was sweet.

"I'm researching a paper for my women's studies class."

"Really?" I had to remind myself to swallow. Otherwise I would have spit out my drink.

"It's my major."

"And you're putting up with Sonny? All this time, I thought you were finding your own way, but a women's libber taking his shit? No way."

"Shh," she hissed. "I need that internship. I told you. Unlike some people who flaunt their muscles and have tuition, stipends, and steak dinners thrown at them, I need the work/study program."

"Really? You're going to go there?" I raised an eyebrow back at her.

"No, sorry. I know you're talented."

"Believe me, I get it, needing money. I come from nothing. My dad sends me some 'cause he knows I'll repay him. But yes, I get a lot of fringe benefits."

"Can we talk about something else?"

"Sure."

I leaned back in my chair, studying her. Cate smelled good, like citrus and home. I was from Florida—kill me, but oranges, lemons, and mangos smelled like home.

"So, tell me, is this what the big, bad jock does when he's sworn off sex?" Leaning over, she sniffed my drink. "Drinks hot chocolate and stalks chubby girls?"

"What?" I leaned across the table. "What do you mean?"

"Sorry to insult your manliness, but that is hot chocolate? With whipped cream." She swiped her finger across my lip, smoothing away a whipped-cream mustache.

"No, I meant that . . . the other comment. I can't even say it."

"What? About chubby girls?"

"Would you stop?"

"I'm sitting here eating a scone. How many girls do you date who eat, let alone enjoy a scone in your company? I'm betting zero."

"Well, you're not every girl."

"Uh, yeah. I'm the one you befriend when you can't have any others."

I pinched off a piece of her scone and held it to her lips. "I guess I just have to shut you up with pastries."

She opened her mouth and wrapped her lips around the pastry. The tip of her tongue grazed my finger and set my cock aflame. This was something new—she did have a point when she said that. Getting turned on by feeding smart and sassy women baked goods was a very new thing, and I liked it.

She swallowed and took a sip of her latte before asking, "So, you ready?"

"For what?"

"The season."

"You telling me you actually care?"

"Don't tell anyone, but I'm a closet fan of all those big athletic men in tanks sweating all over one another. Between that and Sonny, I'll be stripped of my women's rights status."

"No way." I tilted toward her, sniffing more of her lusciousness, and I hardened even more. She was a fan, and she smelled edible.

"Yep. I like the games. I try to make it to a few each season."

"I'll keep that in mind. I think I'm ready. A lot of pressure on this season, but I'm feeling good."

"Oh shit," Cate said, looking at her watch. "I'm supposed to go to a movie tonight, but I have to go drop all of this in my room first." She stood up and gathered the various papers and printouts, stacking them quickly.

"Come on, I'll walk you."

I stood and tossed my half-full cup in the garbage. Cate snatched her last bite of scone and popped it into her mouth. All packed up and zipped in her leather jacket, she said, "I can get there myself."

"What would be the fun in that? Come on."

I cocked my head toward the door and gave Ashton the peace sign. He winked at me and went right back to staring at Ava's tits.

"Where do you live?" I asked.

"Southern dorms. Right across there." She motioned across College Avenue.

"Sweet. Those are hard to get?" I slowed my pace to match her shorter legs.

"I wanted a single, so it wasn't as hard. I guess no one really wants to live alone in college."

"I'd die for a little peace and quiet from time to time. I live with Ashton, the big guy back in the coffee shop, and Alex White lives down the hall with a guy from the football team."

The wind whipped Cate's hair across her face, and a few dark curls stuck to her lip gloss. I reached over and pulled the strands free, our eyes meeting for the briefest of seconds. If I weren't a hot-blooded man, I would have sworn I heard some romantic melody playing in the background.

The spark between this girl and me was intense. Whoever said opposites attract knew what the fuck they were talking about. Cate with her brains and curvy body was doing it for me in a big way. Me, a guy who'd enjoyed so many mindless girls, I'd lost count.

"Right over here." Cate motioned toward a red brick building marked Southern A. "This is me."

We stood at the threshold of her dorm. I wanted to go upstairs, but she looked like she wanted me to get the hell away.

"What movie are you seeing later?" I asked, desperate for an excuse for the afternoon to continue.

She smiled and stifled a giggle. "It's a porno."

"What? You're kidding."

"No, really. I'm taking An In-Depth Look at Pornography and Its Ill Effects on Women of Every Age, and we're required to go to a porn fest tonight. You know, so we can discuss in detail how degrading it is to women."

I grasped her shoulder, shaking her in fun. "Stop! You're playing me."

"I'm not. Seriously."

"I need to go to this."

Cate shifted back, out of my grip. My hand dropped by my side, but itched to get back to her.

"You can't! My prof would have a field day, and I'm already under scrutiny. It's a senior-level lecture."

"Don't worry. Just tell me where it is, and I'll sneak in."

She shook her head, her dark curls bouncing like crazy around her face. "I can't. Seriously."

"No, seriously, you have to. This is going to be a blast. And I can buy you a beer after."

"I don't do beer."

"Whatever you want, just tell me where and when."

"It's in Cavern Hall at six o'clock," she whispered. "Pretend you don't know me." She turned and opened the door to Southern A. "Thanks for the coffee," she called over her shoulder as the door was shutting behind her.

I walked backward and waved good-bye like a fool in love. When Cate was out of sight, I quickly adjusted myself in my pants and jogged back to the main drag and over to my apartment.

Like an idiot, I logged onto Twitter on my way back to the dorm.

@HaftonFan101:
Move along girls, @BallerSteele still sworn off s$x on the air with @SonnyB_KnocknBoots. #findanewman #Steeleisoffmarket #maybenot?

@HaftonFan101:
Just heard @BallerSteele was spotted taking a number in the coffee shop. #justsayin #manwhore

@HaftonAva:
@HaftonFan101 That was me, slipping @BallerSteele my roomie's number! We are wearing him down!

@CollegeBBallFan:
Can we concentrate on ball? This is our last season with @BallerSteele at #Haftonmensball

@HaftonSweetiePie:

@HaftonFan101   @HaftonAva   Hey,   I   thought   @ BallerSteele was mine? No fair

This was a huge mistake. Twitter was worse than high school. *What is wrong with these people?*

Oh, fuck it!

I shoved the phone back in my pocket. I had a porn fest to go to.

chapter eight

Catie

I slammed into my room and collapsed on my bed, squeezing my eyes shut as I breathed hard. Stanwick was going to kill me, after embarrassing me first. It might even turn into death by embarrassment.

My stupid, stupid girl parts and hormones got in the way for the first time ever. What in the hell was I thinking, telling Blane the place and time for tonight?

Blane Steele, man-whore—albeit celibate man-whore—notorious womanizer, and the object of at least half of my female classmates' fantasies. The same Blane that Stanwick referred to in her class last week. She would demolish him, and then me. All because I had a crush.

"Arrrgh," I screamed into my pillow.

Maybe he would be late, and Stanwick would have locked the doors by the time he tried to slip in. I silently prayed to every deity and pagan idol I knew of for that.

Throwing my legs over the side of my bed, I scrolled through the unread messages on my phone.

Sonny: I just got a message you won't be in this afternoon?

Ugh, *shit.*

Catie: Yes, I sent you an e-mail last week. I have a class project. If you want, I can get an excuse.

Sonny: Don't bother. Come early tomorrow. I need the script to be organized for the fest.

Catie: I'll be there as soon as class lets out.

The guy was such an asshole.

Sonny: Early.

I didn't bother with a reply. Sonny would insist on his way, and I would end up relenting. I switched to my e-mails and deleted all the spam, only to be left with one actual message regarding paid internship possibilities for the summer.

Finally, a bright spot in my crappy day. If I got the internship over the summer, I could also find a job waitressing and stay in Ohio. Then I wouldn't have to go home to my sisters and their wrath, or my mother and her constant harping on me to act like a real woman. I'd miss my dad, but that was the breaks. He would understand . . . they didn't call him Big Anthony for nothing.

After huffing a little while longer, I dragged myself to the bathroom and washed my face, and then changed clothes before heading out the door to Cavern Hall. As soon as I stepped outside, it began to pour down rain; not a light drizzle but huge raindrops that fell from the sky and soaked my sweatshirt, causing my hair to curl more than usual. My little backpack umbrella did little to shield me from the downpour, and I probably looked like a drowned rat when I arrived at the movie.

I pushed my dripping hair from my face as I entered the building, shaking the rain from it and then finger combing the curls into some type of style. Stopping for a moment, I set aside my wet umbrella with the others littering the floor outside the room, and brushed the droplets off my sweatshirt before I walked inside. The room was semi-dark, and I paused before deciding to head to a seat at the far left corner against the wall.

I wasn't sure what to expect tonight because I'd never even seen a full-length porno. Was there a plot? Was there even a point? Or full frontal? Yes, I'd seen the little snippets shown in class, but I had a feeling what I was about to view was nothing like that.

"Good evening, students," Stanwick said as she made her way down the aisle. "Welcome to movie night, or *the night you all wake up to the world around you*, as I like to call it. Ladies and gentlemen, you are about to see why I have made this course my life's work. Women are not animals, or to be used purely for sexual entertainment. Women are people."

She made her way to the front of the room and stood in front of the lectern. "If you think you will find this evening humorous, or think of this subject with anything other than with the seriousness it warrants, please leave. I will excuse you. I'm giving you two minutes before I lock the door and we begin our journey."

Only Cora Stanwick could stand at the front of a classroom for ninety seconds and the room remain absolutely still. She checked her watch and glanced at the audience as the back door creaked open and someone made their way toward the front.

I had been in such deep thought as to whether there would be BDSM or sodomy in the films, I'd forgotten who the intruder might be. When I looked up, I saw a tall figure dressed in a hooded sweatshirt and tight jeans.

"Excuse me?"

"Sorry I'm late," Blane said in a hushed tone and took a seat on the other side of the auditorium.

Stanwick glared at him. "Who are you?"

"I'm here for the school paper, covering how seriously committed you are to teaching future women's studies majors, Professor."

"They didn't tell me they were sending someone over, but it's fine. Please have a seat and stay quiet. This is an important part of the learning process."

"Yes, ma'am."

"And don't call me ma'am."

With that, she walked over to the door and locked it before hitting the light switch, enveloping us in total darkness. Then the first movie rolled.

At first, I had to stifle a giggle.

It was a sunny Sunday afternoon, and there was a cop patrolling for speeders on a long stretch of highway. A woman was out for a drive after church, oddly enough wearing a cat suit and heels. Her makeup looked more like she was a stripper than a devout worshipper. She barreled down the dusty road in a sporty cherry-red convertible, the top down and the wind blowing her already artfully mussed hair. Out of nowhere, blue and red lights came on, swirling around the screen with a siren blaring, and the brunette bombshell looked surprised she was being pulled over.

A well-built cop practically bursting out of his tight uniform swaggered over to her car, and she leaned out the window, her lips all pouty.

"License and registration, please."

"What did I do, sir?"

After a few moments of flirtatious banter, ripe with sexual innuendo, the cop ended up following the woman back to her apartment. As soon as they made it through the door, he slammed her against the wall and pressed his body against hers, kissing her. The kiss was deep and hungry as he practically devoured her, and the camera moved in tighter to pick up every stroke of his tongue. She shoved her fingers into his hair, pulling him closer as he pushed his pelvis against hers, grinding his erection into her, which elicited a wild moan from her lips.

Suddenly, I didn't feel like giggling anymore. The lust was palpable. Passion emanated from them as if they weren't acting. It was a feeling I wasn't familiar with, even though I wasn't a virgin. I'd lost it to kind and sensitive Robby Barnes in high school. He'd lasted thirty seconds, which was for the best because I was barely lubricated down there. It was nothing like the lusty scene in front of me, and I began to squirm in my seat.

I knew it was wrong the way the woman was being portrayed. She was selling her body so she didn't get a ticket. The cop was rough, not treating her with respect. If I had to guess, Stanwick would make all these points.

The cop dropped his pants and—surprise!—was commando. *Duh.* The woman dropped to her knees and grabbed his enormous length, licking and sucking her way around it as if she'd known him for years. He leaned his head back into the wall and growled while gripping her hair and guiding her up and down his length.

Still busy with the blow job, the brunette moved one hand down her cat suit, sliding down her zipper. Then she shoved her hand inside and began rubbing herself. She looked to be in pure ecstasy with the man's penis in her mouth and her own hand on her clitoris.

The sucking sounds became louder, his moans increased in intensity, and then he came all over her breasts, now bared and out in the open.

They both stood and laughed, kissing wildly before chatting about what fun it was to role play. Apparently, they were actually lovers, and they liked to pretend to meet in precarious ways on Sunday afternoons.

So, there's a plot?

The movie didn't end. Instead, the pair went back to their bedroom, where the guy performed oral sex on the woman before flipping her on all fours. He shoved himself inside her, gripping her hair as he rammed himself in and out until they both reached orgasm.

I was uncomfortably turned on. It was wrong, but I was. I wanted some of that heat; I couldn't help it. Some primal force rose in me, waking up my libido, taking up residence in my heart and my girlie parts. I wanted to have hot sex.

Like now.

I reached for my water bottle and took a long swig of the cold liquid in hopes it would cool me down.

Stanwick went to the front of the room and started a second movie. I wasn't sure I could take another. I wanted to run far away—to the nearest sex-toy store or male strip club.

I felt the telltale prickle of eyes on me and looked to the right to find Blane Steele staring at me from under his hood. How long had he been doing that? Was my squirming noticeable?

Luckily, the second flick was focused on bondage, more whips and chains than actual sex, and I didn't suffer any more sexual panic attacks.

Until class was dismissed.

chapter nine

Blane

Cate was right—that professor was a tough one. Crap, I almost shoved my hand in front of my dick for fear she was going to rip it off. I could tell right away she was a jock hater, so I went with a fake identity.

Plus, I certainly didn't need to get Cate into trouble.

Settled in my seat, I caught a quick glimpse of her. She was wearing an off-the-shoulder sweatshirt, a different color than I'd seen her wear before. Her hair was a wild mess of curls, her face glowing. And her ass filled up the seat in just the right way. God, I'd been a legs man until a week ago, but this girl's curves were doing it for me.

Wait, I'm sitting in a women's studies class. I shouldn't sexualize her.

If I was totally honest, her eccentric personality and drive made her sexier. Cate was a ball-buster—except when it came to Sonny—and I liked it. What was the deal with that? Sonny was a fucker, and I needed to have a chat with him. But I suspected Little Miss

Independent wouldn't appreciate that.

I didn't have time to dwell on it. The lights went down and the movie started.

Holy shit, if this was what women's studies was all about, I wanted in. Right away, I knew the cop and the chick were role-playing. God, he banged her six ways to Sunday every week like that, and she was smoking in a non-curvy way.

It was right about when she slid down on her knees and shoved his cock in her mouth, I realized I didn't even have a chubby. *Hmm.* And I hadn't been laid since . . . a while.

Discreetly, I turned my head to face Cate, careful to keep my eyes hidden by the rim of my hood. The little pixie was squirming in her seat. *Jesus F. Christ.* I squinted to get a better glimpse, and sure enough, I could see her chest rising and falling with deep breaths.

Hot. Damn. My girl was turned on, and I was pretty sure that wasn't why we were here.

Before I knew it, the movie was over, and I had no idea what happened after the blow job or how long it had been since I turned to watch Cate—who was now staring back at me.

I turned my head back to the screen and watched the second movie as if it was the NBA Draft. I made mental notes on all the bondage scenes, and what not to do. Ever.

As soon as the lights came up and the bitchy professor announced the discussion would take place the following day during class, I hightailed it out of there to the exit on the opposite side of the room, hoping to meet up with Cate.

Leaned up against the wall across from the door, I didn't have to wait long. She practically ran from the room and stumbled over her own feet, face-planting into my chest.

"Hey! If I knew you were going to be so excited to see me, I would've sat next to you," I mumbled into her hair, the curls tickling my nose.

She made a fist and jammed it into my chest. "Ouch! That hurt me more than you! No fair," she whisper-yelled.

I threw my arm around her and led her toward the main entrance. "Let's get out of here before Professor Meany discovers I'm nothing more than a male athlete. She'd probably strip me down and burn me at the stake in the middle of campus."

"Hush. I had to fight to get into this class."

"I can see why. It's like a precursor to an orgy." I squeezed her tight and tried to keep her glued to me.

"Shhh," she hissed through a giggle. Then she conveniently slid out from under my arm to snatch her umbrella off the floor before we made our way through the revolving door and outside.

The rain had stopped since I'd arrived, and the air was damp but cold. I should have been chilly but instead was a little overheated, and the warmth emanating from Miss Turned-On and the sparks shooting between us didn't help. I took off my hoodie and threw it over my left shoulder before sliding my other arm around Cate again.

"What are you doing?"

"Putting my arm around a lady," I said, not bothered by her threatening glare.

"You're supposed to be celibate. I mean, I'm not saying you want to do me or anything, but I don't think it's smart for you to be seen like this."

"Are you fishing for compliments? Want to hear that I want you?" I turned the tables on Miss Know-It-All. *That's right, I have game both on and off the court.*

"No!"

Okay, maybe my moves weren't so great off the court when it

came to actually liking someone.

"I wasn't fishing for compliments," she said. "You said it yourself, we're buddies."

"After what we just experienced together, we are more than buddies."

"Blane, I highly doubt that. Stop fucking with me."

"There you go again with that mouth of yours."

I still hadn't moved my arm, so I decided distraction was as good a tactic as any.

Cate blew out a huff. "My mom is a hot-tempered Cuban, my dad a full-blooded Italian. Tempers flare on both sides of my family, and even though they're divorced, those two can go at it. Still."

"Mine too. Divorced. Go at it. All of the above. Except for the Italian and Cuban part. My mom is really nothing. A Southerner, I guess. My dad, a nice Roman Catholic boy who left the church the day he got his driver's license. He's a truck driver. Been one forever."

"And you? The big star? Going pro, making something of yourself . . . no degree necessary but you're still getting one."

I squeezed her shoulder. "You sound like my mom."

Cate laughed. "Where are we going, anyway?"

"I don't know. Let's go get a drink. Something other than beer. Are you even legal?"

"Six more months, so no. You?"

"Yeah, I reclassed after eighth grade, so I'm good to go. Almost twenty-two."

She lifted an eyebrow at me.

"I'm not dumb or anything. My dad just knew it would be to my advantage to stay back a year. We weren't going to be able to afford a fancy post-graduate year, so I repeated eighth at a small Catholic place and earned a scholarship to their high school."

"To me, it sounds sweet. Like your dad had your best interests at heart."

"Eh, I don't know. He just wanted to brag about his boy doing something."

We walked a few beats in silence.

"I don't suppose you have an ID?" I asked.

She giggled. "No, I don't. I really don't go out much. Overachiever, good girl. Except for the language and all."

I swallowed, and some unfamiliar sensation lodged near my Adam's apple. Missed opportunity punched me in the gut, and I thought quickly.

"How about my place? I make a mean cocktail, and I can't drink another hot chocolate."

She stopped in the middle of the walkway, the campus now dark and quiet around us. A breeze picked up, releasing leaves that floated down from the trees, and sent her citrus scent wafting by me.

I was lost in her eyes, all big and round, a brown so dark they seemed bottomless. For the first time since I left the palm trees and swamplands of Florida for Ohio, I felt real. Like a real man. A human with a beating heart and a future.

I'm a sap. Just stop it.

"I'm not sure about that." Cate frowned up at me. "I'm serious. Sonny is a powerful person around here, and he made you make promises on the air. Just walking around with you is risky, and I don't want to be the cause of you losing fans . . . or games."

"I'm not doing anything. I'm hanging with a friend."

Almost instantly, the spark winked out in her eyes. "What?"

Most girls would have bitten their tongue off rather than respond to the *friend* comment, but not Cate.

She glared at me. "You're making my head hurt. You're nice, and we're friends. Then you wrap your arm around me, hug me tight, chat about porn, and ask me out for a drink, which seems like more than friends. And now we're back to being friends again."

"It's complicated, like you said, with Sonny and the radio station. I've never done this before, actually liked someone or been intrigued. Whatever this is."

"Well, I guess there's a first time for everything."

"It's fucking just my luck, you know," I said, shaking my head sadly. "I meet someone like you when Sonny throws down the gauntlet, and I can't mess up because I've got Coach breathing down my neck. Everyone's watching me. It's been all eyes on deck since last season, when I decided to finish school before I go pro, and do what's right. I must be jinxed or some shit."

"Exactly," Cate said firmly. "I may be all 'I am woman, hear me roar,' but I'm not about to trash your career over a silly friendship. You do what you need to do."

She stood on her tiptoes, grabbed my shoulders, and placed a quick kiss on my cheek. "Take care of yourself, Blane. See you around. Thanks for walking me."

Surprised, I realized we were standing by the dorms all this time. Cate pivoted and shot down the path to Southern A without saying anything more.

I wanted badly to chase her, hunt her down, but I knew it wouldn't work. I had a championship to win and a professional sports deal to seal.

Cate was right. I didn't have time.

chapter
ten

Catie

My stomach lurched as I strode away from Blane Steele. I ran the back of a trembling hand along my lips where they burned from kissing his cheek.

It had taken every bit of willpower I had to turn and walk away because I knew what would happen. Blane would suck me into the fairy tale of believing we were friends, and then when the statute of limitations was lifted on his sex life, he'd dump me. As buddies, of course.

No, thank you.

Suddenly no longer hot and bothered, I shivered as I entered Southern A.

"Hey, Catie!" a high-pitched voice called after me as I headed toward the stairwell.

I stopped and turned. "Hey, Tess. How are you?"

"I'm cool. I got a job at the music fest. I'm going to be working one of the food trucks for my buddy, Ryan. So, maybe we'll go down together? I'm sure you're going to be there all weekend."

Her fluffy blond hair bounced as she closed the distance between us. She'd gone a little heavy with the flowery perfume she wore today, and it made my eyes burn when she stood next to me.

"I'm there all weekend. Sonny's got me on grunt duty." I rolled my eyes, faking exaggerated frustration. No one had to know how hurt I truly was by the stupid shock jock.

"Why? I heard you on the radio for like two seconds. You sounded great. I was over at my sorority, and everyone cheered when you made the joke about Sonny Be Knocking Boots. What an idiot!"

Tess and I couldn't be more different, but I had no reason to ice her out. We'd been roommates the year before, and she was incredibly tolerant of my obsessive overachieving and idealism. I wanted a happily-ever-after, both in love and in my career. She wanted to bang the alphas and eventually marry the guy from the book—Grey something.

"He's okay," I said with a smile. "You know better than anyone how I'm dying to take over that slot at the station. I know I can't make it my women's-only bitch fest, but I can grow the audience and show the world that women can be funny." I leaned against the door to the stairs and sighed. "But I don't know. Lately I'm not sure what I want more. To have fun or be serious."

Tess pushed her hair behind her ear and stared me down. "What was I always telling you last year, Catie? You don't need to be so serious. That's what college is for, experimenting and trying on different personalities. You can have fun, perfect your on-air voice, and then go be the Howard Stern of women and their rage against the machine."

"I know. I'm starting to think I should've listened to you more last year."

She pulled me in for a hug. "It's not too late to start," she whispered into my hair.

"So, the music fest?" I said as I broke away. "What food booth?"

"The gyro truck, so come over anytime and I'll feed you some meat."

My cheeks burned, and I silently thanked God for my Mediterranean complexion. "Stop it!"

She burst out laughing. "We've got to get you some meat," she said, waggling her eyebrows to taunt me.

"I'm going down around four o'clock on Friday, so I'll swing by your room?" I pushed the door open a bit, trying to escape to my single room and my thoughts.

"Sounds good. We're going to an almost-hump-day party tonight. Basketball guys, I think. Want to go?"

"Definitely not, but thanks for asking."

I slipped through the door and raced upstairs to my room, my mind filled with visions of Blane at the party. Maybe he would have taken me to it if I'd said yes to a drink. *As friends*, I reminded myself.

After locking my door, I stripped out of my clothes, threw on pajamas, and plopped on my bed. Snuggled tight with my pillow, I let my hand wander over my hip. It was round, but not lumpy. My fingers lingered on my stomach; it was neither flat nor distended. My legs were short but toned from walking around campus and playing soccer in high school.

Maybe I should try intramurals; get more exercise. I wasn't hideous, but I wasn't a cheerleader or a supermodel or a ball baby.

Thinking about tonight, I slipped my hand beneath my waistband and across my dark curls, searching for my most sensitive parts. Opening myself to my roaming fingers, I grazed my clitoris and a shudder ran through me. Someday a man would touch me there, and it would mean something, be more than experimentation or a random hookup. His hand and heart would yearn to make me scream because I was me.

I moaned a tiny sigh into my pillow and allowed my fingers to trace my lips before dipping inside me. I'd brought myself to orgasm many times before, but I imagined it would be much different with a man deep inside me, mumbling words of love between kisses. Maybe it would be as hot as the porn movie. Not as cheesy or raunchy, but lusty and passionate.

Between the memory of the first movie and the tentative swipe of my fingers, my heart pumped faster. As my body began to tighten and then fracture, green eyes and stubbly cheeks came to mind. Thoughts of messy blond hair floated through my rattled brain, became my focus. I wondered what it would be like to run my fingers through that hair, to weave my red-painted nails through his mussed locks.

My breath came in short pants as visions of Blane Steele attacked every one of my cells.

One day, a man would think of me like that. And I would attack every one of his cells with my passion for life and my smile. It was a good smile. A bright one, according to my dad.

But that man wouldn't be Blane Steele. I'd told him I couldn't be responsible for fucking up his current season or upcoming deal, but the truth was I couldn't fuck with my own heart like that.

Even as buddies.

chapter eleven

Catie

Friday started with the last and final discussion of the porn fest with Stanwick. I couldn't take another second of dissecting those movies. If we weren't looking at still photos of the bondage one, the man whipping a tied and trapped woman, her face painted with a look of sheer ecstasy, we were chatting about the cop.

The first gave me a pit in my stomach. I didn't even enjoy the idea behind it or that it actually happened in bedrooms. The latter made me ache in ways I didn't care to admit.

When class was finished, I tried to make a beeline for the exit, but Stanwick stopped me.

"Caterina?" she called from behind the lectern. Her voice was as uptight as her look, with her hair pulled up into a bun, small readers perched on her perfect nose, and a fitted suit hugging her lithe body.

"Yes?" Wary, I held in place, not wanting to approach.

"Come here, please," she said as she beckoned me.

Taking my time, I trudged down the stairs to the front of the lecture hall as if I were walking the plank, and I sort of was. She'd probably seen me with Blane on Tuesday night, and wanted to make an issue of it.

"Caterina, who was that boy here earlier in the week? I called the paper and they said there was no such article, so naturally I was concerned. Fortunately, I saw the two of you leave together."

"Um, I tripped and ran into him—"

"Enough of that. I know who he is. Remember, I have a son on this campus. That was Blane Steele, and I want to know how he knew where to find the movie seminar."

"He was curious. I don't know him well. I ran into him and it slipped out in conversation, and then he wanted all the details." My mouth ran like verbal diarrhea, every last detail purging straight from my lips.

"I see. And when you left, what did he say?"

"Honestly, not much."

She gave me the stink eye over her readers. "Caterina, I hope you're not falling for that boy. I know the type, and no good can come from it. Especially for a girl like you."

What the heck is that supposed to mean . . . a girl like me?

"Excuse me?"

"You heard me. Don't get involved. I did once, and look what it got me. A son your age and no man to help, but this isn't about me. You have brains and the power to stay on course. Stay focused, Catie. Don't be a lamb going to slaughter. Don't let him ruin your life."

"I don't like him like that, Professor Stanwick," I lied. "We barely know each other. I appreciate you looking out for me, but I didn't realize we were this close."

She laughed, loudly and boldly. It rang throughout the now empty lecture hall. "I see everything that goes on in my class and my department. You are my business. I'm graduating future female leaders, not love-struck temptresses who date jocks."

"Um . . ." Stunned, I lost my words. I couldn't make a sentence if I tried.

"Besides, according to my son, Steele is off the market."

"Yes, he certainly is. Thank you for the warning, but I'm all good."

"You can go now, but know I'm watching, Caterina."

And like that, I was dismissed.

I ran back to my room as fast as my short legs would allow, tore off my leggings and sweatshirt, pulled up my hair in a messy bun, wrapped myself in a towel, and hit the shower across the hall.

After a quick rinse off, I padded back to my room and dressed to go to the music fest. I put on jeans and ankle boots, hoisted my boobs into a navy racer-back bra, and slipped on a layered shirt—the bottom was a black camisole covered by red lace.

In front of my small mirror, I ran my fingers through my curls with a little bed-head solution. There was no way it was going to cooperate and lay flat, so I went for the opposite look. I dipped my finger into a few pots of eye shadow and made my eyes look smoky and sensual, and then lined them in black liner before adding a healthy dose of mascara.

Hey, I was from New Jersey, not Kansas.

I grew up on my mom blaring Springsteen and Bon Jovi, and I might be all about equality for women, but in my world . . . this was how women dressed. In fact, in high school, I'd secretly dreamed one of the Jonas Brothers picked me out of millions of girls who asked for any one of them to go to their prom. In reality, I went with Billy Reynolds as friends, but a girl can dream.

Sonny might be forcing me to stay behind the scenes, but I didn't go out much and this was the music fest. It was a big deal in the middle of central Ohio where there was nothing to do, and it was something I could legally go to and have fun. There would be a roped-off area for legal drinkers, but the main drag, College Avenue, would be closed for everyone else to enjoy the music and food.

As a final touch, I spritzed myself with Marc Jacobs Water Perfume, a Christmas gift from Clara. Then I grabbed my backpack purse and went to meet Tess.

As I approached her door, she stepped out in worn and ragged skinny jeans, a tight white long-sleeved T-shirt that emphasized her cleavage, an Army-green jacket left open, and high-topped Chucks. Her hair was a wild blond mane. She looked like Manhattan, which was where she came from, the Upper West Side. Her parents were new money, but she tried to look like sexy grunge.

"Hey, girl! Look at you," she said with pink-glossed lips.

I touched my own lips and realized I forgot lipstick.

"Wait! I have the perfect color for you," Tess said without missing a beat. She opened her door and came back with a tube of fire-engine red lipstick.

"No way!"

"Way," she said, grabbing my cheeks and swiping some on my mouth, coloring perfectly inside the lines.

I peeked inside her door at the mirror and gave her a dirty look. "I look like a Robert Palmer girl from the nineties."

"No, you look hot. Marlboro, New Jersey, hot."

"That's not the look I'm going for. I need Sonny to take me seriously, and I don't want to be thought of as some sex symbol." *Did I?*

"You're perfect. Let's go." Tess grabbed my arm and dragged me to the stairs and out the building.

We hit the chilled air, and I considered a jacket but ditched the idea. I would warm up from moving around and dancing. And maybe I would have a drink. Surely someone would sneak me one.

Tess rambled on about Ryan and his food-truck entrepreneurial spirit, and wasn't he so hot?

But I was only listening with half an ear, worried that I was having a schizophrenic break, which I knew happened to people in their late teens and early twenties. I couldn't stop myself from exploring the possibility that I was cracking up.

My life goal was to be the voice of women's angst everywhere, yet here I was trotting to a music fest dressed like a sex kitten and wanting to drink, dance, and maybe get laid.

Again, that last part I couldn't help, what with my Jersey upbringing and all. It was in the tap water.

But the drinking and the visions of myself dirty dancing? I'd spent the better part of the last five years offended by my mom, disgusted with my sisters, and repressed when it came to my own desires. And why? Because women like Stanwick told us as feminists we should repress our sexuality and focus on being like men.

Who thought about sex more than men?

Me—right now. *What the fuck?*

I smiled to myself. I even swore in my thoughts. I'd bet Blane would laugh at that.

And there I was thinking about him again, the guy I'd run away from earlier in the week.

"Okay, there's Ryan," Tess said. "I gotta run. Come by later."

Apparently I'd missed the entire walk and conversation. We'd made it to the foot of College Avenue where it ran into the other main thoroughfare through campus, and Tess hurried over to a rainbow-painted food truck. The van looked more like the piece of crap in *Scooby-Doo* than a restaurant on wheels.

I closed my eyes tightly for a moment and tried to center myself. I breathed in deeply and let out a long breath, ridding myself of anything sexual before I headed toward the radio station's setup. Sonny was standing behind the DJ tables, earphones cockeyed on his head as he flirted with a gaggle of blond girls. All of them were hanging over the table, purring compliments and taking selfies.

"I'm here," I said as I sneaked up behind him.

"Look who it is . . . my intern. Ladies, if you'll excuse me, I have to put this one to work."

I glared at him. "I think it's time you quit that, Sonny. Seriously."

"It's Mr. Boots to you."

"No, it's not. You're going to respect me as a person."

I wasn't sure if it was the crowd in the distance or just the comfort of the public space that gave me a backbone, but I wasn't letting him bully me anymore.

"What? You put on a red ho top and grow a set?" Sonny peered up at me with blue eyes surrounded by ridiculously long lashes, which complemented his perfectly coiffed bed head. If he weren't such a pig, he'd be cute.

"That too. Cut it out. Now, tell me what to do since I don't have a speaking role."

"Oh, I think you're gonna get on the mic this weekend. This is too rich, this banter. But in the meantime, babe, go flaunt your bad self over by the giveaways table and entice people over. The guys are gonna go nuts for that shirt."

"Why don't you put it on, babe?" I sneered.

"A, because red isn't my color. B, I don't want to attract the guys. And C, you should've shown this fire weeks ago, girl. Stop being such a hermit and come out of your shell. I think you may have a chance."

Speechless, I simply stared at him for a moment.

dolce

Holy shit. A compliment from the shock jock.

I'd been busy for hours. The giveaway table never let up. Music blared from the stage as all the local bands got a turn to play for the audience.

Now that night had totally fallen, Sonny was going on and on about the evening's main act taking the stage. Dirty Soul was a local band that had gone big-time after signing a record deal with a national label. They also had a female lead singer who played the electric violin, Carrie Stanford.

I liked them, and would have wanted to meet them or her. As of yesterday, I wouldn't have asked Sonny. In my newfound assertive state, I was prepping to go over to ask when I heard a deep voice.

"Hey, coffee girl."

I turned to find Ashton Denube standing alongside the table. He was wearing a dark gray Nike T-shirt, filling out every inch of cotton, and low-hanging jeans. His eyes jumped with curiosity as he waited for me to answer him.

"Um, hi!" I said, forcing a bright smile to my face. "You want a prize or something?"

"Nah, just saw you standing here and thought I'd come say hey."

"Catie," I said, reintroducing myself and pointing at my chest like a cavewoman.

"Right, with a *C*."

I laughed. "Yeah, with a *C*. So, you having fun?"

"Nah, this isn't really my kind of music, but the chick from Mean Beans asked me. And I'm a sucker for her. You like them?" He bumped his chin toward the stage.

"I do."

"Your guy is here, getting food. I'm going to send him your way."

"Who?"

"Really?" He chuckled. "Blane, silly girl."

"He's not my guy."

"He might have this crazy bet going on, but you should've seen the jerk when you came on the radio. He kept shushing us all. You're definitely his girl."

I shook my head but didn't get a chance to answer.

Ashton flashed me a peace sign and said, "Check you later, DJ girl." He sauntered back out to the crowd, and I forgot all about asking Sonny to meet Dirty Soul.

And what was with all the *girls*?

"Catie, get over here," Sonny bellowed, interrupting my thoughts. "Come on, I don't have all night."

I held my breath all the way over to his table, fearing the worst. Dirty Soul finished a set right as I made it to Sonny's side, and he took the mic.

"Yo, Hafton, you having fun? Who's pumped? You know I am. Tomorrow's going to be another big day. The women's basketball team is playing a preseason game. Go, Hafton Green!"

A few boos came from the crowd.

"I know, I know. Sonny B. agrees. Men's ball is way more exciting, all those muscles and sweat. Have no fear, those bad boys of the hardwood will be back soon. Also, tomorrow we'll have Pimply Teenager on the main stage at noon, and the homegrown rapper Cool Ray at nine tomorrow night."

Cheers sounded from the audience. Ray was hot. He'd gone to high school in Cleveland and was slowly making it huge. His videos were all over the Internet, his songs topping the charts, and he was about to go on a national tour.

"Dirty Soul's going to come back on tonight for all you alternative junkies, but I got a special treat first. Sweeter than a Krispy Kreme, nicer than a brand-new Lambo, meet Catie P. My girl is a sophomore who wants to take my slot and make all you guys tree-hugging hippies. Let's hear what she has to say for herself."

Sonny shoved the mic in my face. "Come on, Catie, don't be shy!"

"Hey, Hafton!" I called out, working the crowd. "How you guys doing tonight? Sonny's right, I'm vying for his spot. What do you think? Shouldn't they graduate him already?"

The crowd roared and chanted, "Graduate, Sonny!"

I laughed into the mic and heard my voice echo off the buildings all around us. Putting a hand over my left ear to cancel the effect, I held the mic with my right.

"What do you think? It's time for a woman to take over the Hafton airspace. Don't worry yourself silly, it's not going to become a big pajama party. I'm still going to play your music and pump up your barbaric sports teams."

I semi-lied; I needed to keep up my persona.

"We're not barbarians," they shouted back.

"I got you," I said and gave another of my throaty laughs into the mic before Sonny pulled it back.

"All right, gang, kiss Catie good night. She has to get up early and study her feminism. Speaking of females, how tight is Carrie Stanford on that electric violin?"

"Tight," the crowd shouted back.

"Well, she's coming back. Dirty Soul will be back in five. In the meantime, I'm going to change it up for a moment. I got the Hills for you."

Covering the mic, he whispered, "Say something catchy."

"Until Sonny is ousted, this is Catie P.," was what I came up with.

Apparently, the crowd loved it. They started to chant, "Oust Sonny! Oust Sonny!"

"Good one."

Sonny smirked at me before he pushed a lever to make the music louder. The sultry beat tumbled from the speakers as I made my way back to my giveaways table.

"I thought you watched sports," a low voice said in my ear.

A warm hand grasped my shoulder and turned me. Standing behind me—now before me—was Blane Steele.

At the sight of him, my heart raced, my throat tightened, and my neck was only one part of many that went damp. Clearly, another schizophrenic episode.

"I can't tell all my secrets," I quipped.

"You told me, so that must make me special," he said, his green eyes twinkling.

I got a good look at them and his blond eyelashes and eyebrows because he had his hair pushed back with a pink sweatband.

"Guess I fucking walked right into that one," I said. "You should move back a little; Sonny's right there."

I gestured to the sweatband. "What's with the pink all of a sudden? Stanwick getting you to join the class?"

He reached out to touch my mouth, dragging his finger's roughness along my painted lip. "You did fucking walk right into that one, and I know he's right there. He let me back in your inner circle. And no, I'm not going to be joining Stanwick's lectures anytime soon. It's October. Breast cancer awareness month."

"Oh," was all my jock-rattled brain could make out. I squeezed my fist, pinching myself a bit, trying to shock my brain back to reality.

"You sounded good. Glad Sebastian gave you the mic back."

I averted my eyes, trying not to look at his perfect face with the delectable-looking stubble on his cheeks. I rolled my neck, which was actually stiff from staring up more than a foot to meet his eyes. But then I settled my gaze even with his chest. Although it was covered in a Nike Dry-Fit long-sleeved shirt, I could make out every ridge and plane, and my mouth was no longer dry.

"Thanks," I whispered to his pecs.

Blane lifted my chin with the same rough finger that had caressed my lips.

"Hey, you were great!"

I shrugged and changed the subject. "Are you having fun?"

"Now I am."

"God, you are so cheesy sometimes. Are you having fun?" I raised my voice over the music that was blaring around us. "Don't give me some bullshit line. Do you like the band? The food?"

Finally, I got my nerve and my personality back. That was a short mental episode.

"I do. I like their vibe and that chick . . . woman . . . is rocking out. The food was fair. I got the funnel cake for dessert. Now, that was a little slice of heaven that I'll be paying for tomorrow when I'm running up and down the court at practice."

"That's why I don't play soccer anymore. Didn't want to give up funnel cake."

"Soccer, huh?"

"That was a while ago."

"I may have to challenge you to a goal-kicking contest."

"Then I may have to challenge you to a slam-dunk contest."

"Ha!" His shout of laughter punched me in the gut.

Sobering, I asked, "What are we doing here," voicing my thoughts without thinking, but was interrupted.

"Hey, excuse me!" A guy across the table waved a ticket at me. "Can I have one of those CDs? Here's my ticket."

What the hell? Couldn't they see I was confronting a gorgeous man about why the hell he was talking to me?

I took the guy's ticket and handed him a CD that was complimentary for people dumb enough to buy a VIP ticket. You could hear the music anywhere.

Blane quietly waited at the side, watching me work. I'd just turned back to confront him again when he asked, "What time are you done?"

"What's going on, Blane? I thought we discussed this."

"It's cool. What time are you done?"

"Why?"

"Because I want to walk you back to Southern."

"Really?"

"Yeah. I'll buy you a funnel cake if you say yes." His eyes twinkled. "Mmm . . . yummy, gooey funnel cake."

I couldn't resist a smile. "Yes. Now, go."

I went back to my job wondering how I went from brushing Blane off a few nights ago to now letting him walk me home.

Funny what one will do for funnel cake.

chapter twelve

Blane

Mo had invited us over for happy hour before the music fest. He'd opened up a full bar in his kitchen with one of the freshman team managers running it. The season wasn't in full swing yet, and there was nothing wrong with us kicking back a bit before it got going.

Besides, it wasn't like Coach Conley didn't know what went on. He'd been a college player himself before he blew his knee out and ended up coaching rather than playing in the big leagues.

I was downing my Jack and Diet Coke when Mo sat his ass down next to me.

"I'm gonna tell the team next week," he said in a low voice. "She's keeping the baby, and there's no way I wouldn't cop to being a dad. I'll do what's right. But I'm all-in, in case you were worried."

Setting my tumbler down, I clapped him on the shoulder. "Not worried, dude. You're a good man; you'll do right by the team and your lady. By the way, who is it?"

He looked away, mumbling, "That's the tricky part."

"Maurice?" I growled his full name, sensing that what was about to come next wasn't going to sit well with me.

He ran a hand over his short Afro and let out a sigh. "D-man's sister."

"Shit," I said on a long exhale. "He's going to whip your ass."

"I know. I'm ready for it."

"His mom is not gonna play. She's a tough Puerto Rican, no joke. The last time she came to visit, she nearly beat him over his room being a mess. Now you knocked up her baby girl. What is she, a sophomore?"

Mo nodded. "I think we're gonna move in together. If I don't put a ring or some shit on her finger, their dad is gonna go ape-shit."

"No way I want a front-row seat to your sit-down with D. I think I'll leave my apartment for that."

He lowered his head, and I noticed sweat forming on his forehead.

"Listen, man, you're doing what's right," I said. "But you've got to make a real go of it. My dad knocked my mom up and married her, but couldn't give up the side pussy. Now he's alone and driving a rig over half the year. Don't let that be you."

Mo nodded. "Thanks, man." He stood and crossed back to the bar.

Fuck it, I thought, and followed him.

After another drink, we headed out to the festival. Originally, I didn't want to go because I knew she'd be there. Cate. She'd blown me off big-time, and I wasn't accustomed to being brushed off. But fuck that too, because after chatting with Mo, I had a new plan, and the music fest was the perfect place to make it happen.

We hustled over to the food trucks first before winding our way into the crowd. Ashton disappeared to see Ava, and I got caught chatting up every Tom, Dick, and Jeanette. I'd worn my sweatband for the outing, ready for the season to roll, but it had been a mistake. Everyone wanted to see me, not that I could have hidden at six foot four.

When I finally got away from everyone, I caught a quick glimpse of Ash and decided it was the best time to do what I needed to do.

And I did.

Then I went back and enjoyed the party. Cate's voice echoed off the buildings lining College Avenue, and my brain was not the only organ to perk up. Kill me now, but my dick liked the sound of her voice, the throatiness of her laugh, and the ballsy way she spoke. I smiled to myself, happy as fuck to see her stop bowing down to Sonny.

When she was through talking, I went to find her. Sonny let me back behind the table with a wink—I'd already fixed that shit moments earlier—and I was standing right behind my little vixen wrapped in red lace.

I mumbled into her ear, inhaling her citrus scent, and had to refrain from licking her neck. We chatted until our conversation was rudely interrupted by that jerk wanting his freebie CD.

I wanted to yell, "Get the fuck away," but thought better of it. I would be the one walking her home, and that was all that mattered. My game plan was in motion, and if there was one thing about me—I always knew where the X's and O's were supposed to be.

When the music finally died down for the night, I stood waiting to the left of the radio station's area. Leaning against a tree, I called out, "Cate, hurry."

She flashed me an evil look. No, she wasn't to be messed with when it came to work. The thought niggled in my brain, making me squirm a bit, but I pushed it back.

My silence and patience only lasted another five minutes, and then I sneaked up on my prey again.

"Let's go," I said in her ear. She jumped at least a foot, her head colliding with my chin.

"Shit, you scared me!"

Laughing, I grabbed her by the waist and tossed Miss Feminism over my shoulder caveman-style and walked her straight out of the booth.

"Put me down," she yelled, smacking my back. "What about my funnel cake?"

"They shut down, so I owe you one. And I'm not putting you down until we're far enough away that I know you won't go running back to work."

"Blane, I'm heavy. Put me down." Her voice cracked on the *heavy* part, and I did as she asked.

I grabbed her hand and stilled her movement, forcing her to face me. "You're not heavy."

Her dark gaze skittered over our surroundings in the moonlight as she tried to find something to look at other than me. "I am, seriously. And friends don't carry friends."

"This again."

She started to protest, and I only knew one way to shut her up. I glanced around us, taking in where we were—near the quad, halfway between town and the dorms—and dragged Cate to a nearby cluster of trees.

"Cate—"

"Catie," she corrected me.

"Cate, listen, we're friends but with potential for so much more. Stop bulldozing me. You're a closet sports watcher, and I'm a closet feminist."

This made her giggle.

"And stop with this heavy business. You're a woman, as far as I can tell, and women have tits and ass. Many men like that, including myself." Silently, I added, *But I only realized that a few weeks ago when your curvy ass walked into the studio.*

Her eyes got round, and the sight of her pulse fluttering in her neck made me want to sink my teeth in and leave a mark.

"You can't say stuff like that."

"I can and I will," I protested. Or maybe I argued or demanded; I wasn't sure.

"No. I'm not that kind of woman."

I gently pushed her back against the tree and leaned my body into hers. "Caterina, you can be all woman, have wants for yourself, and still have the desire to be desired. I don't think the two have to be mutually exclusive."

I had no clue where this shit was coming from. All of a sudden, I was spewing philosophy and women's rights dogma as if I knew what the hell I was talking about.

I'd spoken to my cousin Gigi the day before, and she'd made me realize my man-whore rep was worse than I suspected. Then she let me know women are prickly creatures. They want to categorize everything.

"Your girl wants to have a big career in helping women realize their potential, and she's all liberated with the swearing. But she's still a girl, and she may not know it, but she wants to be wanted," Gigi had insisted, and some of it must have sunk in.

I pressed my body against Cate, showing her how much she was desired, and a small gasp escaped her lips. I took it as an invitation and kissed her.

When my mouth met hers, there was no stopping myself. I bit down gently on her lower lip to demand entry, and when she parted her lips, my tongue played with hers and my pelvis pressed a bit harder. I was leaning over her petite frame, so I lifted her onto my feet so she could reach me better, and bent to meet her halfway.

"Blane, Blane," broke through my haze.

I stopped immediately, running my palm over her cheek before sliding my fingers into her hair.

"Sorry." I let out a deep breath. "I had to do that, but I'm stopping."

"I don't think we should do that," she said, the words seeming hesitant.

"I dig you, so why not? I've never liked anyone like this before. I get why you don't want to take me seriously, but I mean it. I like you. You're funny, sassy, smart, and sexy as hell. I want to kiss you again."

"We can't. Sonny."

All this time, we'd been in each other's arms. Now I pulled away to settle my palms on her shoulders and stared her down.

"Christ, if I never hear that asshole's name again, it won't be too soon. I'm sick and tired of him. Every time I'm with you, it's all about Sonny."

"I'm just stating the facts." She looked up at me, her eyes a little glassy, reminding me of Gigi when her high school boyfriend ditched her for someone else at the prom.

"I took care of Sebastian. He's going to treat you right, and he's not going to breathe a word about us. I know how to handle him . . . with tickets and girls."

Cate broke free. "You *what*?"

Shit.

"I didn't do anything," I said, backpedaling. "I just took back my life."

Cate glared at me. "Did you really go and talk to Sonny about my internship?"

"I may have mentioned it, but so what? I was protecting you."

"Protecting me?" she shrieked. "Because I'm helpless? Because I'm poor, tiny, fragile-yet-round Caterina?" Her eyes narrowed and her nostrils flared. "I don't need your protection, Blane Steele. Stay the hell away from me, you hear me?"

She turned and ran into the night. For the second time, I stood there gaping, jilted and helpless because of a five-foot-tall stick of dynamite.

chapter thirteen

Catie

Two weeks had passed since I'd run away from Blane for the second time. The very next day, I'd marched right into the music fest and accosted poor Sonny at the DJ table.

"Blane can go fuck himself, you hear me? Whatever he told you, it doesn't matter. I'm my own woman. You hear me?" I'd kept repeating, "You hear me?" until Sonny finally responded.

His blond head had whipped around faster than if the Playboy bunnies had shown up on College Avenue. The stupid guy had been practically salivating.

"Babe, your fire keeps getting better. We're putting you in charge of the mic for thirty minutes tonight. Hell, yeah!"

"Cut it with the *babe* shit," I'd spat back, and then calmed down. "And what's with the change of heart? Last week, you were super pissed when my heat came out over the air, and now you like it. It's because you're listening to Steele."

"No way in hell, babe, huh-uh. You started out all meek and shit to me, let me boss you around. What the fuck? I was confused because I thought you were all 'hear me, I am woman,' and now you're showing me that spunky side. Me likey."

Of course, he'd butchered the expression *I am woman, hear me roar* while throwing up his air quotes.

But I did get the mic that night for thirty minutes, and I even got to introduce Cool Ray. So there was that. But as I did, I'd wondered if Blane was out in the crowd.

The entire night, I went back and forth between thinking of him and chastising myself for taking Clara's advice to be more demure in my job. I had no idea why I listened to her; she'd made a career of husband hunting while working the Chanel makeup counter at Neiman Marcus. In the end, she spent more time chatting with married men buying perfume for their wives . . . or their secretaries.

Now it had actually been fourteen whole days since that night with Blane at the music fest. I wished I could say the Stealer was out of my system, but no such luck. The memory of our short kiss haunted me during the day and drove me crazy in my dreams. It was my choice to flee—I'd accepted that fact—until yesterday, when Sonny offered up the gig for me to DJ on Halloween.

"Really?" I'd exclaimed.

"Yeah, babe."

"Seriously, Sonny, no more babes. You sure this isn't about Steele and his talking with you?"

I had to ask; I wasn't about to let a guy fix things for me. Nope, that was how my mom operated, which is where Clara got the whole meet-a-rich-fucker idea. My dad wasn't enough for my mom. She thought she was worthy of more, so she left him when we were little and began flaunting her Cuban ass all around town.

Sonny interrupted my thoughts. "Not in the way you think, but those dudes got a rager going on in their building. A pre-season Halloween bash, and I'm not missing it."

On Halloween, I made my way to the studio wearing ratty, worn-in jeans, a black sweatshirt thrown over an orange lace camisole (not that anyone would see it), and Snoopy Halloween socks tucked into my Chucks.

Blane had called me sassy and sexy. I almost laughed at the memory. All it took was one look at my ridiculous Halloween getup, and you'd know I was neither sexy nor sassy.

My mind wandered continuously to Blane and what he might or might not be doing. Was he drinking? Was he by himself or did he have a date? Would he listen to me on the air?

Oh. My. God. I was turning into my sisters. My mom would be so proud.

I walked through the studio doors and gave a quick wave to the security guard before I made my way to the booth.

Music had been on autoplay for the last two hours. Sonny had prepped some playlists, but eight o'clock was coming quickly, and it was my time to take over. I'd be on from eight to midnight. Usually, it was *Sonny's Saturday Hookup,* but tonight it was *Saturday Showdown with Catie.* I decided to ask for callers having relationship problems, figuring it would provide for some kind of showdown.

Clearly, I was winging it, seeing as I had zero relationship advice.

I flicked on the light and sat in Sonny's swivel chair. It was so warm back in the booth, I shrugged off my sweatshirt, leaving me in the Halloween spirit in my camisole.

When the last song wound down, I flicked on the mic. "Hey, Hafton, Catie P. here. Remember me? I'm taking over for Sonny tonight. He had something better to do than entertain all of you. Lucky me, I get to trick-or-treat all night on the air with you. In fact, if you call in tonight, you'll be entered to win a treat. The bakery is giving away a dozen doughnuts to a few lucky callers."

I hit Play on the sound-effects board and the soft hum of a bubbly cauldron joined my voice.

"Right now I've got something from the graveyard, the 'Monster Mash.' Who remembers that one? I'll be back in a few with some more spooky tunes, but here's the deal, Hafton. If you and your significant other are having a Halloween tiff, call in. We'll see if we can get to the bottom of it on this special episode of *Showdown with Catie*."

I inhaled deeply while the "Monster Mash" played and grabbed my water bottle out of my bag. Four whole hours alone in the booth. I should have been ecstatic, but instead, I was sullen. I rubbed my hand along my temple, tucking my hair behind my ear as I adjusted my headphones.

"Get it the fuck together," I muttered to myself, and hit the On Air button.

"Who has big Halloween plans tonight? Partying? Trick-or-treating? Or staying in for a romantic night for two? I doubt the last. Well, I'm here for you, playing Halloween hits, taking calls, and giving out doughnuts. One more tune to really get us in the mood." I flicked Play as I switched the mic off, and Michael Jackson's "Thriller" flooded the airwaves.

The lights on the phone flickered, and I blinked my eyes in disbelief. People were actually calling my show.

I took another swig of water and swished it in my mouth before swallowing, then closed my eyes and took a series of deep breaths.

Vincent Price began his monologue at the end of the classic scary song, cueing me that it was nearly over. I shot a hard glance at the Disconnect button, making sure I knew where it was as there was no one at the station to preview callers. If someone got inappropriate, all I had to do was click it.

"Hey, Catie P. here tonight. Who's this?"

"Hi, Catie. My name's Michelle."

"Hi, Michelle, how are you doing this Halloween? Are you dressed up?"

A little sniffle came over the line. "Yes, I'm a cowgirl, a sexy one." Her voice was hoarse and hesitant. "I was supposed to go to the Halloween Hoedown, but my date didn't show."

"You know what, Michelle? I bet you make one heck of a cowgirl, sexy or not, and you should go hit up a different party. Callers? Who's listening that has a wicked party going on? Give me a ring at the studio, and I'll connect you with Michelle."

She giggled. "That's so cute, Catie. You think?"

"I know! Hold on the line while I take the next call, and I'll be back to get your e-mail address so I can send you party details."

With that, I clicked Hold and picked up another call. Loud music pumped over the line in the background.

"Catie?" a guy screamed over the music.

"Yeah?" Somewhat nervous, I hovered my finger over Disconnect.

"Sonny here. Don't ruin my show, babe, while I'm busy knocking freaky boots."

This time I laughed. "Well, if it isn't our fearless leader on the line. Are you having relationship problems, Sonny?" I figured while the cat's away, the mouse would play, and I was going to get out all my zingers.

"Hey, turn that down for a sec," Sonny hollered over the line. "You need a Twitter name, Catie girl! We wanted to tweet you from this party, but we couldn't. Tell the audience that Monday we're starting a contest for the most creative Twitter handle for you!"

Before I could respond, he was gone.

"Oh boy! Looks like I have to get on Twitter, Haftees. While I think about that and chat with Michelle, here's another Halloween hit for you, 'Werewolves of London.'" I gave a wolf howl into the mic and said, "Call me!" I was turning into a regular tease or flirt, or whatever the name was these days.

Letting my breath go, I went to Michelle and wished her well. After I got her e-mail address, I flicked through a few calls. One was a potential party for my girl, and I dashed off an e-mail to her.

The call lights continued to blink, and as the song finished, I picked up another random call.

"Catie, who apparently needs a Twitter name here. Happy Halloweeen," I said, laying it on thick. This was my chance, and I needed to grab it.

"Hey." The voice was deep and hypnotic, and I had to shake my head so hard, my earphones almost came off. I definitely needed a call screener next time I took over the show.

"What can I do for you tonight?" Not asking for the caller's name, I finally squeaked out a question.

"I'm at a party by myself, no date, and I find myself missing someone I wish was here."

"Hmmm, I'm sure there are a lot of people at this party, other friends," I quipped.

"Yeah, but not one in particular."

"Is it a male or a female friend," I asked my caller, pretending to be coy.

"Definitely female." His voice was scratchy and raw, as if he'd been yelling a lot.

"You should reach out to her." Christ, I banged my forehead into the mic and a loud thud echoed through the studio.

"I am."

"Really?"

"Yeah, I'm talking to her right now. Come to my party if you know who this is."

He rattled on but I hung up, disconnecting his call. I quickly hit Play on the deck and Fetty came on.

"Who's going to whip it nae nae tonight?" I heard myself say, announcing the song, but I didn't register the words coming out of my own mouth.

Slouched back in the chair, I took stock of what just happened. Blane Steele called my show and asked me to his party. At least, I thought so.

But I couldn't go, and I didn't. I stayed on the air and gave out a few dozen doughnuts instead.

And signed up for Twitter.

@SonnyB_KnocknBoots:
Welcome @CuteCatieP to Twitter! #Hafton #HaftonNEWS969 #happyhalloween

@HaftonSweetiePie:
Who was that who called @CuteCatieP tonight? I swear it was @BallerSteele #cheater #happyhalloween

@BallerSteele:
Happy Halloween #Hafton! Who's ready to cheer the Green Boys to a 'ship? #dontworryaboutmylovelife

@Hafton101:
Rumor has it that @SonnyB_Knocknboots has gone soft and let @BallerSteele out of the bet. Maybe he's in love? #steelenolongercelibate?

chapter fourteen

Blane

Sunday mornings in the field house had turned into a regular thing for Mo and me. We'd meet there around eight, bust each other up in one-on-one, and hit the gun before eating our weight at the diner.

Sober and clearheaded, but fucked in the head all the same, I made my way to the court on the Sunday after the Halloween party. The air was chilly, and despite living for three years up north, I was cold. I tossed my hood up, pulling the strings tight, thinking maybe it would squeeze some sense into my head.

For Christ's sake—forgive me, Lord—I was a wanted man, and there was no need to get caught up on some little chippie.

But there was. She might be a little sprite in stature, but she was a giant when it came to personality. And curves.

The back door to the field house clanked shut behind me as I made my way to the locker room. Banging my palm into my locker, I threw my bag in, and grabbed a pair of my practice shoes and made my way to the couches to lace them up.

dolce

The TV was on and the place was immaculate with its dark green wooden benches and matching leather couches. The lockers lined up along the wall with a small monitor above each one, flashing our picture and number. The place was obscene, considering I grew up in a trailer park outside Jacksonville.

The good thing was the locker room still smelled fresh and clean with the regular season two weeks away.

"You in here, Steele?" a grumbly, ragged voice called.

"What the fuck, Mo?"

I stared at my teammate and friend in disbelief. His face was a mangled mess. His eye was almost swollen shut, and if his skin wasn't so damn dark, he would have one hell of a shiner.

He slumped down on the couch across from me. "Demetri found out."

"Yeah, I can see that. What the hell? When?" I leaned forward on my knees and waited for him to answer.

"Well, you were all pussified over the radio chick, so it must have been when you slipped out to call her. I went outside to toss some trash, and fucking D sneaked the hell up on me and gave it to me good. Then he said it was over and I better do right by his sister."

"She told him?" I relaxed back into the couch and made myself comfortable, not sure if we were going to play.

Mo nodded. "That's why my voice is all screwed, 'cause she and I got into such a screaming match. Fuck, I'm an idiot. Who the hell gets into a screaming match with a pregnant chick?"

"Woman. I think woman may be more appropriate."

"Shut the fuck up with all your feminist bullshit. Sonny was right . . . you're going soft."

"Listen to who's talking," I shot back.

He laughed. "Don't! It hurts when I squeeze my eye like that."

"Wimp."

"Want me to give you one? Might make you look tough to your fans."

"Please, I took care of Sonny. Told him he'd get an exclusive after we won the 'ship if he laid off the intern and me, let me see if there was something there. Of course, I also suggested he lighten up on her at work, and then like a fool, I accidentally mentioned it to her. So there's no chance now."

Mo smirked at me and then grimaced, reaching up to gently prod at his eye. "You're even worse than me when it comes to the ladies. Didn't they teach you any moves down south?"

I stood. "Shut it. I have plenty of moves; I'm just getting in touch with my Southern gentleman side."

He stood and twisted his torso a few times. "We gonna play?"

"You up for it?"

"Hell yeah."

We wound our way through the locker area and out to the tunnel.

"Hey, did you make up with D's sister? Angela, right?" I asked as we walked toward the hardwood.

"We made up, and I'm doing the right thing."

I slapped him on the back. "Good boy. Now, get ready to lose."

We played thirty-three and then banged out three hundred shots on the gun before breaking for breakfast.

Walking down the hill toward town, Mo said, "So that's pretty big expectations, we got to win the 'ship for Sonny to stay on your good side."

"Yeah, I know. Big mistake."

dolce

"Hey, Hafton, I got your Fighting Green starting lineup ready to go. Let me hear you scream!"

The announcer's voice echoed through the field house as I jogged in place in the tunnel. It was the season's opening night, and we were playing a cupcake of a team—for us—Central Michigan State. It was a non-conference game, and we were favored to win by a lot.

Adrenaline and nerves rushed through my veins. I tugged at the waistband of my dark green uniform and adjusted the sweatband holding my hair back with my mind on one thing. Winning.

"Here they come, put your hands together! At center, six-foot-ten marketing major Demetri Portacalas."

D-man ran out, breaking the banner, and rushed the bench with two cheerleaders shaking their ass all the way with him.

"Coming next, another senior, Alex White, standing tall at six foot five and playing small forward. White's a local guy and an agriculture major."

Alex took his place next to Demetri, both of them jumping up and bumping shoulders in midair.

"Our main man, Mo, Maurice Dawson, a junior taking after his alumni brother, a six-foot-seven power forward."

Mo pumped his fist in the air and kissed both cheerleaders on the cheek before taking his place and bumping shoulders with the others.

"In the back court, point guard Ashton Denube, another junior, six foot four and lethal with his ball handling."

Ash blew kisses to the crowd and flexed his arms like the showman he was, and hugged Coach. Conley hated his antics, but wouldn't show it on the court.

"Annnd, filling out the back court, junior logistics major and advancing the ball every game, six-foot-four Blane Steele."

When I ran out, a pair of ginger cheerleaders latched onto my arms and stopped me at center court. They waved their pom-poms in the air and turned me around for everyone to see before they let me on my way to bump chests with the other four guys on my team.

The scoreboard flashed, music blared—definitely not the song from *Grease* Sonny had suggested before the season—and the crowd roared.

My blood pumped hard. I lived for this moment before the ball went airborne at center court and the action would begin. This was my time, my game, my court, and my championship to win this year. I hadn't risen from nothing not to take what was mine, and I had the best guys to do it with. I was fucking ready; bring it on, Central Michigan. My Fighting Green were hot and on point, and I was pumped to take them there.

D-man got the tip and knocked it to Ash, who passed to me. It was an easy open shot from there. Three–zip, Hafton. We ran back on defense and when Mo blocked a shot, we were back on offense. Ashton brought the ball up, slipping it to me at center court, and from there I drove right to the hoop, finishing with a dunk.

The hoop lit up and the student section started yelling "the Stealer," but there wasn't time to get distracted. I was back on defense in a hurry. We played a man-to-man defense, and no way the guy I was guarding was getting his hands on the rock.

"Hey, Blane! Call me," some ball baby yelled after I blocked a pass and stole the ball.

Chants of "the Stealer" continued to echo in the field house. I tossed the rock back to Ashton, who drove down the court and sent a heated pass to Alex, who hit the backboard with it. Mo was right there waiting for the alley-oop.

We didn't hold the bad guys at zero, but we were up by eighteen at the half when I tossed a towel around my neck and ran toward the tunnel. Little slips of paper rained down over our heads. All phone numbers; ball babies were there for the taking.

Like an idiot, I automatically lifted my head to flash them a smile, and out of the corner of my eye, I caught a familiar curvy figure leaning against the wall in Section 108. Her hips filled her jeans, and her curls hid most of her face. Every part but the smile on her lips, a smile I wanted to kiss the fuck off.

Like I said, I was an idiot.

"Steele, what the fuck is he doing in here?" Coach Conley growled as I burst into the locker room.

"Who?" I yelled back, but my question was answered when my gaze landed on Sonny's face.

"I don't know what kind of antics you two shits are up to now," Coach yelled, "but I'm not in the business of betting on girls or championships. Get the fuck out of my locker room, Sonny. I have a game to win. In fact, I have a shit-ton more to win, so don't ever come back here again!"

"Give me a winner, guys! See you at the after party. Peace out." Sonny flashed two fingers as he shot through the door.

Coach turned his furious gaze on me. "Steele, if you didn't have twelve so far, I'd have your ass. I thought I told you to behave when it came to the fucking radio jock."

"Oh, he is, Coach," Mo offered. "He told Sonny off, and the good little girl—"

"Shut it, Mo," I interjected before he spilled everything. "We're not here to discuss my personal life. We've still got a game to win out there."

Coach nodded. "Right, get your heads out of your asses. We should be up by thirty. Get out there and give them a show, put some points up on the board . . ."

He rambled on some more, spitting and swearing as he slapped his clipboard into the bench and loosened his tie. A few of us dropped trou and put on dry tights while he spoke, me being one of them. I hated wet balls. Nothing pissed me off more than crotch rot in my spandex.

Now fresh as a daisy, I trotted back out to win a game, but not without glancing up to Section 108 and winking at the stunned little missy still leaning against the wall, one foot propped against the cement.

chapter fifteen

Catie

I raced to the library after the game. Actually, I had a paper for Stanwick to finish, but mostly, I wanted to avoid any contact with Blane. Watching him lead the team to victory tonight was one thing; interfering with his game was another.

Plus, there were a million ball babies he could choose from. Blondes and redheads, tall and even taller ones, gorgeous and even more gorgeous girls. He liked me because he thought I didn't like him back, but I was so not his type.

I opened my laptop and clicked on the document in progress. My title was *Maybe Pornography Isn't All Bad?*

Stanwick was going to fail me. I'd decided to write a counter argument to her theories. Not because I got all hot and bothered from watching porn, but after some investigation, I realized pornography or stripping was the only way out for some women. Single moms, women trying to get out of abusive relationships, girls with druggies for parents—the system didn't work for these young women, and working at Mickey D's didn't pay the bills. Taking their clothes off and having sex on camera gave them the notion they were controlling the situation and calling their own shots, and allowed them to pay the bills.

I was in the middle of typing a chapter about the *Casting Couch*, an Internet show, for lack of a better word, where a very convincing man interviews women on their sexual preferences and knowledge of porn, and promises them jobs that pay upward of five thousand dollars. Of course, the dude must sample the goods before sending in the girl's résumé (was that what they called it?), and the two ended up exchanging oral favors and having sex on camera.

It should be noted, I wrote, *I use the term "girls" in the most positive way because the young women on the couch are very much, in fact, young in age and maturity.*

However, I didn't think the couch was one of the better outcomes of the porn industry. It was more a horrible fad, perhaps even a diss to the women making real pornography flicks.

I was banging away at the keyboard, defending my position, when my phone dinged.

Unknown Number: I saw you, closet fan.

I smiled to no one, just my laptop and my lukewarm cup of tea. I didn't intend to answer. I knew who it was, but I went back to my paper.

Unknown Number: What are you doing? We're having a party. You can't keep turning your nose up at my invitations. They're legit. And we don't check IDs.

I spent ten minutes trying to construct a sentence for my paper, but my concentration was broken. All I could think about was Steele in his uniform, his arms glistening from sweat as he winked at me. Finally, I swiped my finger over my phone and hit Reply.

Catie: Great win! Thanks, but I can't come tonight.

Unknown Number: So you know who this is? You at a better party?

Catie: :) No.

I hit Contacts on my phone and added this number under the rightful owner's name, because apparently I was a masochist.

Blane: What are you doing? Studying? It's Thursday; you've studied enough.

Catie: How did you get my number?

I wasn't going to admit I was sitting alone in the library. If I had learned one thing from Grace, it was to never come across as desperate.

Blane: Mr. Boots, of course.

Catie: Stop it.

Blane: You coming? Don't make me come and find you. That's a lot of coming separately.

Catie: I'm not coming. You don't need to come alone and get me. I'm sure your party is packed with willing come-helpers.

I banged my head into the desk. What was I doing? I didn't know how to talk sex in real life, let alone sext.

Catie: Great game, though.

Blane: Don't do that, Cate. Don't shut me out. I'm coming.

Did I answer? No.

He wouldn't find me.

I certainly wasn't falling into that trap or down that hole, or whatever they called the abyss of hot jock boys.

I toggled the phone on Ignore and went back to my analysis of porn with an ache a mile wide in my gut. I wanted to like boys; I really did. Despite my feminist leanings, I craved something more than the lonely existence I had established for myself, but I needed to reevaluate my goals.

I definitely didn't need the campus player.

With that settled, I grabbed my notepad and scratched down some notes for what I wanted to research the next day, and typed the last few sentences of the casting-couch portion of my thesis.

My eyes were tired, and my head hurt from demanding it concentrate on the task at hand. I was taking a sip of my lukewarm tea when I felt the hair lift off my neck and a calloused hand run along my collarbone.

"Found you," a low voice whispered into my ear. "Told you I would come and get you."

I turned slowly and there he was. Green eyes, matching dark green headband keeping his hair out of his face, and low-riding worn-in Levi's with a button fly—yes, I spent a few too many beats staring at that region. It was in my line of sight right now, after all.

"Blane?"

"That's me!" He slapped my laptop closed and shoved it into my bag.

"What if that wasn't saved?" I hissed at him.

"Come on, Cate. You know you're an every-ten-seconds saver. It was saved."

He grabbed my bag and my almost-empty cup of tea and said, "Come on."

"What? No, I can't just go with you."

"You can and you will."

He guided me out of the seat by my elbow, and I went willingly, saying "no" but showing "yes." When I was on my feet, I wrapped my arms in front of my boobs, keeping my stance firm as I raised an eyebrow at him.

"Cate, hon, I'm not going to corrupt you. I'm not going to rape you or even take you back to the heathens occupying my apartment. Now, come on. I won tonight, and I feel like celebrating with you."

I raised my eyebrow even higher.

"Not that kind of celebrate . . . G-rated celebrating."

I tried to stop it, but my frown had a mind of its own.

"Come on," he said in a wheedling tone. "It'll be fun. Stop with all that *he likes me like a buddy shit* in your head. I see it running around under your big head of curls."

"Fine, I'll fucking go," I said.

"There's my foul-mouthed sailor."

Leaning down, he nudged my shoulder with his. Then he draped his arm over me and urged me toward the exit as he tossed my tea in the garbage and then hiked my bag up on his shoulder.

When we came out of the library, there was a dark blue pickup double-parked on the sidewalk.

Blane opened the door. "Your chariot awaits." He slipped in the driver's seat and buckled up. "You can take the boy out of the swamp, but you can't take the trailer park out of the boy."

"I like the truck. I wouldn't expect anything less masculine or chauvinistic."

"Exactly. Stereotype much?"

He put the truck in gear and turned onto College Avenue, and then headed to the main road out of town.

"You good?" he asked, adjusting the heat and tilting the vent toward me.

I nodded. "You?"

I noticed he had a leather jacket on that shifted with his every movement, and I imagined his muscles flexing underneath.

"Am I allowed to ask where we're going?"

"Yeah, but I'm not telling."

"Okay, as long as you still promise not to rape me."

Without warning, Blane whipped to the side of the road and threw the truck into Park on the shoulder. His eyes were wide as he turned to me.

"Cate, I was joking, but I hope you know I would never do something like that. It was a bad joke."

"I know."

"Are you sure?" He stared deep into my eyes as if he was trying to show me the secrets of life.

"Yeah, women throw themselves at you. No need for rape."

When he sucked in a sharp breath and banged his hand into the steering wheel, I said, "Okay, that was a bad joke too."

"Good, so we're clear. I'm a good guy?"

"The jury's still out, but at least we know you don't take advantage of short, chunky girls in the woods."

"Cate," he growled.

"I'll stop," I said, only to shut him up. I didn't think I would survive another minute on the side of the road in close quarters with the man of my dreams. The way the ends of his hair curled up and caught the moonlight hypnotized me.

Yep, this feminist is now an alpha-male basketball junkie.

Blane put the truck back in gear and pulled back in the lane. We continued driving in silence until he turned down a rural road, dark with no street lights, that seemed to lead into a farm.

"Can we be here?"

"Don't worry."

We bounced down the rutted dirt road, passing a pasture and a barn, and finally came to a stop outside a sports court. It looked so out of place, a cement blacktop in the middle of nowhere with a hoop erected on either side.

"What's this?"

Ignoring my question, he said, "Come on," and flung open his door.

I followed suit, my hand shaking a bit on the handle, my heart fluttering even harder. And it wasn't just the thought we were trespassing that made me shiver all over.

Blane opened a trunk positioned at one side of the court and pulled out a basketball and a blanket. He tossed the ball all the way from the other side of the lawn and it whooshed through the hoop, nothing but net. But he didn't go and retrieve the ball that bounced and rolled to the other side of the grass lining the court.

Instead, he came and took my hand to lead me to the center of the court. With a flick of his wrists, he arranged the blanket on the ground and then said, "Sit down."

I did, surprised that the wool blanket kept my butt warm on the cold surface. Or maybe that was just my butt fat.

Blane dropped down behind me, straddling me before pulled me back against his chest. I went willingly, but held my breath.

This kind of stuff didn't happen to me. This was reserved for the movies and pretty girls.

"Nice, right?" he asked, his chest humming against my back.

I felt every syllable float between us. We were so close, I could feel each ripple of his abs. Surely, he felt my body shaking with nerves, my heart beating a frantic pace.

When I gave a small nod, he said, "This is a booster's house, so don't worry."

"Oh," I said softly, not knowing what else to say.

"He lets us come out here, and he knows I keep the blanket."

At that, I tried to pull away. *Keep the blanket*? All too quickly, I realized I was being introduced to the Stealer's Grand Plan of Seduction.

"Stop!" he said, and kissed along my neck. Like a fool, I allowed him access when he was trespassing all my feelings.

"What is all this?"

"The Stealer's Grand Plan of Seduction." When I pulled away from him, he said, "You said it out loud just a few moments ago . . . like when I spoke my thoughts aloud when we first met."

I scrambled to my knees and turned to glare at him.

"No grand plan," he said with a grin, holding his hands in the air in surrender. "I've never brought a woman here."

I gave him the cocked eyebrow again, worried for a moment my eye might stick like that, because that's what my mom would say. *Oh God, did I really just think about my mom right now?*

"Seriously," he said. "I keep the blanket here for me. I usually come out here after important games and look at the sky so I can thank whatever fucking lucky star for looking down on me. Boys don't just get out of the trailer park, Cate. Guys like me don't have the chance to go to school, to finish and get out, and then meet with agents and go pro. It just doesn't happen. It's a frickin' fairy tale, and I can't fucking believe it."

That's when I fell in love with Blane Steele. I'd secretly watched him play last year and had only met him in person at the beginning of this school year, but I was all-in. Hearing him speak about how lucky he was touched something deep inside me.

Of course, the love would have to remain my secret until the day I died, and I would lie to myself in order to keep having moments like this. Any normal woman would know this was a disaster waiting to happen. Boy meets girl, he has fun, she falls for him, and it ends in heartbreak. But I couldn't be bothered right now with that.

"Maybe you're just that talented," I said. "Does it have to be a lucky star?"

"Cate, my mom was a teenage girl knocked up by a truck driver. This shit doesn't happen in my world. We live in a trailer park, where all it takes is a tropical storm to rip our house off the ground."

He pulled me back into his lap again and propped me up against his hard chest, and leaned forward a little to breathe in my scent. My heart stopped for a moment as his lips ran along my neck, sucking, licking, and nipping.

"And you too," he whispered. "I met you, and I thank the fucking stars for that too."

I pinched his leg.

Wrapping his arms around me tighter, he said, "I mean it. I was sitting there at Sonny's, thinking about how I was sick of the meaningless nameless hookups, ready for something else. I didn't know what the fuck else, but something else. And poof, there you were. All swearing and falling and knocking shit over."

I warmed all over at his words. They were so genuine and sincere, I couldn't help but allow myself to believe them. Letting out a little sigh, I relaxed some and leaned back into him.

"I think it's that one." Blane pointed toward the sky at a sparkling star, bright in the midnight-blue sky. "That's the one that brought you to me."

I lifted a hand and pointed it at another star, this one bigger and brighter. "And that's the one that's been watching over you your whole life."

How could a girl not get swept up in this romantic game? With Blane's aftershave stirring my senses, his hard thighs pressed against mine, and his minty breath warming my collarbone? I was doomed.

"What about you?" he asked. "Who looks out for you?"

I smiled, even though he couldn't see my face. "My dad."

"Yeah?" He brushed my hair back and ran his tongue along my earlobe.

"My parents divorced a while back, and I was always closer with my dad. He owns a little Italian bistro, and when I was younger, I wanted to live with him full time. But my mom said no," I said, thinking *I would eat my way into being a cow with him*, "so I stayed with her and my two sisters, who are perfect. And well, I'm me. Flawed."

"I don't know about flawed, but definitely huggable." Blane flipped me, tackling me to the ground, and squeezed me tight.

Squeals pierced the dark night, and it took me a moment to

realize with surprise that they were mine.

I wanted him to kiss me, to place one of those delicious swipes of his tongue on my lips like he had my neck, but he didn't. He just grinned as he tickled me silly and then walked us back to the car, his arm around my shoulders.

My head bumped against his solid chest as we walked. I wanted so badly to stop and turn to him for a kiss, but I didn't. I took what I could get from the man, and if it was only kisses on the neck, then so be it.

chapter
sixteen

Blane

"Hey, Hafton! Sonny B. here, taking over the daytime airwaves this Friday in gray and dreary Ohio. Let's see if I can brighten up your day. Phish is in town tonight, and guess who's going? That's right, yours truly will be knocking boots before, during, and after. Oh, did I just get naughty on the air? I did. Lucky me, I get to take four lucky listeners with me tonight. Let's play a little Truth or Dare, or just dare, shall we? How about I play Phish's 'Sample in a Jar' and when I come back, we'll announce our first dare."

"Turn this fucking shit off," Ashton called from the sinks in the locker room after practice. "I can't listen to that white boy's trustafarian hippie wannabe music."

"No way," Demetri hollered back. "Bet you a hundred bucks DJ boy is going to dare something here about our man or his princess."

Shit.

Coach had put us through a grueling practice on that Thursday; he wasn't happy with us, and we would feel it later. We weren't *hungry enough* and *taking too much shit for granted*, he'd said, and he was right. We were acting like fools, he'd said.

I knew he mostly meant me, especially when he leaned into the locker room and called me into his office.

"Yes, Coach?" I took a seat in the plush leather chair across from him, my mind elsewhere, mostly on what kind of dare that fucker Sonny was going to come up with.

Coach Conley frowned as he looked at me for a moment. "Steele, you know I'm in your corner. Admire you for what you did last year; not many kids would stay and finish their degree when the pros come calling. I get that it's important, but this year you're acting like a royal ass. What the hell is going on with the DJ? In our locker room, acting like he's part of the coaching staff? He's been looking for a way in for years, hounding my guys." Coach leaned his elbows on the desk and stared me down. "Christ, he used to make Jamel insane with bribes and deals just to get inside my domain."

I focused on his shiny gray hair, not wanting to meet his eyes. One day, I hoped to coach. There was nothing that I loved more than ball. If I wasn't playing it, I wanted to be rolling in it.

"I know, he's gone a bit crazy—Sonny, I mean. But I got it under control," I lied as the hallway erupted with shouts outside Coach's office.

"Oh no, he did not just do that!"

"Shit, that man has brass balls."

Coach stood and went to the door, propping it open with his elbow as he yelled, "Care to enlighten me?"

"Um, sorry to interrupt," Ashton said contritely, his eyes twinkling as he faked an apology. He should have been an actor instead of a ballplayer.

"And now you did, so spill it."

"It's Sonny. He just offered up a pair of Phish tickets to the first dude to get his intern to go on a date with him."

"So?" Coach demanded. "What the hell does that have to do with you?"

I ran my hand over my head and tugged hard on my hair, fearing I was going to pull out every hair on my head. Fucking Ashton, he was going to go into all of it. I knew it.

"That's Steele's lady. He likes her. She's at the bottom of this mess with Sonny, sir."

Sir? What a fucking actor.

Coach turned toward me. "What the hell is this? I called you in to get to the bottom of what I was hearing about you promising a 'ship to Sonny so he'd allow you to get laid again. He told me you needed to get back on *your horse again*. His stupid words, not mine. But you really want to hit on his intern?"

Ashton tried to quickly pass by the office, but Coach caught him by the shirt and pulled him in. I gave him an evil eye and mouthed, *I am going to fuck Ava.*

I wasn't, but let him think that.

"Well?" Coach shut the door, and now it was the three of us.

"Don't shoot the messenger." Ashton batted his long eyelashes and ran his hand over his recently shaven head.

"Steele?" Coach looked at me.

"Sonny has this intern," I said. "Cate . . . Catie P., and I met her when he threw down the original bet. He was making her do all this ridiculous crap for her job, and I called him on it. That's why he called me a feminist. I just defended her and he went crazy. Turns out, she's pretty fun . . . and a women's studies major. Ironic, huh?"

"And sexy," Ashton interrupted. "All woman, Coach, if you know what I mean."

"Okay, that's enough from you, Denube," Coach growled and redirected his laser focus on me. "So, this intern? You're hooking up with her or what?"

"Steele wants to date her," Ashton offered helpfully. "So, he promised Sonny the 'ship and full access to the team if he lifted the no-girls ban. And now get this, the intern doesn't want Steele back!"

Coach reached out and opened the door. "Okay, you can leave, Denube."

With the door closed again—and I was more than certain, Ashton's ear pinned to the wood on the other side—Coach said to me, "I'll be damned. Steele likes a woman."

I nodded like a chump.

"Not going to work this time. First, she's a women's libber—they don't like the athletes. And second, we don't promise championships to anyone. We work for them, so get the hell back into practice tomorrow and be the captain of this damn team like you're supposed to be, and make these guys work for it. Forget the fucking girl for now. You hear me?"

I nodded again.

"Okay, get out of here," he said, dismissing me.

As I walked toward the Union Building to get some lunch, thoughts whirled in my mind like drinks flying on spring break in Daytona. I liked a girl. A woman. A chick. A young lady. Whatever. I liked Cate.

Talking to her grounded me, which was good, because at the moment I needed grounding. I'd turned down a shit-ton of interest from the pros the year before to stay in school, to finish my last few credits and graduate. Was it worth it? I didn't fucking know. At the end of the day, I was going to play ball. It's all I wanted to do.

And now I wanted to be with Cate, but that wasn't going to be so easy. First of all, I didn't even know how I wanted to be with her, and second, there was Coach and what he just laid down.

The dare came back to mind, so I turned toward the radio station instead of the student union. I burst through the front doors and made my way toward the studio and banged on the door. Not waiting for an answer, I walked right in, into a zone defense all by myself.

Another bullshit Phish melody had just ended, and Sonny was making love to his mic when he saw me.

"Oh, looks like we poked the bear, Hafton. I wouldn't have believed it myself unless I saw it with my own eyes, which I'm doing right now. The Stealer just stormed into my booth, eyes blazing. I guess he heard my latest dare. Did you know Mr. Steele has a thing for our intern? He's our Catie P.'s protector and, perhaps, suitor?" He raised an eyebrow at me, challenging me.

Asshole.

"Okay, Haftees, let's do something about this little challenge in front of me. Last pair of tickets is up for grabs for the first girl to get *The Stealer* tattooed on her body."

I slammed my hand onto the table, shaking the equipment, and imagined it was my fist making contact with Sonny's pretty-boy face.

"If your little honey, Hafton's 96.9's own Catie, is the first to mark her body with your name, we know it's meant to be, Steele. It's only a matter of time!"

Sonny shoved the mic back in its holder and hit Play, sending some awful music blaring into my ears, and I turned to leave. I couldn't even talk to the jerk.

His challenges and dares were giving me whiplash. First it was *don't fuck around*, then he messed with my intern, goading everyone on campus to ask her out, and now ball babies were going to be running around with my name tattooed on their bodies.

When my mom named me Blane Steele, I was pretty sure she thought I was going to be a porn star. Thank fuck, shaking my junk wasn't my big break out; playing ball was.

Although the thought of having a bunch of women running around with my name inked on their skin made me feel like I was some kind of gigolo, a role I didn't have to be.

At least, not anymore.

chapter seventeen

Catie

"Caterina?" Stanwick called my name with disdain. "Please stay after class."

Stanwick waited for me at the bottom of the steps, her hair scraped back in a severe bun, her stance stiff and off-putting, a smirk on her lips.

"Yes?" I clenched my hands, stilling their shaking.

She towered over me in her pumps, and I found myself wishing for height for the millionth time.

"Caterina, I need to reconsider having you in this class."

"If it's the paper, I plan to document my stance even further. I'm just trying to see their choice to go into pornography from their side. The girls—"

She stepped toward me and whispered, "It's not that, Caterina. Although I do find the whole premise despicable. It's this job you have at the radio, and the consorting you're doing with the shock jock and the basketball player."

I swallowed my self-disdain for liking boys. "What?"

"Do you live in a bubble? Even I heard the incorrigible Sonny Be Knocking Boots this morning." She said his name on a snarl, her teeth biting off each syllable.

"Um, no, but I don't know what you're talking about."

"Walk with me, Caterina, to the window." She motioned to the large window at the opposite side of the room.

We made our way over to the window. Through the small panes, I saw men, lots of them, standing and waiting. Some held up signs with slogans like Go out with me, Catie P. or Pick me, Catie P. I especially liked Go Phishing for a real man, Catie P.

"I don't know what this is all about," I admitted to Stanwick.

"This morning, Sonny B. promised a pair of Phish tickets to the first guy to get you to go on a date." She raised a perfectly plucked eyebrow at me and waited for me to explain.

"Oh," I said, feeling like a thousand-ton elephant was sitting on my chest.

"You don't see how disgusting this is? To set you up with the highest bidder, a man—any man—who is just in it for a contest? That is morally degrading and an embarrassment to this department. I thought I could let it go after your lackluster night of dating advice on Halloween, but now this."

"It's radio," I said weakly. "They need ratings."

"Then does it make you happy to know that right now, dozens of college girls are running around town looking for an open tattoo parlor?"

"What? I have no idea where this is going, Professor Stanwick."

"During class, I received a text from another student alerting me to Sonny's second dare of the day. The first young lady to get a tattoo reading *The Stealer* gets a pair of tickets to the Phish concert."

"Phish?"

"This isn't about Phish, Caterina. It's about you disgracing the entire female gender with your sorority-girl antics, your ball-baby tendencies."

Surprised, I gasped.

"What?" she snapped out, pulling herself up a little taller. "You think I don't know the lingo, that I live in a bubble? Why do you think I teach in this department and have spent my life making it a nurturing and fair place for women? I don't think I can permit this type of behavior from someone in my class."

"But I didn't do anything, Professor Stanwick," I said, desperate to plead my case. "You can't blame me for Sonny's actions."

I wanted to stomp my foot and swear up a holy mess, but I knew better than to show my hot-headed temper at this moment.

Stanwick narrowed her gaze on me. "You are consorting with the enemy. Don't think I don't know it. You are dismissed to go change your paper's thesis and clean up your associations. Otherwise, you will force me to take necessary action."

I walked out without another word, dragging myself and my foul mood out of the building. I forgot the barrage of bachelors waiting for me, and as soon as I exited the door, I was bombarded with shouted invites.

Tucking my chin to my chest, I whispered, "Excuse me," and tried to escape.

"Catie, come on! One night, one concert!"

"Look at me, Catie!"

Fucking Sonny. He'd incited a riot, and was probably sitting in his booth watching through some sick fuck's Facetime feed, plotting like President Snow in *The Hunger Games.*

"Get the hell out of my way," I said a bit louder, and took off toward Southern A.

I walked quickly, practically running until I stormed through the door to my dorm. When someone called my name from the couches in the common area just inside the door, I paused to see Tess coming toward me.

Ugh. "Hey, Tess, what's up?"

"Someone's waiting for you in my room!"

"Oh God, Tess," I whined. "You didn't let one of those freaks inside, did you? Tell me you're not so desperate."

"You mean the nuts trying to win the Phish tickets?" Shelby strode over to stand next to Tess. She had a smile so broad, I thought her face was going to crack.

I shrugged. "Yeah, I guess this thing's got a bit crazy. Sonny from the station did some stupid dare. You didn't let those people in?"

The last part came out low and angry, a deep bellow from somewhere in my chest. It was part Italian stallion, another part Castro. I was livid, not to mention I was about to be thrown out of my major because of Sonny.

"No, not those freaks," Tess said, beaming. "A good kind of freak. A really tall freak." She started to bounce up and down like she had to pee, becoming more and more excited as she spoke.

"Are you okay?" I reached out to steady her from what looked like a mild seizure.

"A tall freak, Catie! Did you hear me?"

"Fuck." I grabbed my forehead. "The tall part escaped me the first time."

"Come on." Shelby grabbed my shoulder and spun me toward the stairs.

I barely knew her; she lived next to Tess and would sometimes eat with us. Now her long red hair blew back into my face as she dragged me to meet a tall freak.

Why couldn't I go back to being a lonely short freak?

Tess unlocked her door, and Shelby gave me a quick shove inside the poster-decorated dorm room.

Who is that? I thought, overwhelmed by the oversized male faces staring at me from her walls. *Edward? Or Jacob?*

"Cate?"

I shook my head free of my inner musings about *Twilight* and focused on the tall man in front of me.

Tight black skinny sweats hugged Blane's legs, and a dark green T-shirt clung to his chest. His hair was wild, as if he'd been running his hands through it. He held a hand over his chest and worried his lower lip while he waited for me to look up into his eyes. When I did, I found worry and confusion.

"So you heard?"

He nodded. "Stupid Sonny."

Tilting my head at him, I narrowed my eyes. "You wound him up him even more when you tried to get out of your bet. Because of me."

He stepped closer, still rubbing his chest, and laughed. "I got him this time, though."

"What now? You can't fix this for me, tough guy." When I jabbed him in the chest, he yelped. "Oh, don't be such a baby!"

"I'm not. I don't have a lot of time to explain, but we have to get into town real quick."

"Why? I can't go out there. These asses are following me around, asking me on a date so they can see Phish! *Phish!*"

I burst out laughing and started to pull off my winter coat, which I only just realized I was still wearing, and truth be told, had worn all day. I'd stayed bundled in my down coat of armor for hours.

"Leave it on," Blane insisted. "We have to go."

"Would you stop! Where the hell do you want to go?"

"Never mind, but you may want to change into something more comfortable first."

"Stop, Blane. What the hell is going on? I can't hang with you. I'm about to lose my feminist card, and I have to go fix this with Sonny." I looked down at my jeans and sweatshirt. "And what's wrong with my clothes?"

How dare Stanwick question my feminist tendencies? I was in the middle of telling a dude off for trying to tell me how to dress. *Take that!*

"We're going to fix this Sonny thing. Look."

Blane whipped off his shirt, and I would have been drooling over or licking his chiseled abs if my eyes weren't squinting at the script tattoo under his right pec that read, *Cate with a C.*

"Oh my fucking God, are you nuts? Have you gone crazy?"

He grinned at me. "No, consider this me asking you on a date to go get a tattoo, and I consider my taking your arm your way of saying yes. Call Sonny, because winner, winner, chicken dinner, I won the tickets. It's only fair you get a tattoo too, and now you can get *The Stealer* tattoo and get more tickets."

"Did you not hear me? What's wrong with you?" Not waiting for his answer, I sat down on Tess's bed. "I think I'm going to faint."

He sat next to me and ran his palm up and down my back. "Cate, it's no big deal. It's a tattoo. It's a dare. Let's go. We can have fun."

Squeezing my eyes shut, I breathed deeply. "Steele, I can't get a tattoo with your nickname. Forget the fact that I don't have any ink—"

"Why is that?"

Blane was still rubbing my back as he interrupted me. I felt myself melting with every gentle stroke along my spine.

"Look at my shoulder." He bent lower to show me a tattoo of a big bird with its wings spread. "It doesn't hurt."

"No offense, but you have the kind of body that lends itself to removing your shirt."

He tackled me to the bed, keeping me pinned in place as he spoke into my ear. "Now I'm issuing my own dare, my fair lady. We're going for the tat, and before I was going to suggest you get it on your wrist, but now it's your back. Your gorgeous back that I'll get to see naked."

I didn't get a chance to answer because Tess and Shelby came stumbling through the door, "Let's go, Catie! Tattoo time."

My eyes flew open wide as I gaped at them. "Have you been listening all this time?"

"Damn right," Tess said with an unapologetic grin. "The nun of Southern A is in my dorm with the Stealer, so I'm listening."

Before I could utter a word about Sonny, or Stanwick and my degree being in jeopardy, I was shoved into a big hooded sweatshirt and escorted downstairs.

chapter eighteen

Catie

We tumbled through some random door on College Avenue, the chimes ringing weakly beneath the heavy metal thundering from the speakers. My head throbbed, but not nearly as hard as my heart pounded. My hand was in Blane's, and we were *on a date.*

Not really.

In reality, it was a ridiculous dare—just a contest—but my naive heart didn't know that. I was pulled tight to Blane, my body plastered against his, and in my mind, this was a date.

Which was why I'd permitted him to drag me all the way to a tattoo parlor and was about to permanently mark my body with his nickname. All of a sudden, I was a young girl trapped in a woman's body, and he was a teen heartthrob.

A muscular dude covered in tats seemed delighted to see us. "Steele, great! You're here. I've been telling girl after girl we're closed. Couldn't put off business that much longer." Turning his grin toward Tess, Shelby, and me, he asked, "Which one of you is the woman of the hour?"

I stood there quietly, hoping Shelby would offer up her body. This guy looked like he knew what to do with it.

"This one." Blane shocked me when he tossed me over his shoulder and carried me to the back.

"There are a million Italian women wagging their wooden spoons in your face right now. We don't do cavemen," I yelled, upside down and thrashing.

"Well, I do," he shot back.

"Should we come?" Tess and Shelby's combined voices carried down the hall.

"No!" Blane and I shouted at the same time. Finally, we were on the same page.

In the back room, Blane set me down on my feet, still grinning as I glared up at him.

Getting himself comfortable at the tattoo table, the big guy said, "I'm Colby. You can thank me later for turning all the other chicks down. Pick your poison." He tossed a few CDs toward me.

"I guess you don't have any Tori Amos?"

"No," Colby said and went back to his tools.

A soft hum startled me.

"Don't worry, I'm gonna be quick," he added under his breath. "Don't say that too much to the ladies."

As Colby laughed at his own joke, Blane took the CDs from my hand and picked out some Enya.

Soon "Enigma" filled the room, and Blane slipped his hand under my shirt and drew circle eights on my back. "Ready?"

For what? Sex?

How could he be so sexual in this moment?

"This is just a dare, you know." I studied his boyish features, so incongruous atop his huge frame, trying to use my brains rather than my emotions.

"It is and it isn't, but let's do it anyway," Blane said. His fingers ran up and down my spine, causing goose bumps to pop out along their path. "At the end of the day, I'm always about winning."

"So this is about Sonny." My heart beat faster as I watched Colby practice writing *The Stealer* in script.

"No, Cate. It's about you. Don't think for a second it's about anything else. You think you aren't desirable, but I disagree. I'm winning you." Blane gripped my shoulder and pulled me close, dipping his face into my hair as he breathed me in.

How many times had I told this cat to scat? Now he was being all tender and loving, as if I left milk out every night for him to lap up.

I scanned the room, checking for hidden cameras. This must be some type of prank they were going to upload to YouTube later. *Feminist goes gaga for the jock.*

"Take your shirt off, Cate."

And like a victim of Stockholm Syndrome, I did. Laid on my stomach on the table, with my boobs smashed painfully beneath me and Blane Steele rubbing my shoulders, I got my first tattoo. *The Stealer*, scrolled across my left shoulder.

Of course, Colby did the honors, snapping a pic on his iPhone and tweeting it to @SonnyB_KnocknBoots as fast as he could before I snapped back to reality.

"We should turn on the radio," Colby said as I tried to pay him, shoving some cash his way. He waved me off. "On the house."

"No radio," I countered.

Colby shrugged. "Fine by me."

Blane grabbed my hand and pulled me out to the front room where Tess and Shelby were waiting. Impatient, they pawed at my sweatshirt, trying to pull down the shoulder and get a glimpse of my tat.

At the sight of my sour face, Blane grinned. "Come on, Cate, you have to have some fun in life. Right?"

This from the guy who knew he was going to make millions next year. I, on the other hand, was going to have to look for a new job tomorrow. And a new major.

Blane's phone beeped, and he pulled it from his pocket.

"Hey, what are you doing?" I asked.

He shoved his phone in my face. "We're making headlines. Look."

@Hafton101:
Rumor has it that @CuteCatieP is the winner of the Phish tickets?!?! Doesn't she work for the station?

@HaftonSweetiePie:
I got one too @CuteCatieP, and mine is better.

A picture of a "The Stealer" tattoo was embedded with the tweet. *Oh God. I hope Stanwick isn't on Twitter.*

chapter
nineteen

Catie

Convinced I'd been roofied, I found myself at a party at Alex White's place two days later. I was wearing black leggings tucked into my boots and a deep burgundy off-the-shoulder long-sleeved tee with a chocolate-brown cami underneath. The shirt was baggy enough to hide a few of my extra curves but kept slipping off my shoulder, revealing my most recent lapse in judgment.

"Damn, girl . . . he wasn't lying!" and "You did it!" and "Look at that fresh tat!" were the most overheard comments of the evening. I cursed my love of off-the-shoulder clothing, blaming New Jersey and Sarah Jessica Parker. It might be an oldie, but we grew up on a steady diet of the movie, *Girls Just Want to Have Fun*.

Music blared all around me. A DJ spun tunes, and a makeshift dance floor had been erected in the living space. The team was on a high; they'd won their second non-conference game by forty-two points.

Blane's larger-than-life personality ruled the room.

"Cream puffs," Mo called out. "Nothing but a bunch of babies."

"Damn straight," Blane yelled back. "Loser cream puffs!"

"Go, Green!" Alex chimed in as he headed toward me.

"So, you're the little girl causing all the commotion," he said, knocking his chin in my direction. His dreads were pulled back in a ponytail, and he was holding a bottle of beer that looked small in his huge hand.

"Be nice," Blane growled. "I'm the one passing you the ball."

"Shut the fuck up, Steele," Alex shot back, "and let me say hello to DJ girl."

"Hey, DJ girl is my nickname for her."

Someone came up behind me and ground their pelvis against my hip. I jumped forward and nearly knocked the beer out of Alex's grip. Twirling around, I found Ashton standing there, smiling as if he'd just won the lottery.

"Watch it, basketball boy," I said, tossing his own barb back at him.

"Ooh, her claws come out." Alex slapped Blane five, and they laughed like wild hyenas.

"Move out of my way," Mo shouted over the chaos. He lifted me and spun me around. "Hello there, pretty lady."

"No. Just no." Blane shook his head at Mo.

Demetri, the most enormous of them all, growled his agreement. "Definitely no."

"I hear you!" Mo held his hands up in the air and backed off. "Look, I'm behaving."

I turned to look at Blane, and he mouthed *later*. I guessed he meant there was a story there.

"So these are the guys—Alex, D, Mo—and I hear you met Ashton," Blane muttered, pointing at each as he said their name.

I recognized them all from my season of clandestine basketball watching. Now I was in the middle of their party, all of them gathered around my less-than-perfect body and chatting me up as if I were a good friend.

This was not my life.

"Now if y'all will move along." Blane took my hand and led the way until we settled near the far side of the dance floor.

We'd never collected our Phish tickets, and I'd ignored every text from Sonny. I forced myself not to think of my internship or Stanwick. Apparently, I didn't want little things like my job or my major to get in the way of my new groupie status. In the span of a mere forty-eight hours, I'd apparently lost all direction in my life.

"Take it easy, man," Blane said to a freshman rookie, a tall, lanky black guy getting hammered on Crown Royal. "We have another game on Tuesday. I know you think you're not playing, but you never know."

When "The Freaks Come out at Night" rocked the speakers, Blane grabbed my hips and jostled me around playfully. Then he snatched my Diet Coke and tossed it in the garbage before dragging me out to the makeshift dance floor.

As he slowly ground against me, I squeezed my legs together, trying to dispel the tingles forming at the juncture of my thighs. Seriously, I was going to get pregnant from him this close to me, shaking his hips. When he lifted his arms, his shirt rose enough to expose the V formed by perfectly toned stomach muscles.

I ducked my head and stared at my boots, hiding my smile, and checked to make sure there were no wet spots on my pants—and not from peeing.

Blane lifted my chin with his finger, and I had to tilt my head all the way for my gaze to meet with his eyes. At best, the top of my head was even with his chest.

Let's dance, he mouthed.

"Now you ask? After you already pulled me out here?" I stood on my tiptoes so I could reach his ear.

He snatched me up close and lifted me even with his face.

"Put me down!"

"Admit you can dance. You're part Cuban, right? So, show me some moves," he said as he slid me down his body, back to the floor.

Looking up at him, I knew I had to keep my feet on the floor, my heart in check, and my head in the real world, not in this fantasy I was building. But I could do that in a few minutes.

For now, I pushed my hands into my hair and lifted it off my neck, trying to flip it seductively like I saw once on TV. Then I shook my ass and let it all go, closing my eyes and pretending I was standing on my bed, all by myself with no one watching.

The freaks do come out at night.

After a few more songs, Blane led me back to his apartment. It was only a few doors down the hall, but it wasn't close enough. My heart beat a rapid pace, and the very tips of my fingers and toes tingled. I was a lovesick schoolgirl when it came to the Stealer, and at the moment, I couldn't bring myself to care.

He'd stolen me.

"It will be quiet in here," he mumbled as he squeezed my hand.

That's what I'm scared of.

I didn't mention that, though.

When we entered the darkened hallway of his apartment, he flicked on the light near the kitchen. Soft light flooded the common area, and I made out an obscenely large television and a bunch of gaming consoles and controllers.

"Do you want something?"

I shook my head, my feet practically planted in the cheap linoleum.

"Come here." He wrapped his arm around me and pulled me close. "You good? I don't want you to second-guess this." He ran his hand up and down my back, his palm so warm it almost singed my skin through my shirt and camisole.

"I'm okay." The words floated from my lips on a whisper.

He leaned down and brushed his lips across mine, his hardness pressing into my abdomen. I opened my mouth to protest—my abs weren't firm and I didn't want him to notice—but I couldn't get a word out. When my lips parted, Blane took that as an invitation for his tongue to enter my mouth. He swept along my lower lip and sought the roof of my mouth, enticing my tongue to come out and play.

The smallest moan started in my chest and rose all the way up to mingle with our kiss. Blane tightened the hand on my back in response, bringing me closer as his other hand pushed into my hair, gathering it and pulling it behind my neck.

"Oh God, Cate, I've been wanting to do that for a long fucking time." He released his hold on my mouth to let his words out on a hurried breath.

He didn't let go of my hair, and kept his gaze focused on mine as he spoke. Then he tilted my head back and grazed my neck with his teeth. My skin prickled under his touch, an intoxicating mixture of gentle and rough, and I ground myself against his leg, no longer caring about my too-soft abs. I wanted this man—somehow, some way, any way.

The way I'd felt hot and bothered during the porno was a faint memory, and nothing compared to this. At the moment, I felt sexy in my own right. Here I was, a sensuous woman with desires and needs and wants, turned on by a man.

"You make me so hot, Cate." He took my hand and grazed it over his crotch. "Feel that? I've been like that since I saw you in that coffee shop. Fucking weeks aching for you."

Gazing up at him, I whispered, "You don't have to say anything swoony, or whatever you usually say with all the girls."

"No, don't ruin this moment with that bullshit. I like the way you challenge me, take me on. Don't waste any breath on bullshit."

I leaned back up on tiptoes and kissed Blane. It was the first time I'd initiated any kind of kiss. In all my life, I'd been reactive rather than proactive when it came to intimacy. My fiery temperament only came to life when I was verbally warring with someone.

With my hand lingering on his hip, I gave it permission to roam over his ass. He groaned when I squeezed.

"Take what you want," he said into my mouth.

I climbed his leg and locked my hands around his neck, but the height difference didn't give me enough leverage.

Leave it to Blane; he scooped me up. I instinctively wrapped my legs around his middle, and he set me on the counter behind me. With my butt on the very edge, Blane was able to fit between my legs, rubbing his crotch against mine to apply just the right amount of pressure to elicit another moan from me.

A wave of vertigo washed over me as his erection made contact with my leggings. His button fly rubbed against the spot—the one my own finger found from time to time. Except when I touched it skin to skin, I didn't get anywhere close to the sensation I was reeling with right now, even through denim and cotton.

We were still kissing, Blane breathing out and me breathing in. He pulled away and sucked on my lower lip before moving to my neck and planting those little bites, like the other night on the court. My head lolled left and his mouth made contact with my right clavicle, devouring it with kisses and nips. With no thought from me, my hips surged forward and moved from side to side, grinding my clitoris into oblivion.

Whoever said sex is like riding a bike was wrong. I rode a bike, and when I got on, I always had to reacquaint myself with the whole process. But this, this precursor to what I hoped would be sex, this I'd never done. It made no difference; I knew what I was doing right away.

My pelvis surged forward and sought what it wanted. *Blane's penis.* His very hard and what I presumed to be big dick.

"I want to spread you out on this counter, but let's save that for another time," Blake whispered into my ear.

He could have said, "I like peas and carrots," for all it mattered. The mere sound of his voice automatically kicked up my libido.

Blane picked me up again and my legs went around his waist again, keeping the contact as he carried me straight to his bed. I didn't even have time to protest.

Once he'd spread me out before him, Blane caressed me with his eyes. I'd never felt more exposed, and I was still fully dressed. Like some sort of tiger, he pounced next to me and pulled me against him, and our mouths met again. This time, I attacked his lips and tongue like a tigress, and growls came from my male counterpart. I slipped my hand inside his T-shirt to his shoulder and hoisted myself a little higher.

"Shhh, slow it down, Cate. I can't go as far as I would like tonight."

"Why?" I whimpered like Jenna Jameson in one of her original bad pornos.

"Haven't you heard me? I like you. You do it for me." His hair flopped into his face and he shoved it back behind his ear. He stayed leaning over me, propped on his elbow to hold his weight.

I turned and tried to hide.

"No hiding, Cate."

He leaned over and gave me a closed-mouth kiss, taking his time, allowing his palm to trace its way up my skin. He broke free again and took off my shirt, and nerves shot through me. I tried to roll and twist, to cover myself. In my mind, I wanted sex—but with clothes on.

"Huh-uh, none of that either," Blane said softly.

He reached back and pulled his shirt off and was back on me in a second. Skin to skin, he tugged on my ear with his teeth and ran his palm over my bra and sides, down to my waist and back.

"You're beautiful," he murmured, and I blushed. "Sorry about the calluses; occupational hazard for me."

"Feels good," I mumbled back.

"Let go of those negative thoughts I feel tumbling through you," he said, lifting up and looking deep into my eyes. "Seriously, Cate, your heart is banging too hard and your pulse is racing with negativity. This isn't stressful; it's all good. Me, you, and no shirts."

I felt my grin grow wide, and I didn't even turn my face.

"I've wanted this for a while, a long while," he said, and began kissing me again.

My hand trembled as it finally landed on his bare back. It roamed all over his hard muscles, my nails lightly scratching his smooth skin.

"Harder," he said on a moan, and I obliged.

I felt him slide my bra strap down, and his hand caressed my tattoo. It made me glance at his chest, and when I saw my name, nerves sprouted like weeds all over again.

My name is on his chest.

I couldn't think on it for long because suddenly my bra was off and my nipple was in Blane's mouth, and my pelvis was rocketing off the bed.

"Oh my God," I think I said. I couldn't be totally sure, but it sounded something like that.

As he sucked and licked and nipped, I moaned, loud moans I didn't think I was capable of making. *Porno-worthy moans.* I rolled my eyes at myself, but I couldn't stop the moans if I tried.

His fingers wrapped behind my head and tangled in my curls. He held me close, his thumb leisurely grazing the nape of my neck. I didn't think this was an erogenous zone, but let me tell you—it is.

Blane's lips left mine, but they didn't leave my skin as he slid down my body. He nipped at my collar while he plucked at my nipple with his finger. Then he blew warm breath on the spot, causing my nipple to pucker even harder. He sucked on one and then the other before traveling farther down.

I wasn't sure he should be going down there like that on me, and I shrieked out his name on a moan.

He stopped tracing my belly button with his tongue and looked up. "You know I'm a Southern boy?"

"Blane, seriously, I've never done that."

"Even better. I'll be a perfect Southern gentleman."

I squeezed my eyes shut as I felt him sliding my pants down my thighs and pulling off my boots so he could finish the job.

He crawled back up my body, planting a gentle kiss on my mouth, but his lips didn't stay there long. They trailed over my stomach, latching onto my hips, and caressing my sensitive skin while holding me steady with his hand. I was hot and cold, my skin on fire from his touch yet chilled where he abandoned. His tongue continued to swirl over one hip while he lightly squeezed the other, although my hip bones weren't prominent like other girls'. I had hips, soft ones, and

Blane's lips and fingers were worshiping them.

Pushing aside my own insecurities, I squeezed my eyes shut and pretended I was the supermodel he made me feel like I was.

I blew out a long breath as the tip of his tongue neared the juncture of my thighs, spreading warmth to where I was already blazing. His breath followed the wetness of his tongue, coming out in pants along my prickled skin. I tried to still myself, but my hips rose and reached for his mouth.

"Oh my God, I'm sorry. I didn't mean to do that," I whispered, ashamed and more than a little embarrassed.

"I liked that a whole hell of a lot, Cate," he said just before his tongue landed on my hot spot.

He swiped over my clit, and I'd never felt such sensation in my life. My spine tingled and my toes curled with tension. His finger entered me, hitting another spot, this one inside me, and when he flicked it, every last inch of me shot off the bed. *The G-spot.*

My legs went rigid as his tongue made love to my clitoris— teasing, tormenting, and testing my patience. I wanted it harder and rougher. I needed it slower, to last longer. I craved it all.

I turned my head toward the pillow as my knees began to shake, and my hair fell over my face. A blast of exhilaration hit me, and I screamed Blane's name as my orgasm ran wild through my body.

His tongue rode out the waves rippling through me, caressing each one out of me, and lapping up my orgasm until I finally lay spent and happy on the bed. He crawled back up, keeping his weight on his forearm, and lifted his finger to his mouth. He licked it partially clean and then brought it to my lips.

"Open," he said, and I did. Wanton and desperate, I opened wide and licked his finger clean of my own juices.

And I loved every fucking second. *Like a whore in a movie.*

"Hey, what's wrong?"

Too embarrassed to share my thoughts, I shook my head. Turning my face away, I sought refuge in the pillow again, thankful my hair provided cover.

"Huh-uh." Blane gently turned me to face him. "What's wrong? Did I do something you didn't like? Did I hurt you?"

He frowned at me, making little crinkles form beside his eyes. Using his free hand, he shoved his hair behind his ear, and since it was damp with sweat, it stuck.

I shook my head again.

"Cate, talk to me. Please."

"It's just . . . that was so dirty."

"What?" He rolled off me and tucked me into his side, pulling me close, my boobs smashing into his rib cage.

"It's just I've spent the last few years all determined to be some champion of women's issues, and here I am, no better than some ball baby, coming on your hand and licking it off. I should be disgusted with myself. I'm no better than a two-bit actress who takes her clothes off for one of those porn flicks." Ashamed, I buried my face in his chest, not wanting him to see my tears.

"Hey." He lifted my chin with his finger and swiped over the tears with his thumb.

"You're not some two-bit actress, Cate. You're an adult, a woman who likes a man, and I like you back. And we're being intimate with each other. The door is locked and we're enjoying each other's bodies in the privacy of my room. That's healthy, normal, and right."

He kissed my forehead.

"I think I should go."

"Listen, I don't want you to go. We can put our clothes back on and hang out. We don't have to go any further; I respect what you want."

"I'm so confused," I said with more conviction. "I should go."

"I'm not gonna force you to stay, but I want you to—"

I stood and snatched up my clothes, yanking them on as I averted my face.

"I have to go," I said again, wallowing in my own self-recrimination.

"Cate, wait. Please?"

Blane rolled off the bed and threw on a pair of sweats he grabbed from the floor. "I understand you're working through a lot, but don't leave like this." He cupped my cheeks and pressed a kiss to my lips. "I like you, so leave like that. Take your time and think about what I said. But—"

"No buts," I blurted.

"Oh yes, buts." He lightly tapped my ass. "I'm driving your butt home," he said, snagging a T-shirt and his keys.

chapter twenty

Catie

On Monday, I mentally chastised myself through all my morning classes.

Stupid, fucking girl. How could you fall for the boy, the class man-whore of all the men out there? You're no better than the same girls you sit in class and despise.

The very class I was sitting in, the one where Professor Stanwick stared me down from behind her readers.

To make matters worse, some other part of my psyche decided to take issue with the browbeating.

But he's a good guy, gentle and caring. Blane is the first person to see me, touch me, make me feel like a woman.

I dropped my head into my hand and tried to put all my bullshit thoughts out of my mind. Stanwick was going on about something in the news. Today's lesson was on the guy who started *Girls Gone Wild*.

"He took advantage of young women," she said, "some inebriated or under the influence, who wanted to be celebrities. He claims he had their permission, but he's no better than the guy who hosts the *Casting Couch* series. In fact, our very own Catie is doing a paper defending the likes of this man. Isn't that right?"

I lifted my head and shot up in my seat. In an instant, my inner guilt shifted from bemoaning my love life to second-guessing my pig-headed ideas.

"I-I'm sorry," I stammered, "but to defend him or people like him wasn't my intention. The paper is exploring the women who get involved and why."

And I still have to go to my internship. What a shit day.

Stanwick narrowed her eyes on me. "There are so many other avenues for women to make a living for themselves, I can't for the life of me understand why you would subscribe to defending those women."

"*Those women* don't have the same choices we have. Many of them can't afford higher education," I shot back.

"Stand up, Ms. Presto," Stanwick ordered. "Listen here, missy. This is a top-ten women's studies program. We don't support pornography and we certainly don't defend it. We also don't stand by our students giving dating advice on the air, or canoodling in the corners with student athletes who do nothing but sexualize women. We especially do not support these antics being splattered all over Twitter."

Not done tearing me to shreds yet, Stanwick gave me the deathblow. "You are dismissed from this class for the rest of the trimester. You were not as mature as I believed you to be when I allowed you to take this class. You may see the counselor to look into other courses or majors. Perhaps cinematography, with your strong interest in pornography?"

"What? You can't do that!"

My cheeks burned as my classmates stared at me, enjoying the showdown. Heat seeped to my scalp as a combination of Italian and Cuban anger licked at my belly, but I shoved it down. This was not the time for a temper tantrum. God, Stanwick was being flat-out unreasonable standing there with her arms crossed in front of her chest.

"Yes," she said smugly. "I can and I just did. Good-bye, Miss Presto."

She turned and effectively dismissed me as she went back to her lecture, tapping her pen on the SMART Board, refusing to glance my way.

With my shoulders hunched, I snatched up my things and walked up the aisle between the theater-style seating of the classroom to the exit, hanging my head like a dog sent to the corner. My vision suddenly blurry, I made my way out into the damp day. With an hour until I was due at the station, I slumped onto a spot under a tree, the ground cold on my ass as I dug my heels into the soft grass. I tilted my head back against a tree and sat crisscross applesauce, and closed my eyes.

Images of myself as a young girl, pudgy and in pigtails, flashed behind my eyelids. Memories of running through Grandma Cee's yard with Dad chasing me and calling "you're it" played on a continuous loop. We'd play until I was exhausted, and then my dad would toss me over his shoulder and carry me into Grandma's kitchen. She'd put out my very own cookie table—almond biscotti dusted with powdered sugar, ladylocks, mini cheesecakes, chocolate chip cookies, and a glass of milk.

We'd sit and laugh until my mom came and picked me up. Then she'd raise holy hell.

"Cee, you're making her even fatter! Don't you see, she's short and busty like your side?"

My dad would shush her and whisper in my ear, *"You're so beautiful, mi Caterina. Don't you listen to her."* He'd kiss my cheek and lift me up from the chair to spin me around. *"See you next week, baby doll."*

Every time, my mom would grab my hand and waggle it in the air. *"Even her fingers are pudgy,"* she'd say.

"Glory, stop," my dad would yell at her.

She'd rush me out of there and my poor dad would always yell, *"Kiss Grace and Cedes for me."*

Now as I sucked in the chilly air and breathed out tiny puffs of smoke, I yearned to go back in time. Memories continued to spin in my mind. My mom leaving for a week with a guy named Gus, and then coming back to move us out of my dad's house. Her poisoning my sisters against my dad, and the way she hated how I wanted to spend time with Dad and Grandma Cee.

My lousy mom went from rich man to rich man, bleeding them of money for Botox and plastic surgery, and maxing out their credit cards. My sister Grace chased married men, and my younger sister, Cedes, made a life out of being clueless. I was the one who was supposed to be smart and successful, the one who was proud of my feminine curves and big brain. *The outcast.*

Stanwick was right . . . I should be ashamed. I had no right aspiring to be a warrior for feminism when I was nothing better than a hussy, falling for the college athlete who would make tons of cash as a pro.

I tugged at my hair in frustration. Why did I have to repress my desires to be a feminist? Couldn't I have a career and sexual fantasies at the same time? Were all female CEOs celibate?

I stood up and brushed off my ample backside before I made my way to Starbucks, avoiding Mean Beans and who might be lurking there. I was determined to take a hard look at my life, to stay away from Blane and his allure, and to prove my professor wrong.

But I didn't know how the hell I would do that. Stanwick was a big powerful surge in the feminist movement while I was barely an electrical volt, but she didn't get it. Those porn actresses and strippers didn't have choices like she had, or like my female classmates and I did. No, they were stuck in a no-win situation where they believed opportunities like the *Couch* and being in front of the camera gave them a semblance of control. At least, that's what I assumed.

My life sucked. I'd been kicked to the curb by my professor, I was tangled up with both Sonny and Blane, and I was sympathetic to adult video stars. All because of that stupid fucking dare.

My first step in fixing my life was ditching Sonny. I needed the job, but I would find something else. At least, I kept telling myself I would—on repeat in my brain the whole walk to the station.

Sonny was the one who'd gotten me in this whole mess to begin with, and I needed a clean break. If it weren't for his shitty treatment and imbecilic behavior, I could continue to fetch his coffee and would have had the chance to take over the segments he didn't want. But Sonny was who he was, and I couldn't deal with him anymore.

I walked into the station and waited until Sonny had a break, chewing on my thumb the whole time. When I finally had his attention, I dove right in.

"Look, this has been great and I appreciate all you've done, but it's not working. I keep getting sucked into one mess after another here. My professor hates the show, and I'm nothing but a thorn in Blane's side. You deserve a funnier, sexier replacement, and I need to make my own name for myself. And I never want to call someone Mr. Boots again, Sebastian."

His eyes grew wide and he actually protested for a moment, but then when his words fell on deaf ears, Sonny switched gears and thanked me for my help.

A short while later, I walked out of the radio station, even more determined to come up with some type of retaliation against Stanwick. I walked home in a daze, revenge ideas mixing with plans to make money.

The only thing I came up with was deciding that when I went to Mean Beans the next day, I'd see if they needed someone more competent than Ava.

"Heya, Hafton. Sonny here, and boy do I have stuff for you. First off, I have to send out a big smooch to my girl, Miranda, over the airwaves. That's right, ladies, Sebastian Jones may be in love. Go over and see my woman, Miranda; she works at Book World in the romance-and-mystery department. Look for the fiery red hair and the long legs tucked into knee-high boots. Boots, people! Sonny be wanting to knock those boots for a long time. Anyway, lurve you, lady, and thanks for the dinner over the weekend. This tune is for you."

Michael Jackson's "Baby Be Mine" filled the air as I sat alone in my room and picked away at my stats homework, half distracted by the text that had been sitting on my phone.

Blane: You okay? You coming to the game tomorrow?

It had been sitting there for hours since two o'clock, and I had yet to reply. Blane wasn't good for me. Forget the fact that hanging with him had basically gotten me thrown out of my major today; he was moving on soon and I wasn't.

"I'm back, Sonny B. here on WHSU 96.9, spinning the jams and keeping you company on this lonely Monday night. Are there parties going on? Tweet me, babes! As for me, I'm manning the station alone because our fearless intern is looking for a new internship. That's right, cute Catie P. is off to greener pastures. I can't wait to hear about her adventures, and I can't help but think we will." Sonny's laugh rang out, and then he was back. "So, I'm all alone here. Anyone looking to fill my shoes? Tweet me too."

This time Sonny played some hip-hop, and I turned down the volume and tried to concentrate on my stats homework again. My phone dinged.

> *Blane: Cate, please answer. You left the radio station? Did Sonny do something?*

This time I answered. There was no way I wanted Blane getting involved. I was too proud for that shit.

> *Catie: No. I'm good. Figuring some things out. Don't think I'll be at the game tomorrow.*

Yeah, right. Who was I kidding?

I turned off the radio, deleted my Twitter account, shut down my phone, and ignored my misgivings as I went on a very important mission. I took the campus bus to the outskirts of town and saw my destination at the end of a strip mall. The neon-green sign flickered in the darkness.

Adults, XXX blinked on and off as I swallowed any reservations and pushed the door open. Blane might have formally introduced me to what my clit could really do, but I needed to get to know her much better than I had in the past.

Inhaling deeply, I thought back to the porno fest. As soon as it was over, I'd wanted to rush out and get a vibrator right then, recognizing my lack of familiarity with my own needs. Stanwick and her crusade, along with my inability to enjoy sex without feeling like a slut, had landed me in the last place I expected to find answers.

Bells jingled overhead as I walked in and tried to pretend like I belonged here, like this was a regular outing for me. Immediately, I felt stupid and insecure in my clunky boots and sensible winter coat.

I really need to harness my inner Italian. I'm in a sex store!

Yeah, right. The Mediterranean side of me was a double-edged sword. It was my damn hot-blooded temper that had put me in this no-win situation—out of my major, out of a career-minded job (although the manager at Mean Beans had promised me some hours), and out of touch with my sensuality. And looking for answers in an adult toy store.

A guy with huge gauges in his earlobes and his nails painted glittery black looked up from behind the counter. "Can I help you?"

Avoiding any eye contact, I mumbled, "Um, just looking around."

You can do this.

Any liberated woman should be concerned with her orgasm, right? Wasn't that what *Cosmo* splashed on their covers every month?

Maybe I should have started with a few copies of *Cosmopolitan* and *Marie Claire* at the newsstand before venturing to the adult toy store . . .

Nope. Not stubborn, fire-breathing me.

I took in the glass case next to where I was standing that displayed some intricate glass . . . dildos? Was that what they were? They looked like penises made of glass with ticklers of some sort.

"Oh. My. God," I said under my breath, and fixed my gaze to the ratty carpet as I moved quickly toward an aisle.

I peeked down Aisle 1 before deciding I could explore it. This was a tame section full of costumes. Maid outfits, sexy policeman uniforms, and accessories like handcuffs and boas filled the shelves. Rounding the corner, I saw Aisle 2 was more of the same. Edible undies and chocolate sauce for the body seemed benign enough.

Aisle 3 was a bonanza of exactly what I was looking for— vibrators. Not the top-of-the-line museum-quality ones like in the glass case, but your everyday vibrators. There were small ones and really large ones, vibrators shaped like a tube of lipstick, and dildos of all colors, anything from neon-tinted to run-of-the-mill flesh-colored ones in hues from peach to black. I practically tiptoed to the middle of the aisle, and my hand wavered on its way to snag a small version, a purple pocket rocket.

"That's a good one. Powerful," came a voice from behind me.

Pretty sure I peed myself a little, I stood totally still, gripping the vibrator but afraid to turn around.

"Excuse me, I just have to grab something from right in front of you."

A hand reached around me, and its long fingers with black-tipped French-manicured nails sorted through the pocket rockets before settling on a green one.

"Got it!" the sultry female voice sang in my ears.

Curious, I turned to find a stunning blonde standing behind me, long and lean, her hair tousled in waves. Her face was flawless, her makeup heavy and perfect, and from the look of her dewy skin, she wasn't much older than me.

"Good," I choked out. Then out of nowhere, I asked, "You recommend this one?"

"Your first?"

I nodded and dropped my gaze, noting the carpet was a deep red covered in hot pink kisses.

"Hey, don't be shy. I can help you," she said quietly. "That's a good one for a quickie, but if you really want the full effect, you should get this one." She reached across me again and pulled something called "The Rabbit" off the display hook.

When I took the package and eyed it warily, she laughed at me. "It's a bit much, but I promise you, it will get the job done."

"Thanks." I was humiliated. Not because I was purchasing a vibrator, but by the fact that I was so unfamiliar with my own sexuality. The memory of rushing out on Blane flickered in my head.

"I'm Sarina," the sexy woman said to me, her hand outstretched.

"Catie." I took her fingers in mine and she shook my hand firmly.

"Want to ask me anything else?"

"You come here a lot?" Suddenly, I was intrigued by this woman, who was clearly comfortable with her own sexuality.

"I do. Sometimes more than others. This is actually for my boss." She waved the vibrator around casually, like it was a box of Oreos.

"Your boss?" *What kind of boss needs his or her employee to pick up vibrators?*

"I make adult films, and we had one of these break on the set." She pitched her voice low, apparently not from shame, but so she wouldn't attract unwanted attention to us.

"Wow," was all I could get out.

"It's a living," she said with a shrug. "I don't normally go around sharing that information, but you seem nice, and look like you could use a helping hand."

"I'm not a virgin," I said quickly, shooting that misconception down right away.

She giggled. "It's okay if you were, but I get it. Inexperienced in finding your own orgasm?"

"Something like that. More like I panic from intimacy. It makes me feel dirty."

She ran her hand down my sleeve and looked me in the eye. "Sweetie, you should never feel dirty when it comes to your needs."

I nodded.

"You checking out?"

"Yeah, I'm going to get both," I said sheepishly.

We walked together toward the register, where the guy with the black nails sat reading some nudie mag. As we paid for our purchases, Sarina and I made small talk about the weather, the impending snow and shit, as if we were in the grocery store checkout line rather than buying sex toys.

As we walked outside into the cold and said our good-byes, a light bulb went off in my head. This was the type of woman I wanted to write about in my thesis paper—a woman in the porn industry living in the same small town as Stanwick and her stuck-up ideals.

"Hey!" I called to Sarina, halting her as she walked over to her SUV. "Can I come with you? Check it out?" I ran over to where she stood and said, "I'll stay out of your way. I'm just curious."

There went my impetuous Italian side again. Here I was, Cute Catie P., the nun of Southern A, asking to visit the set of a porn movie.

Sarina frowned down at me for a second, considering. "Sure, but if Frank asks, tell him you recognized me from the videos. I don't want him thinking I run around telling people what we do right here in the middle of boring Ohio."

"Of course."

Her SUV beeped as she popped her car locks and asked, "Want a ride?"

I grinned. "My mom always said not to ride with strangers, but she also probably wouldn't be a fan of porn, so fuck her." I slid into the passenger seat, a little excited at this crazy adventure, and away we sped.

Twenty minutes later, I laughed when we pulled into the parking lot for a big warehouse. "It is kind of weird, this going on right here in the farmlands of Ohio."

"Cheap space, low cost of living, and a good supply of actors," Sarina said as if it were common knowledge.

We walked inside to a live set, and I was introduced in between takes to Frank, who sat in the director's chair. I swallowed while taking in my surroundings. If I thought I didn't know much before, I was way wrong. Sitting there that night, I realized I knew nothing. With my legs crossed and my hands demurely in my lap, I took in the scenes, some scandalous and others quite enticing.

I felt my pulse pick up a few times, and squinted to get a better view. A few times, I looked away, embarrassed for the actors in front of me, but I always ended up turning back to the set.

After a while, I decided it was time for me to head home and figure out how to use my vibrators. Sarina and I exchanged phone numbers and I took the bus home, my new toys tucked into my backpack.

chapter twenty-one

Blane

Tuesday, Coach called us early to the field house for a team meeting before the night's game. He made it clear we were to win, and win big.

"Listen to the radio guy, Steele. You can't afford any distractions," Coach said, directing his comment at me. And he was right; I couldn't afford to be distracted.

We hit the hardwood and warmed up as a team. When the buzzer rang, we were shooed down the tunnel back toward the locker room to wait until the official introductions.

As I wound my way to the overhang, I saw her.

She might have said she wasn't coming, but Cate was there in Section 107 leaning up against the wall, her eyes anywhere but on me. She was pretending to focus on our opponents from Indiana. I almost yelled up to her, but she wanted to remain anonymous. And I didn't need the distraction.

I had a game to win—actually, a season to win. There was no

denying, I also wanted to explore whatever this was with Cate, but she needed to be into it. I was fine with inexperience or not taking shit too quickly, but this whole not allowing herself to enjoy pleasure was bullshit. Not me at all. I was one hundred fucking percent behind getting it on and getting it on good. I wasn't going to feel guilty for having wants or desires, and she shouldn't either.

Fucking nuts. How could she be all pro-women, but be so repressed? It didn't make sense. And what did we really have? One night of passion, a few funny conversations in a coffeehouse, and a shared disgust for Sonny?

"Y'all ready to win?" I shouted as I banged my fist into the locker, setting my thoughts aside.

This was what I had—a locker room full of sweaty guys willing to leave it all out there on the hardwood for me. My life was hanging on the precipice, and these guys fucking knew it. We were a family.

"Damn straight," Ashton yelled back.

"Amen!"

"You know it, Steele!"

The rest of the team joined in, shouting obscenities and promises for destruction. Demetri and Mo slapped a high five, putting aside any personal shit before heading out to the hardwood. The locker room resounded with cheers, chants, and slaps until Coach Conley blew his whistle.

"Let's go tonight! I want you dunking and putting on a show for these dudes. Scare 'em right up front. Give *them* your goddamn cockiness, not me, you hear me? You're never a shoo-in for a win. You have to work for every damn point, men."

"Yes, Coach," chorused throughout the room.

Then we were on the move again, through the locker room and out the tunnel, ready to hear our names called. I felt good; loose and pumped. I'd like to say hearing my name and all the cheering that followed didn't do much for me. But it did.

Midway through the first half, Coach gave me a break, benching me for some rest since we were up by twenty-five points. The beating we were putting on this cupcake team was insane. I'd gone hard for the first three minutes, putting up two dunks and serving up five assists. Then I'd banged a three from way downtown, and the bad guys missed on their offensive run.

Alex snagged the rebound and threw a heated pass to Ashton for another three. The dude was fouled, smacked on the arm as he lofted the ball into the air. The shit sank right into the net, but he pulled an and-one foul.

Of course, my man made his extra point from the line. From then on, it was easy. With sweat trickling down my back and over my arms, I passed with fury and dribbled with intensity. This was my house and the love of my life all wrapped up in one.

I had loans from the bank counting on me going pro. My car was sold to me on borrowed money. My mom wanted a new place, even though she wouldn't say anything. My dad wanted a star.

There was a lot riding on this. It was a good thing I fucking loved being on the court.

Seated on the bench, I swigged from my Gatorade bottle and looked toward Section 107.

Gone. Cate was gone. *Oh well, like I thought. We didn't have much. Or did we?*

I stared for a beat or two and then my head was back in the game—games, actually. Because this was all I had.

With a ball in my hand, I would do what I needed to.

Wednesday, I tried to find Cate, but she wasn't in any of her regular haunts. I leaned my chair back at Mean Beans and pretended to listen to Ashton, but I was on the lookout. I ducked when Ava's friends popped in and eventually left, successfully avoiding chatting anyone up.

I might have also traipsed by the women's studies building, but nothing.

I couldn't spend all day on the hunt; we had practice and team meetings. It was the beginning of the season, ultimately the most important season of my career so far. This would be the one everyone was watching; my performance would be judged and graded. The rest of my life depended on this season.

Thursday, I hit the weight room for some light lifting and stretching. Some Bush from the nineties blared over the plates clanking into the bars and the bars hitting the racks. I was in a wall sit stretching my legs when Mo squatted next to me.

"What's happening?" He turned his head toward me.

"Living the dream, Mo."

Our thighs quivered and my forehead dripped onto the floor. I pushed my sweatband higher on my head, swiping the sweat with it.

"You are, buddy, and don't you fucking forget it."

He was right. I came from a trailer park. When that Catholic school gave me a scholarship in ninth grade, I didn't know how much my life could change. Now I did.

I glanced at Mo. "You're right, man. I don't know, feel like I'm floundering a bit. Shit, you got a kid on the way. Who's going to be waiting for me when I'm making all this money next year?"

I stood, straightening my legs and shaking out my quads.

Mo snorted. "My man, you're gonna buy your momma a house and make a good life. And shit, you're gonna fuck a lot of women looking for the one." He stood and smacked me in the side with the back of his hand. "Don't let the rest of us down, especially the one with a fucking baby."

We didn't talk anymore; Coach called us in to watch tape for the next day's game. Sitting in the dark room, my mind wandering, I wondered if the Stealer might have stolen his last heart.

Fucking Cate. She was cute, yeah, but smart and sexy too.

And she was ignoring me.

chapter twenty-two

Blane
Mid-December

"Sonny B. here. Most of you are packing up and heading home for the winter break, but I'm staying right here in Hafton, and my girl, Miranda, and I are going to decorate our tree tonight. Have no fear! I'll put a picture up on Twitter for all you jealous lovaaas."

"Grandma Got Run Over by a Reindeer" played in the background as Sonny made love to the mic.

"You know who else is here over the break? The Hafton men's and women's basketball teams. That's right, folks . . . I wonder if they get freaky together? Let's hear your thoughts, Haftees, give me the 4-1-1. Call me or e-mail the station, and we'll be back with any and all scoop. Oh, and give a nice hello to Johnny, our new intern, if you call."

"Grandma" finished and some Bob Marley-style steel band song played.

"God, that guy's taste in music is ass. I'd know he was white from a mile away." Ashton tossed a foam ball against the wall over and over again. A constant whir and whack echoed throughout our apartment.

"Hey! Enough with the white-boy jokes," I said. "And dude, fucking cut that out with the ball or I'm getting a new roommate."

"It's true," Ashton said with a grin. "Present company excluded. You like good rap. I do worry when you start with the rock, but I know it's hard to take shake that out of the Southern boy." He took aim and zinged the ball my way.

"Thank God. I was getting a headache from all the back and forth." I snatched the ball before it slammed into my chest. "So, what's got you all twisted in knots?"

He hung his head. "Fucking Christmas is in two days, and I got no poontang."

"You're vile, man."

"Hey, it's the truth. My girl, Ava, went home, and you should be proud 'bout me hitting it with just one lady."

"You're growing up." I flashed him a wicked grin and lobbed the ball at his shiny bald head.

"How 'bout you?"

"Sonny's leaving me alone, maybe since we've won every non-conf game, but he's not mandating I stay celibate. So I guess I'll go out looking. Wanna come?"

"What? In your pickup?"

"Yeah, we can be like, *y'all looking for a good throw?*"

Ashton burst out laughing. "Dude, you been hung up on that intern ever since she went MIA. Don't you fucking tease me. We're not going on the prowl in your truck."

"Plus, you have Ava." I looked at him and raised an eyebrow.

"Exactly, white boy. Good thing you're smart."

This time I laughed hard, and Ashton laughed with me a moment before giving me the eye.

"So, what's with Catie?" he asked, not giving up on it. "Where the hell did she go?"

"Not a fucking clue. She left the radio station and hasn't been back, according to Sonny, and I haven't seen her around. She's got a new phone number too."

"Ouch, cold dusted by the lady, huh?"

"Shut the fuck up, Ash. Let's play some *NBA 2K*," I said just as Sonny came back on the air.

"Okay, Haftees, let's hear it. What the heck are you doing this Christmas, and don't bother calling in if you're heading to Aspen to chase some snow bunnies. We don't want to talk to you."

"He's a train wreck," Ashton said, pulling out the game controller.

"Sonny B. here. Who's this?" Sonny's radio voice echoed from the speakers.

"Hey, Sonny, it's Jules in Southern B! I wish you were still single, and I'd stay and decorate with you."

"Be still my beating heart. Miranda, are you listening to this? If so, cover your ears." Sonny lowered his voice to a conspiratorial whisper. "Me too, Jules. Me too."

Stupid Sonny.

There was a click, and he went to another caller. "Sonny B. on the line, who's there?"

"Hey, Sonny. I'm heading home, but I'm going to watch a ton of that new adult star, Ariel Stone. Have you seen her? She's new on the scene, and fiiine."

"Now, really? Let's keep this discussion PG here, buddy. But e-mail me. Don't forget."

Click.

"I'm going to roll another tune. This one goes out to my guys about to get busy with their conference games and winning us a 'ship."

Nelly's "Air Force Ones" overtook the station, and Ashton clicked it off with his foot.

"God, it's enough of that ass. Who you want to be on the game?"

"The Magic, of course." They were my favorite team, and I had the game set to play all their superstars.

"Bullshit, you and the fucking Magic. I'm going old school. Lakers."

A while later, as we began the second game of our virtual basketball war, Ashton said, "We should google that Ariel chick. Sounds like we both could use a release."

"I don't do porn anymore," I said without thinking, and then winced. *Big mistake.*

"What?" Ashton threw his controller down and pounced on me. He had me pinned to the floor, his hand at my throat as he growled out, "You don't do porn?"

"Not anymore," I gurgled. "Can you let me go?"

"I'm outta here," he said, and he scrambled off of me. "You might be fucking contagious. Don't do porn, *pfft.*"

chapter twenty-three

Catie

I handed the bar bouncer my brand-spanking-new fake ID, a little early Christmas present for myself. I'd gone home for two days for the holidays, and it had been forty hours too long. Thankfully, I couldn't stay longer due to my new work demands.

As soon as I'd entered my childhood home, my sisters were on me about my failures.

"Thought you were going to be some big champion of women, Catie? And here you go getting the boot," Grace had taunted me over the kitchen table.

Cedes cornered me in the bathroom, slapping my bare butt with her towel as I dried off. "Good thing you were sent packing. You look like you've been hitting the scones."

"Shove off, Cedes," I snarled. "And here I thought you were starting to be nice. You're a bitch."

My mom spent the first day glaring at me, pinching my waist as she chastised me for wasting my dad's money on a "foolish education."

She'd continued to offer up the prospect of working with Grace as some sort of solace.

As usual, I ended up drowning my sorrows in rice pudding and cannoli at my dad's restaurant while he ran around and filled the Christmas take-out orders.

With my head low, I'd walked down the snow-covered path to a waiting taxi, where I slumped in the backseat the whole way to the bus station. As the bus carried me back to campus, across Pennsylvania and parts of Ohio, I glanced wistfully at farmhouses decorated for Christmas and wished for a new family.

Now as I entered the Golden Goblet, a newish wine-and-beer bar at the edge of campus, I realized how much I yearned to be loved for myself.

I brushed the snowflakes off my coat and set it behind my bar stool, one that had seen the imprint of my ass all too frequently over the last week. At first thought, a wine-and-beer place seemed like a weird fit on a college campus, but after I'd been there once, I got it. They sold beer by the case and wine by the jug. It was the kind of place big groups of fun-loving people went to get their buzz on and have a good time.

I went by myself—mostly to relax—or to meet Sarina. She helped me with the ID and everything else I didn't know jack about.

It was New Year's Eve, and the few other women I knew were home. Tess and I had stayed in touch since my life had imploded, but she'd gone to Shelby's house for the holiday. They went on for fucking forever about skiing, bonfires, and hot rich guys before they left. Of course, the women from the women's studies program had distanced themselves since Thanksgiving when my expulsion from the program became official.

I hadn't officially seen the guys since Thanksgiving either. Of course, I'd watched a few games from behind the scenes or on TV, but when I thought I saw a basketball player in the vicinity, I went the other way. Luckily, we were knee-deep in studying for finals right about then, and I was busy.

Sort of.

I discovered the Goblet allowed you to order wine by the glass at the bar the night I arrived back at school from Christmas, tired and bone cold off the bus. After that, I started coming regularly before going to work on my current project, which required being loose. Sarina and I met here every few days, and she'd fill me in on what I needed to know. It was quickly becoming a formidable bond between the two of us—two women from opposite ends of the social spectrum with nothing in common.

Tonight, I ordered a prosecco; after all, it was New Year's. When in Rome, and all that. Sarina was at a party. She'd invited me but I declined, offering to pick up a shift for her at the studio.

Staring into the bubbly set before me, I smoothed my hair behind my ear. I'd straightened it using my new flat iron, and the lights above the bar were reflecting off its shine. I took out my new smartphone and checked my e-mails. There were a lot, so I scrolled down for a while.

Sarina's picture came up on the screen, her long blond curls waved around her face and neckline, her blue eyes cool and collected, her lips a shiny hot pink and puckered.

> *Sarina: Hey, girl! Hope you have an awesome new year. You're the best!*

I smiled. She thought I was the best, and I thought she was even better. What would Stanwick think about that?

dolce

Catie: Have fun, lady! I'll see you this week? Happy NYE!

Sarina: See you tomorrow!

I sipped my drink slowly and thought about my next stop. In a million years, I could have never imagined spending a day in my life doing what I was doing. Yet here I was, doing it on New Year's Eve. My dad would have a fit, my sisters would never stop talking about it, and Blane . . . he would be disgusted.

Or not. I didn't know.

Sadly, I'd lost a portion of my financial aid when I was dismissed from my major. A component of my aid package was based on the intrinsic value I brought to Hafton's women's studies program. The monies were derived from a fund, earmarked by the benefactor for the sole purpose of crafting women leaders.

Luckily, my mind continued to form a plan that started with Mean Beans and ended during my trip to the adult store. My original plan was to find part-time work and seek revenge on Stanwick. Little did I know the two concepts would merge and begin to sustain me in this journey.

Hafton was on a trimester calendar, and when the first trimester ended, I left campus for a studio apartment. It brought a little bit of a savings for my dad when it came to room and board, and it provided me with the privacy I required. And craved.

Sitting at the bar, deep in thought as I made mental notes for the book I was writing, I didn't hear someone slide in next to me.

"Hey."

Frowning, I swiveled toward the voice. "Mo, how are you?"

The large guy planted on a stool to my left took me by surprise, especially as he sat there in a black leather sports coat, his dark eyes focused on me.

"I'm good. We play tomorrow, so I have to head out soon, but I brought my lady out for a New Year's beverage . . . forgetting she couldn't drink because she's knocked up. I'm an idiot like that."

He tipped his head to the back of the bar where a stunning mixed-race woman sat sipping on a glass of club soda. Her hair was down, wavy and wild, and her cleavage practically burst out of a black halter top. She certainly didn't look prego to me, but what the hell did I know?

"I'm sure you're having fun anyway," I responded, swallowing a lump of regret.

I'd only talked to Maurice once before at the team party back in November, and he seemed nice enough. But that wasn't my scene anymore. Actually, it had never been my scene. I'd only hung out with cool college athletes once.

Mo studied me. "So, what's the story? My man says you dropped off the face of the earth, and here you are toasting the New Year by yourself?"

"I'm doing some soul searching, finding my own way, figuring shit out—pardon my language. Blane didn't need all that baggage. He's got a life of grandeur ahead."

"Keep telling yourself that, Catie." Mo patted my shoulder and stood up. "I have to get back to my lady. Happy New Year."

"Same to you."

I tossed a twenty on the bar and got up. It was time for me to do what I needed to do.

With my bag tucked under my shoulder, I entered the warehouse.

"Hey, Frank," I hollered as I headed toward the back, my boots clunking on the cement floor.

"Hey, girl. Thanks for coming in tonight, Ari."

"No problem."

Seated in the back, I slipped out of my coat and oversized sweatshirt, leaving me in only a sheer T-shirt as the script called for. I quickly pulled my hair in a bun on top of my head and fitted my wavy red wig on top. I'd curled it the night before. Sometimes I wore it straight and glossy, but tonight I was doing a coed type of scene, and I felt wild hair was best.

"I'll be ready in fifteen," I called out, swiping on some red lipstick before grabbing my fake eyelashes out of the case.

Grace had no idea what she was actually recommending them for when I called her for advice; she was so excited I wanted faux eyelashes. Sarina had explained they were a must in the industry.

My sisters had also been flat-out excited when I said I was heading back to school early from the holidays. Apparently, my presence stressed Mom out, which spoiled the holiday for my sisters. *Bitches.* I could only imagine what they'd say if any of them found out why I'd hurried back to school.

"Hey, Ari," I heard from toward the door.

"Hey, Ricky," I called back. *Tricky Ricky*, my partner for the night.

That's right, I was now a full-fledged member of the porn world— Ariel Stone in the flesh. In only a few short weeks, I'd been dubbed *Queen of the Titty Fuck.*

Oh, the power of the Internet.

I was living out my thesis, making a quick name for myself on the Internet and paying my bills while doing it. And all the while, I was writing a book, a book that would twist Stanwick's knickers. When I was tossed out of the program, I'd gone into deep-research mode, and my thesis paper had transformed into a full-length book.

Bitch.

Meeting Sarina has been a lucky break for me. Turned out, she was a single mom living in the middle-of-nowhere, Ohio. Originally from Arizona, she'd followed some guy to the Midwest, and he had his fun with her until he knocked her up. Then she was stuck all alone with nothing more than a GED and a screaming newborn. She'd tried working at a grocery store for a while, but the hours sucked and the pay was worse.

Then she met Frank.

After that night she first took me to the set, we met for coffee. Over a big piece of cake, of which she only took one bite and I ate every last crumb, I told her all about the three S's that had ruined my life.

Stanwick.

Steele.

Sonny.

After hearing my story, she agreed to introduce me to her world and help me expose the harsh realities of why women stayed in the porn industry. How it helped put food on the table and afforded women time to be with their children.

I squeezed my eyes shut and took a deep breath before dusting a fine layer of pale pink glitter onto my cheeks. It had been Sarina's idea for me to try out in a skit, and the thing went berserk with five-star ratings. She'd suggested I keep going but hold true to my hard limit—penetration—and make some money on the side while learning exactly what went on in the adult-film industry.

I knew it would isolate me from the entire women's studies world, but I couldn't help but feel compassionate toward Sarina and her friends. They were women too, and how could I really write an exposé without going undercover?

So Ariel Stone was born and the real Caterina Presto was found—the Catie with a new purpose. I finally had a mission, a cause, a place to call my own. I'd been looking for that my whole life.

I also knew it was the last thing on earth Blane Steele needed in his life with the league calling. Maybe it was self-punishment on my part; I didn't fucking know. What I did know was Blane would have no use for me when I finished with this project.

As if Blane Steele wants me in his life.

I frowned at my reflection, hating when I thought about Blane at work. Sometimes I got so wrapped up in thinking about what would happen if he knew about this, tears stung my eyes.

Tonight, I shoved any thoughts of the six-foot-four baller out of my mind and took a deep breath. It was a new year and a new me. What had started out as an experiment to prove Stanwick wrong, a way to prove my theories correct, was slowly turning into a way of life.

"Let's go, kids. I got a party to get to," Frank hollered across the room.

"Me too," Ricky yelled back, rolling his eyes.

Frank had turned out to be an okay guy. He produced the videos on the cheap and passed a lot of the profits over to us; it was how he kept good talent. We made money, and he made more movies and even more money.

I dusted a little glitter over my boobs and puckered my lips, making sure my lip gloss was even before I headed out to the set.

As I lounged in a sexy pose on a red velvet chaise, Ricky approached—more like sauntered for the camera—while rubbing his hand over his clothing-covered erection. His dick bulged in his skinny black pants, and he made all kinds of weird moans and facial expressions for the camera. I thought he looked like he was in pain, but Frank had assured me that was what ecstasy looked like.

To me, that wasn't what Blane looked like during our one moment. The one I ran away from because I was ashamed of what we'd done.

Look at me now.

I kept trying to imagine what it would be like to actually be turned on by Ricky with his mouth shaped like an *O* and his body now angled over me, his breath puffing on my face.

"Look what the cat dragged in," I said, repeating my lines. "If it isn't another hard dick. Oh my . . ." This cued my long sigh and husky breathing as I ran my fingers along Ricky's bicep.

"Baby, you have no idea," he said, his voice all deep and manly.

I almost giggled because the dude was as gay as they came, or maybe he was bisexual. Whatever. His penis was huge and hard, so he must like women a little.

I was wearing tight leather leggings and a sheer white T-shirt marked Property of Athletics Department. It was a ridiculous outfit, made more so by the high-heeled athletic shoes I wore on my feet.

Was this what men wanted? It must be, since I was making big money doing it.

Ricky ripped off his gray hoodie. *An effort to make him look like a college student?* He unbuttoned his pants and pulled them off, his tight black boxer briefs were next, and then his penis was in my face. I oohed and aahed as I touched it, acting like it was full of holy water and I needed to be baptized in the worst way.

He cupped my hand and stroked his length with my hand over his, working his shaft at a quick clip. I could have been microwaving oatmeal or sitting in stats class for all the excitement I felt. In one undisciplined second, my mind went back to my night with *him* before I yanked it back to the present.

Ricky leaned closer, bringing his penis front and center.

Moans and grunts mixed with choruses of *Oh, baby* and *I'm gonna blow.* The slap of skin provided the percussion to this perverted symphony as his hand and mine worked his penis. Leaning closer, he let go of my hand and yanked down the neckline of the V-neck I wore, exposing my breasts so he could run his penis between my cleavage.

I twisted and squirmed as if this was taking me to new heights of pleasure. Before long there was a splatter all over my boobs as Ricky grunted and pumped his hips, and he reached down to rub his ejaculate over my glittery skin.

"And that's a wrap," Frank yelled. "We'll have this puppy out tomorrow, call it something like 'Rose Bowl Splash.' The college guys will devour it on game day."

Ricky handed me a towel and kissed me on the cheek. "Have a great new year, Ari," he said, and then he hightailed it out of there.

I wiped off and tossed my wig in a bag before I threw on my coat and went straight home for a shower. A long, hot, disinfecting one.

chapter twenty-four

Blane

"Hafton, are you ready? Are you pumped? Sonny B., that's me, and I'm here tonight at the field house, coming to you live for Hafton's first conference game of the season. Can the Green take on those big, bad guys from Akron? I think so. Even though you losers didn't get tickets to the game, put your hands together and up in the air, wave them like you actually do care for our starting lineup!"

Sonny's voice boomed through the locker room's speakers as we kept moving while we waited for our names to be called.

I bounced on the ball of my feet, jumping up and down and rolling my shoulders to stay warm and loose. It was the first Friday after winter break, and we were on point. I needed to play and burn out some aggression.

The holidays had been a fucking bust. First, Cate kicked me out of her life. Then my parents visited, ended up banging, and weren't speaking afterward. Same shit, different day . . .

I'd been going on adrenaline and riding the high of a few easy wins, but wasn't in the mood for any bullshit when I walked into brunch by myself. My mom had sat there waiting like the cat that ate the canary, a huge grin on her face.

Shit. I'd seen that look before.

"Christ, don't even say it," I'd said, sliding into the booth at Denny's. She loved that restaurant, and although it wasn't my favorite, I liked to make her happy. "He's not going to fall for you like one of the guys in your books. You two were done before it started, Mom."

She laughed like it was some funny late-night TV joke. "Honey, I know that. But that ass is stuck on me, and now I'm making him squirm."

"Mom, you have got to stop playing these games. I get it. It makes you feel like you have the power, but you don't. Relationships aren't about power. They're about being equals."

"They're not kidding," she said, studying me with a smile. "You've gone soft. I like it, Blane. You're one of the good ones."

"Mom, stop. Stop messing around with Dad. Move on. Don't go back to your mobile home and plot how you're going to torture him more. I love you, and I know deep down, you hurt. Just move on."

"Let's talk about you, honey. Any young women in your life?"

The waitress came and took our orders, bringing me a tall glass of milk and my mom a coffee. Apparently, she'd ordered those while waiting for me.

"She needed some space. I'm respecting that and then going back in."

"Good. I never thought you to be a quitter."

"Ugh, Mom, enough. How about we talk about your pets?"

That was a safe subject, so that's what we discussed.

We ate and said our good-byes, and when Christmas rolled around, I didn't tell her Dad stayed to have dinner with me.

It had been a lonely dinner for two at the diner. Two despondent men acting macho over two plated Christmas dinners. Afterward, I'd gone home and downed some Crown Royal with Mo, who was envisioning the following year when he'd be a dad, and no doubt dressed up as Santa.

As a team, we'd lost some of our focus over the holidays, so when we got back, Conley had verbally whipped the shit out of us on a daily basis. Tonight we needed to be focused, to run like a well-oiled machine, or however the expression went.

"And last but not least, they're calling our starting two-man, my good friend and the guy you wish you all knew, third-year player Blaaane Steele!"

Sonny's annoying voice trailed behind me as I ran out to the crowd screaming my name. I ran through the line, bumping shoulders and chests with my teammates before removing my warm-up jersey.

We went right in for the tip, and the ball was flying to me. I kept the ball to myself and took it right to the rack. Two–nothing, Hafton. The bad guys got the ball and went for three, the ball swishing through the air, and we were down one. Back and forth was pretty much how the first quarter went. I imagined Sonny's colorful commentary kept the radio listeners entertained.

It was only a four-point game at the half, and I knew by the way

Conley was staring at me, his eyes nothing more than tiny slits, he wanted me to take over in the second half.

I tossed my warm-up jersey over my head as I made my way to the tunnel. Foolishly, I looked up when I heard, "Stealer! Hey, baby, be mine!" It wasn't the girl screaming who caught my attention; it was the short stack leaning against the wall right under Section 108.

I shook my head to get the vision out of my mind. The next twenty minutes were crucial. I needed to listen to Coach; my judgment couldn't be clouded by a tiny black-headed minx. But after . . . that was a different fucking story.

"Y'all are my fucking men!" I pumped my fist in the air as I entered the locker room, raging obscenities.

"We gonna take our game back?" Ashton banged his fist into the locker.

Coach yelled, "Shut it, gentlemen. Not enough of a show out there. Where's my team? You all stay out too late last night? Give me a W!"

We took over the second half with an attitude adjustment. I moved the ball down the court, feeding the guys with dimes. One by one, they hit buckets. I had a gorgeous outside shot that swished through the air and sailed into the net. We ran a man-to-man defense where each of our guys guarded one of theirs, and we basically rendered them scoreless in the second half.

We won by twenty-five and poured out of the court on a sea of cheers.

"Unstoppable! Yeah, boys," Ashton chanted as he pounded his fist into his locker.

Sweaty clothes flew through the locker room, most landing in the big industrial hamper, and steam filtered above the showers as the cheering continued.

"We partying tonight," D screamed. "Yeah, boys. Fucking A-right, Green for life!"

"Get after it, next week, we're gonna kill it! Yeah!" Mo slapped his towel against the wall and swiveled his hips, waving his dick in the cool air.

We were a bunch of pigs, but winning pigs.

"Put that fucking thing away," Demetri said sternly.

"Don't be so fucking crazy, it's all your sister's," Mo taunted him.

"Shut the fuck up, Maurice, while I'm still in a good mood."

"Let it go," I told them, not in the mood to break up a fight.

"Where's the party?" Alex strutted in, toting a few freshmen behind him. "They're ready to get laid on our coattails." He pointed to the scrawny nineteen-year-olds.

"I got my lady waiting," Mo said as Demetri eyed him up. "Speaking of ladies, I saw your DJ girl over New Year's, Steele."

I was drying my ass with the towel, and didn't bother covering when I turned around. "What did you just say?"

"I saw Ms. Cute Catie."

"Where?"

"Put your cock away and I'll tell you."

I snagged my towel off the floor and tied it around my waist. "Well?"

"At the new wine joint."

"She's not twenty-one. What was she doing there?"

Ashton smirked at me. "I thought you were over her."

"Be quiet," I said to Ashton, then circled my hand at Mo to spill it.

"She was alone, man. Spewed something about you not needing her shit right now."

I glared at him. "What's up with you waiting two weeks to tell me?"

"Oh boy, you got it bad for Cute Catie," Alex said, taunting me. "I'm going to tweet her."

When he grabbed his phone off his locker shelf and started banging away at the keyboard, I kept quiet. I knew what he would find.

Puzzled, he looked up at me. "She's not on Twitter?"

"Canceled her account. For the best," I muttered.

"Now that we got that out of the fucking way, where's the party?" Alex asked, still scrolling through his phone.

All of a sudden, his head flew up, water spraying from his dreads "Whoa, listen to this. @Hafton101 swears he saw an Ariel Stone lookalike at the game tonight. What the fuck? I have to go home and google her. I heard her titty-fuck shit is hot as hell."

"I'm heading out," I called, dressing in jeans and a Henley.

"What the fuck? Where you going?" Ashton called after me, but my Timberlands were already at the threshold.

"Catch you later."

Snow had covered my pickup during the game. I turned the engine over and got back out, pulling the collar up on my coat before I brushed off the windshield. After jumping back in the driver's seat, I put the truck into gear and hightailed it to the far end of campus. The Golden Goblet sat at the very end of College Avenue, and from the looks of it, wasn't a place I'd ever go. But Cate had been there two weeks ago, and maybe it was a regular thing for her.

I left the truck in a spot behind the shopping center and hustled through the cold, shivering because my hair was still wet and it was fucking freezing. I practically ran to the door of the joint. Once I got inside, I ran my fingers through my hair, trying to make myself look presentable. I hung my coat on a hook and paced toward the back, surveying all the tables.

Nothing.

As I headed to the bar, I saw her. She was sitting on a stool, her hair tied up on top of her head, her sweatshirt falling off one shoulder.

I walked right over, no warning, no patience. Running my hand over her bare shoulder—her right one, the one without my name—I spoke in her ear.

"Thought you weren't legal."

She flinched and jumped in her seat. "Blane?" She gave me an annoyed look and quickly slipped her phone into her purse.

"Hi," I said sheepishly.

"What are you doing here?"

I leaned against the vacant stool next to her. "Looking for you. Where have you been?"

"Mo said he saw me?"

I nodded. "Where have you been?" I repeated my question, wanting . . . no, *needing* an answer.

"I got thrown out of my major."

"I heard. Sonny told me, but that's all he would say."

"I moved off campus, and I've just been trying to stay under the radar." She kept twisting her wrist and looking at her watch.

"You meeting someone?"

"Actually, yeah. I have to go; someone's picking me up."

"I miss seeing you," I admitted foolishly.

"Miss you too, but I have to go."

I curled my fingers and ran the back of my hand along her cheek. She wasn't wearing much makeup, and she looked beautiful. "Saw you there tonight."

A smile started to form on her face, but she quickly schooled it. "You know I'm a fan."

"Let's have another drink." I pointed toward her empty glass.

"I can't."

"I got you; I'm not who or what you want. I'm just a baller or whatever. A stupid guy who will make a ton of money someday, thanks to my athletic skills."

"Stop." She placed her hand on my chest and fire licked through the Henley, her fingers sending a jolt to my pulse. "It's not you; it's me. I'm figuring stuff out, and you don't need that."

"Let me decide that, not you."

"Seriously, Blane. I have to go. Great win tonight."

She planted a small kiss on my cheek, her lips ghosting over my five o'clock shadow before slipping away. I wanted to sink my tongue into her mouth, but she was on the move.

"Wait!" I said. "Can we get a drink tomorrow?"

She swallowed hard, and a strange expression flitted over her face before it was gone.

"Coffee maybe?" I was grasping at anything.

Cate sighed. "Sure. How about Starbucks off campus?"

"Really?"

"Yeah. Two o'clock?"

"Good," I said, taking her elbow. "Let me walk you out."

"No, you go ahead. I'm going to use the restroom first."

I wanted to wait and see her out, but she'd looked like seven shades of green when I suggested it. Having been raised by a single mom, I knew not to push it.

So I ran back to my truck, ratcheted up the heat, and headed back to what I was sure would be a rager at my apartment. When I scrolled through Twitter while I waited at a red light, my suspicions were confirmed.

> *@HaftonBabe:*
> *Where is @BallerSteele? I'm waiting for him at his place.*
> *#nolongercelibate #GoHaftonGreen*

chapter twenty-five

Catie

I didn't know why I agreed to meet Blane, other than I was a sadist. Or was I a masochist? I didn't know which was which, but I clearly liked to inflict pain on myself.

I couldn't stop thinking about Blane as I got dressed. I even straightened up my bathroom before tossing everything Ariel-related into a drawer, out of sight.

Not that I was planning on bringing Blane back here, but he couldn't know about this. Ever.

I wasn't ashamed. In fact, I was scared by how much I felt in control over the situation. The money aside, I was making my own rules. For the first time in my life, I wasn't in anyone's shadow, and I was standing tall in my choice. It wasn't at all what I thought would come of the experience. Originally, I wanted to understand why women started in the industry, and why they stayed.

Now I got it. What else would they do?

Catching a glance at myself in the mirror, I smiled. I was still the same short, curvy woman, but there was something different. I felt more desirable, but not because of the sexy videos. No, those left me needing a shower. It was the control. My mom wasn't there telling me how stupid I was, and my dad wasn't comforting me with food. My sisters weren't judging, and Stanwick wasn't chastising me.

My phone pinged just as I was heading out to walk to Starbucks. Standing in the vestibule of my shabby apartment building, I plucked it out of my coat pocket and read the incoming text.

> *Tess: Hey, girl! Where have you been? Would love to see you.*

> *Catie: I'm here. Want to do lunch this week?*

> *Tess: Sure. Did you see what's going on all over Twitter? Sonny's in love.*

I smiled to myself. What an idiot.

> *Catie: Yep! Dumb guy. Of course he is.*

> *Tess: And you? Have you seen you-know-who?*

> *Catie: No.*

> *Tess: Fine. Oh, heard from Shelby you got an ID! Want to do lunch next week at the Mexican place and have a margarita?*

Why not? I was only taking two classes since I was thrown out of my major, making me ineligible to take what I wanted this trimester. And only two classes on my schedule left me a bit of free time.

Catie: Sure.

Tess: Text me on Monday.

Catie: OK.

I shoved the phone back in my bulky coat pocket and pushed the door out into the cold winter air. The sky was gray and hung heavy with moisture. It would probably snow tonight, and I would be happy to snuggle at home in pajamas. Frank didn't film on Saturdays, choosing to take his wife out instead, so it was my night off. Otherwise, I worked double-time during the week, filming as much as I could. The money was an insane motivator, the notoriety not even a close second for me.

It was also free speech and such. I was so sick of Stanwick tossing out my ideas. These ladies did what they had to do, and no one stopped them from doing it.

My boots crunched through the leftover snow on the sidewalk as I hustled to a hot cup of coffee and an even hotter tall drink of man. A chill ran down my spine at the thought of what I was doing. I bundled myself tighter in my scarf and picked up my pace.

Why couldn't I have aimed for a soccer scholarship? Instead I was thrown out of my major, kicked to the curb, and turned into an overnight porn sensation.

"Hey! Cate."

I turned to see Blane getting out of his pickup.

"I would have picked you up," he said as he rushed over to walk in with me.

"Not necessary. A little fresh air does me good."

I tried to form a friendly smile, but couldn't help the sizzle traveling through my whole body at the sight of him. He looked good in bulky Timberlands, with a puffy coat unzipped over skinny sweats and a thermal shirt.

"I see you're still sporting your sweatband from last night." I sniffed deeply as he held the door open, allowing the aroma of fresh-roasted coffee beans to give my tired head a much-needed jolt.

"Can't take it off now."

"I don't even want to know what it smells like."

"Hey, I run it through the water in the shower."

We stepped in line, and like a missile, his hand landed on my back in a fiery explosion. I tried to scoot away, but he pulled me into the circle of his arm and whipped out his phone to snap a selfie.

"What are you doing?"

"Sonny lifted the ban; I'm sure you already know. The whole campus is wondering where Cute Catie is, and I'm giving them proof she's with me."

His fingers worked overtime on his phone before he said proudly, "Done."

"I don't even want to know what you just did," I whispered before breaking free from his hold.

"Hey, Steele, awesome game last night," the barista yelled.

"Yeah, unreal," the girl at the register said, practically swooning at the sight of him.

"Thanks, y'all," he said as we stepped up to the counter. "A cappuccino, fully leaded, and a bottled water."

I gave him the stink-eye. "You don't have to order for me."

"Cut the feminist crap. You're just an everyday woman now."

Little did he know.

"I drink a skinny latte now, for your information," I snorted back.

"That explains your curves being smaller. I liked them better the other way."

He turned back to the swoony counter girl and said, "Give me two of those scones too."

"Stop, you're making a scene," I mumbled, noticing a lot of customers glancing at their phones and then looking up at us.

"Hey, Blane, will you take a selfie with me too?" some girl ran over from the fireplace to ask.

"Sure." He winked at her and said "smile" as she hit the button on her phone.

I frowned at Blane as the girl scurried off, holding her phone in the air triumphantly.

"Glad to know you're not putting all your eggs in one basket."

"Oh, I am. I most certainly am, Cate."

That's exactly what I didn't want to hear.

We sat down in a couple of overstuffed chairs near the corner, the fire to our right and the bathrooms to our left. Too late, I realized there was no avenue of escape.

Blane cracked his water, took a swig, and leaned close to me. With his hand on my knee, he said, "Cate, what the hell? What's up?"

"I needed space," I said, giving him an overused excuse. Next I'd be giving him the old, *It's not you, it's me.*

"Come on, you may have acted all small with Sonny, but that's not you. What the fuck?" His hair was wet from snow, and his eyes were flecked with small slivers of gold inside the green. He wasn't smiling, though. He looked concerned.

If only he knew sitting with me could ruin his career.

"It was bullshit," I said, averting my eyes to gaze unseeing at the fireplace. "I was thrown out of my department and I had to think shit over."

He smirked at the swear words I let fly. "I get that, but we had this one time . . . one night, whatever you want to call it. I don't usually do romance, but it felt great. And intimate. And then you bailed."

"I know, I don't know. Ugh." I leaned back, resting my head on the back of the chair for a moment as I closed my eyes. "There are too many mixed messages out there, and they're driving me wild."

"You're a witty, sexy woman, and I'm an interested man. There's no mixed messages here."

"And then what? I give you it all, all of me, and then what? The NBA, and tall, gorgeous women throwing themselves all over you?" I grabbed my latte and took a big gulp. My stomach tumbled with my nervousness; the lonely scones on the table weren't even calling to me.

"Whoa, let's back up. Did you hear me? You're a woman and I'm a man, and we're both young. I can't say shit about next year, but right now I'd like to hang out with you."

He took another swig of his water, and I watched his Adam's apple bob as he swallowed. Strangely, I wanted to run my tongue along his neck.

"Why?"

"Come on, you can't be that naive, Cate. You're sweet, sassy, built like a woman should be. Any guy would be silly not to want to hang with you."

"Are you doing that whole swoony thing again?"

"I'm trying it out for a while. Is it working?" This time he smiled and a small dimple appeared on his right cheek.

I wanted to lick there too.

"It's sort of working," I admitted.

I gulped coffee and tried to swallow the lump in my throat. I'd already tainted my own reputation and stood to do worse when my research came out, and now I was considering tossing this guy's future in the trash.

"So, what the hell have you been doing all this time? Watching women's basketball?"

Nerves skated over my spine like a hockey player on steroids.

Or a basketball player with NBA aspirations.

I looked away, shifting a little in my chair. "Um, I've been up to a little of this and a little of that. Made a few new friends and got an ID, but you already know that. Experiencing life."

That wasn't too much of a lie. Exactly.

"So, can we do a little experiencing together?"

I raised an eyebrow at his dirty suggestion.

"Not like that. Right away. G-rated or whatever. I can take you on a picnic. Isn't that what girls love?"

"I wouldn't know. I've never been on one."

"Then we should do it."

"Blane, it's the middle of January. When it's warmer, maybe?" I nipped off a piece of the scone and popped it in my mouth.

"Ha! Yeah. How about an indoor picnic? Next week? We're traveling the beginning of the week to Ann Arbor, but when I get back?"

I thought no, but yes came out of my mouth, and my heart sank to my boots.

Maybe I could keep this whole project a secret until I was out of the business? I was stashing the money and planning to shift my focus to pure research soon, needing more anecdotal input to flesh out my data.

"Good." Blane squeezed my thigh, bringing me back to the

present and making my panties wet.

How was it that Ricky masturbated in front of me and I felt nothing, and this guy touched my leg and I was ready to go? All the way?

"Now tell me, have you been watching my games?" he asked and then finished his water.

I felt my smile reach my ears.

"I knew it!" Blane slapped his hand into the small table in front of us, causing a commotion.

"Shhh, I've already been delisted as a feminist. Now they'll call me a ball baby!"

"Let's see what's happening on Twitter," he suggested, and I slapped my forehead.

"Fuck."

He cracked up and swiped his finger up the screen on his phone.

> *@Hafton101:*
> *Looky here - @BallerSteele is out with the former #CuteCatie. Are they an item? (@SonnyB_KnocknBoots) What about the 'ship?*

> *@SonnyB_KnocknBoots:*
> *Hey, #CuteCatie, come back and see me - fill me in - I have this new intern who spends his day watching porn*

> *@SexySarina:*
> *Aw, look at the cute couple #steeleandcutecatie <3*

Blane started typing away, and I peered over his shoulder.

@BallerSteele:

Working on it, @Hafton101 (On both the #ship and #CuteCatie)

"Looks like they're already talking about you." He ran his knuckles over my cheek, and I shivered.

"You cold?"

I shook my head.

"Here." He picked off a piece of the scone and ran it along my lips. I opened willingly and let it fall on my tongue. "We could take a picture of our tattoos." He swiped the hair off my shoulder and tugged at my sweatshirt.

"Oh God," I grumbled. "That seems like a lifetime ago. But it wasn't."

"It definitely wasn't, and it was fun."

Blane ran his nose along my cheek before backing away. Then he winked and leaned close again. I was getting dizzy from all the back and forth, or maybe just from him. Who the hell knew?

He whispered near my ear, his warm breath stirring my hair. "Let's do this again, Cute Cate."

I smiled like a fool, swallowed, and nodded.

"I have to go; Coach wants us in for a team meeting. But I'm driving you home."

"Okay."

That's how easily I gave in to him.

Ball baby.

chapter twenty-six

Blane

She wasn't the same Cate when she first showed up on Saturday. Quiet, reserved, or whatever the fuck you call it. She wasn't the foulmouthed sprite I knew her to be.

But it didn't take long for her to warm up, the pulse in her neck to start fluttering, and a few four-letter words to come out of her mouth. *I had her at hello*, or whatever the movie said. I think my high school girlfriend made me watch it before she put out.

Monday morning, I arched my back in my seat on the bus and adjusted my earphones. A little old-school Guns and Roses blasted in my ears as I shut my eyes and concentrated on ball. And a little more Cate.

I'd have to invite her personally to the game on Friday, so I could know where she'd been hiding.

Okay, enough Cate.

I visualized my crossover and my spin move. I actually saw it happening in slow motion against our upcoming opponent, and felt a rush of adrenaline.

Someone tapped on my shoulder, and I turned to find Mo behind me on the bus.

"Ready to ball out?" He slid the cans off my ears.

"Fucking A right," I shouted.

"Listen, man, the baby's due in April," Mo said in a low voice. "I'm yours until then, but I got to have a plan. We need this 'ship."

"I know, my brother. I know. You're gonna do good and make your bro proud. And me."

"You too, Steele."

We both settled back with our music until we arrived and were hustled off to a practice.

My mom called just as I was heading to my hotel room for the night.

"Hey, Mom," I answered, shutting the door behind me.

"Guess what? I got a bigger advance than I thought, and Gigi is coming to stay with the dogs so I can come up again in two weeks!"

Sitting on the edge of the bed, I blew out a long breath. Of course she was. My dad was also scheduled to come in two weeks.

"I assume you know Dad is coming?"

"Yeah, I'm going to stay out of his way . . . okay, baby?"

As if.

"Of course. Listen, I have to get some rest. Big game tomorrow night."

"You do that, honey."

We hung up, and I texted Cate on the new number she'd given

me, but I didn't hear back.

The next morning, I woke up early and did a few rounds of pushups and sit-ups in my room. Ashton, who had come in sometime after me, was dead asleep in the other bed. I slapped his ass when I was done.

"Come on, we got a team breakfast and a light practice."

"Shit, fuck," he mumbled, but got up and walked to the bathroom with his dick in his hand.

"Dude, you have got to stop that," I called out, but knew he wouldn't.

I checked my phone after lunch and saw I had a text from Cate.

Cate: Sorry. Was working on a project late last night. Good luck today! :)

I didn't respond; Coach would have my hide if my mind wasn't on winning this game, which it was. It was a nationally televised matchup, prime time on ESPN, and I was fucking ready to ball out.

Doing my usual thing at warmup, stretching my wingspan and my hammies, I heard a lot of boos. Part of being on the road. It didn't matter; I took possession after the tip and didn't let my foot off the gas.

"Push it," Coach yelled from the sidelines, and I did.

We put on a show, the starting five. We were up by twenty-two at the half, and hit the locker room with chants and slaps.

Back at the new half, we all took turns getting rest on the bench. Conley rotated us like a pro, veins bulging in his neck as he screamed plays to two of the new guys rotating in and out, and then to us. I ended it with a quick pass to a newbie, Slick, and he dunked at the buzzer.

Another one in the bucket.

"Winner, winner, chicken dinner," I yelled in the showers after the game.

"Dude, I need some chicken and some bird," Alex yelled back.

"You're sick," I called back.

"No, that's you, lover boy."

He was sort of right.

Wednesday, I picked up Cate at her new place at five. She came running down the steps in jeans and a puffy coat, her hair tucked into a dark green Hafton knit cap. I smiled to myself at her repping the team.

"Hey," she said.

"I could've come up to the door, but if you're not ready for me to be in your place, I'm cool." I winked as she buckled up.

"It's just . . . never mind. Chalk it up to excitement."

I wasn't sure what it was going to take for her to come out of her repressed shell, and I certainly didn't know why I wanted to try, but fuck it.

"Congrats on the game," she breathed out, her words making little puffs of smoke in the car.

Reaching out to turn up the heat, I said, "Yeah, it felt good to give a beating that bad on the road. Speaking of which, you coming on Friday? I can get you a ticket with an actual seat."

"I'm not sure yet. I want to, but I have to see if I can."

What the fuck was that all about? I raised an eyebrow.

She focused on fastening her seatbelt, not meeting my eyes.

"Seriously, I'm working on this project with a partner, and they only have certain times available."

"I got you. I'm hurt, but I got you."

"So, what are we doing?"

"It's a surprise."

I reached over the console and flicked on some music. "Sit back and enjoy the ride."

She turned the dial, and whose voice came shooting through the truck? Yep, Sonny.

"Yo, Hafton, I'm single. Miranda and I had a bad breakup. Who wants to console me? Call me here. Now."

Some awful *twerk it on the dance floor* vibe came on, and we both laughed.

"I can't believe I quit," she admitted.

"I don't get why you let him push you around."

Cate pushed her hair behind her ear, but kept her gaze focused on the road. "It was complicated. Basically, my sisters are different from me. They're all girlie and like to woo the guys. Clara, the oldest, told me to soften my approach at work."

"Doesn't seem like you to give a fuck." I caught a quick peek of her out of my peripheral vision. She was biting her lower lip and scrunching her face, deep in thought.

"I guess I was struggling with who I was before all this . . . getting kicked out of my major. I don't really know."

"Well, I'm glad you're finding your way," I said honestly. I thought about if I didn't have ball. Who would I be?

Then Sonny interrupted my thoughts again.

"Sonny B. here, who's this?"

A male caller said, "Dude, if you're single again, you have to check out Ariel Stone. I'll—"

I didn't hear the rest because Cate grabbed the dial and switched the station.

"I can't listen to him anymore."

"That's good, 'cause we're here." I stopped in front of a barn and put the truck in park.

"What's this?"

"A barn."

Rolling her eyes, she said, "I can see that."

"Another booster, they all love me. They're banking on tickets wherever I settle. Come on." I threw open my door.

Cate jumped out of her side of the truck, and I came around to grab her arm. Her head was even with my rib cage, and she was practically sinking into the wet grass as we walked toward the door. With a flick of my wrist, I slid open the large slatted door, and right there in the center of the barn was a picnic.

I might have asked Mo for help, who in turn might have asked his woman for some guidance.

"This is so beautiful."

Cate stopped in her tracks and stared in front of her. Strings of tiny white lights hung from the ceiling, giving the barn a romantic light. A large, soft blanket lay on the floor, an invitation to sit down and relax if there ever was one. A bottle of wine chilled in a bucket, and a small spread of finger foods sat with a pair of wineglasses and small plates on one corner of the blanket. On the other corner was a plate of chocolate-covered strawberries, artfully arranged into a heart, sitting on top of another folded blanket. A small cooler waited beside the wine.

"I didn't really do much," I said with a shrug. "D's sister Angela helped; you know, Mo's lady. But I asked her to," I quickly added.

"It's really too beautiful," she said haltingly. "For me."

"Come on." I took her hand and led her to the blanket. We sat down and I threw the second blanket over our legs. Thank fuck the barn was heated. These boosters were some rich mo-fo's.

I poured some wine for Cate and snatched a beer from the cooler for myself. I'd already eaten a shit-ton with the guys after practice, which was good because this girlie food wasn't going to cut it.

"Cheers." I knocked my bottle into her glass and passed her a plate.

We ate and made boring small talk. I told her about Mo knocking Angela up, the fight with D, and how things had settled.

"Kind of crazy, isn't it? Having a baby in college?" She ran her hand through her hair, shifting it behind her ear.

"I guess, but Mo's graduating and he's gonna make good money, so I guess she'll tag along."

Cate seemed to think for a beat. "But she may want to finish her degree. Have a fallback."

"There's my little feminist . . . a short stack, but mighty."

"Seriously, you don't know what will happen in life. She could follow Mo, and then he could leave her high and dry later."

"He could, but I don't think he will. They're having a baby. He's doing the right thing."

She shrugged and took a sip of her wine.

"You've changed so much in the last few weeks, drinking and now just settling for my answer. When I first met you, you would have made me drive you to Angela so you could pound some sense into her head." I stroked her arm. "Is everything okay?"

"Yeah," she said softly. "Like I told you, I'm figuring stuff out."

"Tell me about this project."

She smirked at me. "I would, but then I'd have to kill you, and I think the team would be pretty upset."

"Don't do that."

"Tell me about you," she said, changing the subject. "What's coming up on the schedule? What does Coach say?"

Secretly, I loved Cate's interest in sports. It wasn't fake. She liked to see us play enough to sneak around to do it, and she always asked about it.

I didn't love whatever was going on inside her head and this secret project. Seemed to me she was in over her head, but who was I? A dumb jock. What the hell did I know?

"My mom and my dad are coming the same weekend," I told her. "Next week to see the game against Pitt."

"Really?"

"Not by coincidence either. My mom is a glutton for romance . . . and punishment. She's chasing my dad around again."

Cate huffed. "At least they can be civil. My parents can't be within fifty feet of each other without tearing each other's eyeballs out."

I laughed hard and took a long pull of my beer. "My parents will fuck and then pull each other's eyeballs out. I don't know what's better. And this is a big fucking game."

Tired of the small talk, I set aside my beer and pulled Cate close until she landed on my lap. I reached over to grab a strawberry and ran it over her lips. Her tongue peeked out to taste the chocolate.

Holding the strawberry just out of her reach, I said, "I want to kiss you." Or maybe I asked, because I didn't know what she wanted, and I wasn't sure what I wanted. I'd never had to think about it before . . . or ask.

"You're quite the romantic," she said, her brown eyes jumping with curiosity.

I liked that about her. I excited her and she didn't even know it.

"My mom writes romance, did you know? She must've rubbed

off on poor me."

She didn't say anything, just stared at me like she was trying to understand the opposing team's plays. My cock was hard as shit, and my heart raced like I was at center court. I both loved and hated it. My whole life was ahead of me, and yeah, I wanted more. But was this it? This tiny outspoken woman from New Jersey who seemed to be so sure, yet unsure of herself?

Was I settling? I almost laughed out loud at how fucking ridiculous that sounded. I was on a date; it wasn't a honeymoon or a lifetime of promises, no matter how deeply she looked into my eyes.

I tossed the strawberry aside and leaned in to kiss Cate. "Is this okay?"

And there it was, that *sensitive* part of me. I'd been raised by mostly my mom, and she and my dad might be fucked up but she didn't raise me to be that way. She'd be mortified if she knew how I'd made my way through women like they were sweatbands these past few years. One thing for sure—I'd never forced myself on them, but I definitely took what was being offered.

And here I was asking if a kiss was okay.

To me, it felt way better than okay.

My tongue sought refuge in her mouth, fucking it while my hand stroked her back. Her soft moans vibrated against my tongue, and I swallowed each one as if I were starving.

I ran my hand up her spine, halting at the base of her neck to hold her close. I didn't have to put too much pressure, just enough to make my needs known. I wanted Cate, needed her riding my cock, but I doubted that would happen.

Eventually, I pulled back and brushed her lips with the back of my knuckles. "You're so beautiful."

She bowed her head at the compliment, and I lifted her chin with my finger.

"I mean it." The tattoo of her name burned on my chest as a reminder of the commitment I'd already made to this girl. I was all-in.

"Thank you. You're not too bad yourself." She reached over and ruffled my hair.

We relaxed and laughed together as we fed each other strawberries. Side by side, we lay back on the blanket and talked some more while I stroked her arm. She nestled her head against my shoulder, and I told her more about growing up with a single mom in a trailer park. She talked about her dad and how much he meant to her. Her sisters sounded like bitches, and her mom was an even worse piece of shit.

It wasn't until her phone pinged that we noticed how late it was. It was close to ten o'clock, and she said she had to meet a friend.

"What?" Bewildered, I poked her side and tried to make fun of the situation, even though jealousy burned a hole in my gut. "Who? A booty call?"

She turned an evil eye on me. "Don't be rude."

"I'm not. I guess, just jealous," I nervously admitted.

"Well, it's a friend who is a girl, and I promised to help her with something."

"Who?"

"You don't know her."

What the fuck?

"Can you take me back now?" Cate ran her hands down her pants, straightening her clothes. "I had a great time, but this isn't something I can back out of now."

"Sure," I said abruptly, not bothering to push my anger from my tone.

And when she turned away, for a second I thought I saw tears glistening in her eyes.

chapter twenty-seven

Catie

For a second or a few hours, I'd felt myself slipping into the warmth of Blane Steele, and then I wasn't. Angry and frustrated, I stomped into the warehouse at eleven p.m. like a bitch in heat. My libido was up, my feelings low.

Frank looked hard and long at me. "What's wrong, Ari?"

"Nothing."

"You sure you're good to go?" He stilled, watching me move toward a dressing table.

"I'm fucking fine, Frank."

"Okay, short stuff."

I flipped him off and tossed my tote on the counter. Then I dropped onto a seat in front of the mirror and stared at my reflection.

Jesus, I was a porn sensation. *Me!* Yeah, I loved dressing like a Jersey girl, but this was insane.

For the first time since I'd gotten myself tangled up in this cockeyed plan, reality hit me hard. It landed in my belly, a hard pit of satisfaction coated in regret. I was proving what I believed to be true, yet destroying the only good thing I'd ever had.

But I never really had Blane. *Right?*

Shit. Enough!

I tugged on my wig and checked my reflection as I tucked in stray wisps of my own hair. Then I ripped off my sweatshirt, leaving just my camisole. I snatched one of the skin-colored pieces of tape off the table and turned to see my tattoo in the mirror.

He was a stealer, all right; he'd basically stolen my heart during the course of one picnic.

Frowning, I smoothed the tape over the tattoo so there would be no way to identify me in the video, and then I swiped on my makeup.

With my boobs pushed up high, nearly bursting out of my cami, I walked onto the set wearing tight jeans and knee-high boots. Sarina came in next wearing a similar outfit, although she would be taking hers off. I was just going to remove my top and bra so Big Bryan could come all over me . . . after fucking Sarina in every hole.

I found it hard to plaster a smile on my face this evening. It was better when I had isolated myself. There were less people to hurt when I didn't have connections outside my adult-film family. Sarina had become more of a sister than my own; I couldn't leave her in the dust.

I was on a mission to prove many of these women weren't the cheap, tawdry sluts we believed them to be. They were women, sisters, moms, and aunts just like all of us, and this was their job, their way of putting food on the table, paying the bills, and placing presents under the Christmas tree.

"One, two, three . . . live set now. Quiet, please," Frank shouted, and that was our cue to begin.

We shot the movie in two takes, and as I was leaving, Sarina insisted on giving me a lift so I wouldn't have to take the bus.

"You okay?" she asked as we stopped outside my building.

"Yeah," I said softly.

"It's normal to have doubts about what we do," she said, apparently reading my mind.

I shook my head and sniffed back a tear.

Sarina reached out to pat my shoulder. "This weekend, I want to bring a few other girls over to your place. They said it would be okay for you to interview them. Lisa's parents tossed her out like garbage when she got pregnant at sixteen. Brittany is like you, a college student who pays her tuition and expenses with the money. She sees this as the ultimate freedom of speech, and is looking forward to meeting you. And then there's Chantae, a lifer. She got into the biz with her ex-husband and never left. She has three boys."

"Wow."

A smile crossed my face. This was exactly what I wanted, to prove my theories, and Sarina was providing me with firsthand accounts.

"Thanks, Ri. Seriously, I can never pay you back for this." I leaned over to kiss her on the cheek before I got out of the car to brave the cold.

"Hey," she called to me. "When you're famous, don't forget me."

Then she drove away, heading home to crawl into her own bed for only a few hours' sleep before her son awoke.

Saturday came faster than I expected.

Of course, I'd sneaked into the field house the night before and watched the game before heading to film. I hid out in Section 305, so there was no chance of Blane seeing me, but he'd texted after the game anyway.

> Blane: *Were you there? I swear I could smell you.*

> Catie: *LOL. Yes. Great game! Loved the dunk in the second half. The one with the and-one.*

> Blane: *That guy hacked the hell out of my hand, but thanks. Where did you sit?*

> Catie: *Never. The section number will die with me.*

Truth was, I couldn't take his eyes stroking me before heading out to tape. I didn't like being duplicitous, even if this was only a fling to him. In a few short months, his opinion had come to matter to me, and this wasn't something I could explain.

> Blane: *I'll be distracted during the next game looking for you.*

> Catie: *No way. I've seen you. You're all about ball on the court.*

> Blane: *Just wait and see. Do you have time for dinner Saturday?*

> Catie: *Maybe. I could do a late one.*

Frank would be off tomorrow night, so I didn't have to work. But

the girls were coming over in the afternoon, and I didn't want to rush them.

Blane: Deal. I'll grab you around eight?

Catie: OK.

Blane: We're going to go to a restaurant and not break into anyone's home.

Catie: I knew that was all a lie! Boosters, my ass—we were trespassing!

Blane: That's for me to know. See you tomorrow, shortie.

Catie: Don't you dare call me that, Jolly Green Giant.

Blane: LMAO.

That was yesterday. Now I raced around my small apartment and straightened up for my company, wondering what they would think of me. Would they accept me?

As I fluffed the pillows on my bed, the doorbell rang.

I pulled the door open to find a diverse group of women in the hallway—tall and short, busty and rail-thin, some wearing makeup and others not. Bright lipstick glared from one highly made-up face, while another woman's head was covered by a scarf.

Sarina made the introductions at the threshold. "Ladies, this is Ariel, also known as Cate. She's going to vindicate us."

I smiled at them, hoping I would do them more good than bad.

"This is Brittany." She pointed at the young woman with bright pink lipstick wearing leggings and an oversized denim shirt, and UGGs on her feet.

"Hey." The girl stepped in and pulled me into a hug.

"This is Chantae."

The woman with the deep mahogany skin and a bright green scarf wrapped around her hair blew me a kiss and walked into my place.

"In the back are Mich and Tish."

These two were obviously identical twins. It felt like double vision looking at them both in braided pigtails, skinny jeans, flannel shirts, and heavily glossed lips.

"You got any coffee?" they asked and sauntered inside.

"And this is Lisa," Sarina said with her arm around a petite brunette with enormous boobs.

I dragged my gaze away from her impressive chest and said, "Nice to meet you."

Lisa narrowed her eyes on me. "So, you're the newbie taking up all my bestie's time?"

"Umm . . ."

"Kidding, babe. Good to meet you," she said, and pinched my arm before she slid past me.

I made coffee and poured generous mugs, passing them all around before making a second pot.

Sarina explained what I was doing with my project, and I chimed in with a little more detail while the women made themselves comfortable on my bed and floor. Their eyes were wide as they listened.

"Basically, my professor wouldn't even hear my reasoning as to why women might actually choose to be filmed in this way. The more

I thought about it, the more I felt how shortsighted she was. Anyway, for her there's only one way to be feminist. In her eyes, if I date an athlete or feel empathy toward women who believe the best solution for them is pornography, then I'm not a feminist. But she's wrong; for some women, it may very well be their only choice."

A round of cheers broke out in my apartment.

"You go, girl," Chantae called out, and the twins punched their fists into the air.

After a few hours of talking, several more pots of coffee, and more than a few tears, the women said their good-byes and filed out.

Sarina kissed me on the cheek as we stood in the doorway, and I hugged her tight.

"Thanks," I whispered.

"No, thank you."

I gave her a kiss on the cheek. "Have fun tonight with your little guy."

Part of me didn't want her to go. I wanted to sit on my bed and ask her about my situation with Blane. Was it serious or casual? What did she think he wanted?

And more importantly, was I being a fool?

She reached out to squeeze my arm. "Hey, babe . . . whatever's on your mind, put it to rest. And you know, if you don't want to make the movies, don't. That's the whole point of this project, right? The power of choice. A feminist is someone who exercises that power."

"You're pretty smart, Ri. You should write the book." I smiled and shooed her out the door.

Leaning against the door after I closed it behind her, I realized Sarina had hit me where it hurt. I was writing about choice. Except, these women had no other choice, but me? I guess I sort of did. I was working on my education and once I had it, would be qualified for something more than the adult-film industry. At least, I thought so.

Maybe I would quit the movie-making part, and would be no worse for the wear. And if I did, maybe I could call my dad and borrow some money?

I tossed the idea around in my head while I jumped in the shower and got ready for my date, or whatever it was. Buddy time? Buddy fuck? Maybe.

There were so many maybes, but that was also part of having choices. I could choose to have fun with Blane or not.

I decided to go with what was behind Door A.

Fun.

chapter
twenty-eight

Catie

My apartment had never seen so much action when my doorbell rang for the second time in one day. This time, two-hundred-plus pounds of steel stood on the other side, and it wasn't Superman.

But close.

"Hi."

I answered the door while shoving my arms in my coat, and then stuck a deep purple beret on my head. I was in my usual outfit—leggings, cami, off-the-shoulder sweater, hoop earrings, and lined boots. Blane looked delectable in a long-sleeved black T-shirt, worn jeans, an open leather jacket, his ever-present sweatband, and Timberlands. He only affirmed my choice to have fun.

When would I ever have the chance to do this again?

Never.

I was hard up and he was desperate. This was my only chance.

"What's happening down there?" Blane teased.

He winked at me, and I pretended to punch him in the gut. He feigned being hurt so he could bend over, and then he tossed me over his shoulder and spun me around.

"Put me down!" I shouted. "I'm heavy."

"Just showing you what it's like up here. And no, you're not heavy." He pinched my ass and set me down. "Ready?"

"Yep, let's blow this joint."

When he said, "I see you're bringing your filthy mouth along tonight," I giggled like a schoolgirl. *Giggled!*

"And I see you went all out with the sweatband tonight," I teased him.

"Can't take it off. No can do, lady."

He shifted it up a notch on his head, and his eyes crinkled just a tad. It was the sexiest thing I'd ever seen, better than the first porn we watched. Taking a deep breath, I calmed my hormones.

We left my apartment and Blane grabbed my hand. At the bottom of the stairs, Mr. Southern Gentleman held the door open and tossed his arm around me when we stepped outside.

"Shit, it's cold!" I exclaimed.

He squeezed my shoulder. "You may have to warm this boy up later."

Rock music came to life as soon as he started up the pickup.

"Sorry, I was jamming on my way over, getting my confidence on."

I smirked at him. "Oh, I'm so sure you needed that."

We drove toward College Avenue, but didn't turn.

"Where are we going?" I asked as butterflies the size of pterodactyls flew around inside my belly.

"Geno's."

"Really? For Italian? I've never been, but I've always wanted to try." A warm feeling that couldn't be more girlie or gooey ran through my veins.

"Me too. It sounds pretty damn good, and I'm in season, so I can eat."

"You know my dad owns a small Italian restaurant in New Jersey. I told you, right?"

He nodded. "Yeah, and I thought this would remind you of home. I know you're sort of a daddy's girl."

"Am not," I protested with a smile.

White puffs of air formed from our breath, and I rubbed my hands to keep them warm.

"Should I turn the heat up? I had it down because the truck was cold." Without waiting for my answer, he flicked a dial on the dash.

After a few beats of silence, I asked, "What did you do today?"

"Team meeting, light practice, watched tape, played Xbox. You know, all in a day's work."

"Ha! I bet."

"And you?"

"Homework and research," I mumbled.

"For your secret project?"

Blane was teasing me, but it only served as a reminder of how much jeopardy I was putting him in. I breathed a sigh of relief over my decision to stop filming. I crossed my right fingers near the passenger door, hoping this whole episode would pass without any detection. I could write my book as if I'd never starred in a porno.

"Yes, but you know, if I tell you, I may suddenly combust."

"Really? We wouldn't want that to happen." A nearby streetlight illuminated the corner of his mouth turning up.

We finally pulled up at Geno's. It was at the far end of town, past the agriculture school and at the bottom of a small hillside. Rumor had it that Geno grew a lot of his own vegetables and herbs right there behind the restaurant.

My dad had told me all about Geno; he was a bit of a legend. Food Network came here at least once a year, and Geno was frequently a judge on their cooking shows. A local, he'd graduated from Hafton's ag school before he went to culinary school in Cleveland.

And then I remembered. *Oh shit, this place is pricey.*

"You sure you want to eat here?" I asked Blane as he reached to turn off the engine.

"Yeah, of course. Why not?"

"It's pretty expensive."

He gave me a pointed look. "I can afford it."

"I wasn't suggesting otherwise. Fuck!"

"I may be blue collar, but I have some money. And guess what? Soon I'll be making a ton of it. Ball is life, and all that."

"But I can't go Dutch here," I protested.

"I have class too, Cate. I wouldn't bring you here to go Dutch. Come on, let's go and forget this conversation ever happened." He got out and ran around to open my door, and we quickly entered the warmth of Geno's.

The smell of fresh garlic and tomatoes filled my senses as soon as we walked in.

"Smells amazing," I said.

Blane leaned in and sniffed the top of my head. "I know."

Good thing he had his hand at my lower back, because I almost tripped over my own feet at that comment.

We were seated at a corner table near the back window where sparkly lights twinkled over Geno's garden, now bare for the winter. Tall torches ran around the perimeter of the garden, lighting up the hillside and sending smoke into the night air. A small pink votive cast shadows on our table next to a sectioned round dish with various dips.

Our server greeted us right away. "Welcome to Geno's. I brought warm focaccia bread for dipping. Can I get you anything to drink?"

Blane raised an eyebrow at me, and I raised one back at him as if to say, *What?*

"Can you bring us a bottle of your house red?" he asked our waitress.

"Sure thing. Get started on the bread and dips, and I'll be right back."

When she was out of earshot, I leaned forward to speak in a low voice. "I guess they don't card athletes."

"It's one of the fringe benefits." He grabbed a piece of bread and ripped it in two before handing half of it to me. "Ladies first, and don't be one of those *I don't eat* type dates."

"If you insist." I plunged my bread into the fagioli bean dip and savored my first bite. "Mmm, this is so good."

Blane tried it too and moaned with appreciation.

Our wine came, and I toasted to the upcoming away game. Blane toasted to what he called my 007 project. Heartburn raced up my esophagus at the mere mention of it.

We sipped our wine and dipped our bread while I smiled more than I had in my entire life. A few times, I pinched my leg under the table to make sure this was actually happening and not a dream.

He shot me a smile. "I think we're set to take the team on the road. We've been playing well, and the team is really gelling. Plus, Coach banned Sonny from the locker room, so my promise to win him a championship is all but forgotten."

"I doubt he forgot," I reminded Blane.

"Who cares? It was worth it to be able to get to know you—"

"Stop," I said.

"What did I do?" His fingers had been caressing my forearm, but he quickly pulled them away.

"Saying stuff like that, that I'm worth this or that."

"You know, for some sort of macho feminist, you really don't advocate for yourself, Cate."

His eyes darkened with emotion, and I started to laugh.

"Jesus, what now? Didn't you just hear me?"

I couldn't stop laughing when the server came back, interrupting our awkward moment. Blane ordered us a brick-oven pizza and antipasto salad to share.

"Seriously, Cate, why do you do that? Put yourself down and then laugh." His hand settled again on top of mine.

"You said *macho feminist*. It was pretty funny." I stifled another giggle.

"And the other part? Putting yourself down?"

A tropical storm of seriousness brewed in his eyes. Dark green swirled with deep gray, and flecks of blue sparked inside the funnel cloud.

"Because you're you, and I'm me. I guess that's why I always sneaked into sporting events and decided to be all pro-women to begin with—I never saw myself as the cool one. I was smart and cute and sweet, but not sexy or sultry. Like the women you're probably used to spending time with."

I stared at the votive slanting shadows on the tablecloth, and steadied my breath. I'd never confessed something like that before, come clean about my shortcomings and how they played into my decisions. Here I was laying it all out there for Blane Steele, the campus stud, all solid muscle and gorgeous hair. He was an icon at Hafton and soon to be iconic everywhere, and I was telling him all my woes.

He squeezed my hand and I looked up. I half expected him to get up and run, but he didn't. He sat firmly in his seat and continued to stare me down.

"Cate, there are no women I'm used to being with. Yes, I would be intimate . . . or fuck," he said, glancing around us before whispering the last part. "But it was always just a mutual getting off, definitely not the kind of thing where we'd spend time together. For the last few years, I've ate, slept, and breathed ball. I need money, need to make a living doing that shit."

My thumb took a chance and rubbed against his.

"I'm a man." He leaned in. "Yeah, I have needs, but I'm stumbling as much as you are with spending time with someone."

I took a deep breath and licked my lips. "Okay."

"Wow, so I've rendered Little Miss Big Mouth speechless."

This time we were both laughing when the server arrived with our food.

Blane gestured that I should serve myself first.

"Looks incredible," I said, scooping some salad full of beans and smoked meats onto my plate.

"I like any and all food. Not picky here," Blane said as he pulled his elbows off the table. He might have grown up without much, as he liked to so frequently point out, but someone had obviously taught him table manners.

"Me too. Sadly. It makes my mom crazy," I admitted. "But my dad would be gaga for this place. I have to call him tomorrow and tell him every detail."

"And you're liking all food makes me crazy in a good way. I'm having the most fun I ever had out to dinner." Blane clinked his glass into mine. "Cheers again."

I turned my head to the side in an effort to hide the blush creeping across my cheeks.

"Hey, look at me," he said, and I turned back. "I meant it, this is fun. Don't be bashful."

"I'm not. It's just I've really never been complimented like that."

"Consider it just the beginning, short stack."

"See? I knew you couldn't go that long without insulting my vertical challenge."

Blane plopped a hot pepper in his mouth, which he quickly regretted, and I burst out in more laughter.

After he chugged half of his water, he narrowed his eyes at me. "You could have warned me, Italian girl."

"What fun would that have been?"

"I'll show you." He pressed his large palms into the table and leaned over to kiss me, swiping his tongue in my mouth.

He pulled away. "How's that taste?"

"Incredibly hot, in a good way." This time I didn't even turn to hide my blush.

We kept eating, and by the time we'd finished the appetizers and wine, I couldn't eat anything else. Blane ate the pizza by himself, and it felt so domestic while I sat with him and he ate. At one point, he pinched off a bite of his slice and fed it to me.

This was all so strange for me. I wasn't playing on my home court, nowhere close.

The server was unobtrusive, the candle flickered prettily on the table, and the wine mellowed me. It was an idyllic evening. But with every second that passed, I grew more troubled.

I was stolen by the Stealer, and pretty sure I was unable to be rescued.

After dinner, Blane drove back toward campus. I was never more uncertain of what to do. I looked out the window as the familiar sights whizzed by, and didn't want this night to end.

"Do you want to come back to my place? No pressure," Blane asked. glancing at me.

"I think so."

"Cool. I don't want this night to end."

Me either.

chapter
twenty-nine

Blane

We parked outside my building and I had to adjust myself when I got out of the truck. I'd been in a perpetual state of arousal since I first picked Cate up. Her smell, her laugh, the way her tits bounced—all of it drove me wild.

But then she'd become secretive about her project, as if she didn't trust me, or she'd make some ridiculous remark, getting all down on herself. It was like having the icy contents of a cooler tossed in my lap.

I knew I had to check my erection at the door because I didn't know what she was down with . . . when we got back to my room. This was a definite first, but strangely erotic.

"Come on," I said, and wrapped my arm around her on the way to the building.

We rushed through the outer door and I guided her to the staircase. When loud music filled our ears as we reached my floor, I stopped in my tracks.

"Shit," I murmured. "Looks like my pad became party central

while I was out."

"That's cool," she said. "Do you still want me to come in?"

Christ.

I couldn't help it, I backed her into the wall and leaned my large frame into hers, revealing just how much I wanted her to come in.

"It's everyone else that I want to go," I whispered into her ear, my breath lingering over her lobe. I also couldn't control leaning in and sucking on that lobe.

Cate's back arched and her pelvis reached for mine.

Whoa.

We ground into each other while I tasted her, plundering her mouth. I knew I should stop. She seemed to be into it, asking for more with her body, but what if she second-guessed herself like last time? My cock could only take so many blows, not to mention my ego.

I pulled back as if I'd been punched in the gut. "Is this okay?"

There I went again with the considerate me. *What the hell?*

Apparently, I wore "gentleman" well, because she nodded.

"Say it, please," I begged her. "I need to hear that you want my mouth on you, so I know you won't worry there's something wrong with what we're doing."

I leaned back a few inches, giving her room while she decided. A couple of seconds ticked by as she looked up at me, and I fought the urge to adjust myself again. My dick was at war with the zipper in my jeans, trying to fight its way out.

"Yes, I do. I want this."

Cate kept her eyes on me, unashamed and full of desire, and I didn't hesitate. I went back in for more of her luscious mouth and her firm tits pressing against my chest.

"Whoa, boy!" someone called out from down the hall. "Look

who the cat dragged in . . . or should I say, the pussy?"

Reluctantly, I pulled away from Cate's mouth. When I rested my forehead against hers, she mumbled, "Is that who I think it is?"

I nodded, and we both turned our heads to the side.

"Cute Catie!" Sonny bellowed in the hall, holding my apartment door open to let the hip-hop pour out of my place. "Are you ready to come back to me? Who knew that in a few short weeks, the audience would miss you."

"Good to see you too, Sonny," Cate said dryly.

"Guess you're pretty fucking glad Mr. Boots here let your boyfriend out of his bargain so he could pursue you." When I shook my head, he flicked his gaze to me. "Don't be shaking your head, pretty boy. You owe me a championship and a replacement shock jock. This Johnny asshole is shit."

He approached and flicked my sweatband at the end of his rant, and then turned his focus back to Cate. "So, what do you say, Catie?"

I hadn't even spoken one word, and the fuck-face was taking over my date.

Cate snorted. "I say don't refer to yourself in the third person, and I'll think about it."

"Really?" Shocked, I turned to Cate.

"Yeah," she mumbled.

I grinned like a fool. "Great! Now that's all settled, Sonny, you can run along and go wherever you were going." Giving him a pointed glare, I added, "And leave Cate all to me."

"Talk soon." Sonny gave me a mock salute and walked off, yelling over his shoulder, "And, Catie, make sure he has enough energy left to win the trophy."

His laughter trailed behind him until he slammed my apartment door. The hallway was quiet other than Jay Z's rapping.

"Come on." I took Cate's hand and led her to my place, a little nervous about what we might discover behind the door. But we'd already survived Sonny, so it couldn't be that bad, right?

"Ho! Look who it is!" Ashton yelled from the couch, game controller in one hand and a beer in the other.

"And look who else." Alex strode over to us, grabbing Cate's hip and pretending to grind up on her.

"Cool it, White."

I shoved him off my date and took her hand. We walked into the common area, which was crawling with ball babies and players. Mo sat in the corner with his lady on his lap, D had some girl cornered in the back of the room, and everyone else was jamming and drinking as Ashton played his video game.

"Want something to drink?"

"Water?" Cate asked me with a wary look in her eyes.

"I'll be right back." I squeezed her hand and made my way to the kitchen for some bottled water.

When I got back, Alex was cozied up next to Cate and they were laughing. Fury burned through me, but I tamped it down. This was all new for her, and he was probably just being welcoming. Of course, he also probably wanted to get in her pants.

Fat fucking chance.

"Thanks for keeping Cate occupied, White, but I'll take it from here." I slapped him on the shoulder and passed Cate a bottle of water after cracking the cap for her.

Alex looked back at me. "Oh, I was just hearing about life in Jersey, near NYC and all that."

"God, you are dead set on going to New York. You already know Mo is going to Brooklyn, and they're not going to take two guys from Hafton again. That was a one-time deal with Tiberius and Jamel."

"Bro, there are two teams in NYC. I'm thinking about my boys, the Knickerbockers."

"I've seen them play once," Cate offered.

"Yeah? Who knew?" Alex said.

When he wrapped his arm around Cate, pulling her tiny body next to his, I glared up at him and his big head of dreads.

"With my dad," she added. "A guy who was a regular at his restaurant gave him tickets once. Dad is a sports fan with three daughters, but I'm the only one who was into it too."

As Cate lifted her face toward Alex and explained her childhood, I clenched my free fist at my side.

"That's what got you into sports?" I said, interrupting their walk down memory lane.

"Yep. My other sisters were easily poisoned against my dad, but not me. I loved how easy he was, and nurturing. I guess it's weird how I found comfort at a sporting event. I loved the hot dogs and the action, and my dad explaining it all to me."

Suddenly she waved her hand in front of her face, clearing any expression. "Ugh, this is getting too deep for now."

Alex grinned down at her. "Well, take a good look at me, girl, because I'm going to be playing at the Garden one day."

"Yeah, for the championship," I reminded him. "Got to win that first, my man."

"You already know, Steele. We got that in the fucking bag."

A tall beauty who looked like an African princess slinked up next to White and purred his name.

"Gotta go, lovers." He gave me a chin bump and blew a kiss at Cate before sauntering off with the ball baby.

"Who's the little girl?" she purred at him as they walked away. "She's not your type, babe."

A frown spread across Cate's face, and I gave her a squeeze.

"Slough it off, beautiful. She's a hanger-on and you're a keeper."

At my words, she looked at me with starry eyes. "For years I thought when women said in romantic comedies their knees went weak, I thought they were bullshitting. But now I know what they were talking about."

For some reason, this excited me. Cate's eyes weren't starry you're-going-pro eyes. They were more what-you-said-meant-the-world-to-me eyes. The kind of shit my mom wrote about, but I also thought only happened in people's imaginations. Now it was directed at me.

And it made me feel like Michael Jordan.

Enough was enough; I had to get Cate alone.

"Want to go back to my room where it's quiet?"

She nodded and I led the way, my hand on her lower back, my fingers itching to run over her bare skin.

Inside my room, I asked, "Are you okay with me locking the door?"

Another nod.

"It's not that I want to go all hot and heavy on you, but I don't want any nosy people poking in," I lied.

"You don't?"

"No, I don't want anyone coming in, and yes, I do want to go hot and heavy, but only when you're ready."

"I think I am."

You think or you know, Cate?"

We stood facing each other, our bodies barely an inch apart, not touching but sparking off each other. I reached out to take one of her curls between two fingers, sliding down its length as I focused on its silkiness rather than her eyes.

"I don't want you running off again, saying what happens between us is wrong or forbidden. It's not. When a man likes a woman and the woman likes him back, it's okay. When there's respect and shit—" Frustrated with myself, I ripped off my sweatband and ran my fingers through my hair. "God, I sound like a freaking psychologist. But I like you, Cate. You excite me, and not just sexually. In a lot of ways."

"I know," she whispered, and took one small step to close the divide between us.

I didn't hesitate. My mouth came down on hers, nipping and tasting. Unable to wait another minute, I ran my fingers over her back, under her shirt but on top of the tank.

"Can I take this all off? It's in the way," I said, still feeling the need to ask permission.

"Yes," she breathed into my mouth.

I broke free and tugged her shirts off. She stood there in a red lace bra, her pulse beating a rapid rhythm in the curve of her throat as she gazed up at me with wide eyes.

"You're gorgeous, Cate." My finger wound a path from her collarbone to her cleavage and back up to her heart. "Inside and out," I mumbled before kissing her earnestly. My cock raged in my jeans, but my brain told me to slow my pace.

I turned her around and backed her toward my bed, gently laying her before me, never breaking free of her mouth. When I finally releasing her lips, she fell back on my bedspread, her dark hair fanning out everywhere, and I stood to admire her.

She was soft where she was supposed to be, although a few places were softer than others, and I fucking loved it. There was a tiny scar above her eyebrow that she didn't bother to cover up with layers of makeup, and her hip bones didn't jab into me when I pushed against her. Cate was a woman, all woman, more woman at a mere five foot and a few than I could handle.

I sank to my knees and ripped my shirt over my head, running my hand down her thigh until it met her boot, then tugged it off and made fast work of the other. My fingers roamed back up her legs to her belly and circled her belly button. She was nothing like any other woman I'd ever been with, I thought, but were they really women or just girls?

I looked up from her navel. "God, Cate, you're all fucking woman."

Her eyes were glassy, and when she bit her lower lip and swallowed, her chest heaved up and down.

"S'okay?"

"Yes," she said, but the word came out hoarse, froggy almost.

I tugged at her pants. "Lift your hips."

She did and I slid them off, revealing a slight pair of red panties. They were snug at her pussy and stretched across her hips, and Christ, my dick surged to get inside them.

I smoothed a hand over the front of the satin and Cate whimpered. Her pelvis lifted off the bed, reaching for me, and that was all the invitation I needed to bend down and lick along the trim of her panties.

With the very tip of my tongue, I ran along the border between satin and skin, leaving goose bumps in my path. I took a deep breath and blew warm air, making the goose bumps more pronounced. It also made Cate's pelvis reach higher and her whimpering louder.

I could barely register the music coming from the party over the sound of my pounding heart. My dick didn't agree with my teasing her, but I knew I couldn't rush this or push her. Waiting would make it better.

I slipped my hand under her, between her ass and the flimsy satin, and squeezed. She moaned, and I let my tongue linger for only a second more before I tugged her panties down.

"Okay?" I asked, and her whole body shook from her nodding.

And then, *pow*, my tongue made contact with the wet, silky skin inside her small bush. I lapped first one side and then the other before landing on her clit. I licked and drank from her pussy with a fever consuming my whole body, somewhere between an extreme state of bliss and sheer torture. My jeans were so tight against my crotch, I was pretty sure my dick wouldn't be in one piece if and when it came time to fuck.

Or make love? Be intimate?

No, fuck.

Gone was the gentle lover. Tasting Cate did peculiar things to me, namely making me the horniest bastard alive.

She quivered under my mouth, and I begrudgingly took a quick break.

"You taste so fucking good, Cate."

I spoke my thoughts aloud before I dived back in, reveling in every inch of her pussy. All too soon, she convulsed and lifted her hips into my face, coming on a scream. I licked her quiet before crawling back up her body.

"God," she mumbled. "I never . . . God, just never."

I kissed her then, hard and hungry, sharing her flavor with her before pulling away.

"I have to take these jeans off. My dick is going to break if I don't," I muttered into her ear. "No pressure, it just hurts," I assured her.

"I'm not a virgin."

"I'm good either way, but you've turned me into stone. Fuck, you're amazing," I said, shoving my jeans and boxer briefs down.

I fell next to Cate and began stroking myself with my leg tossed over hers. Our mouths came together again as pre-cum slipped from my tip, wetting my cock.

"Watch me," I said. "I want you to see what you do to me. Big, bad me falling prey to little you."

I pumped my cock, my mind on eating her as I gripped tighter and stroked harder, my lips fused with Cate's until I broke free. "Do you see how fucking hard I am? My dick is reaching for you, all of you," I muttered while my hand worked a furious pace.

She glanced down at her hip where my cock was leaking and jutting, my groin shifting with every sweep of my fist. Her eyes were darker than normal, her pupils dilated as she looked on, and the pulse in her neck throbbed.

"I'm so hot for you." I breathed on her neck and bit down, careful not to leave a mark.

A whimper tumbled from her lips, and I came like a teenage boy, making a mess all over Cate's stomach. She watched in awe, and it was the most beautiful fucking thing I'd ever seen.

I smoothed my come over her stomach and left one more closed-mouth kiss on her mouth. Then I snagged my T-shirt off the floor and cleaned her off.

"Was that good for you?"

She nodded and tucked herself into my side, her head on my chest. "Was it okay for you?"

I pulled her tight. "Absolutely and perfectly sweet."

My breathing began to slow, and I felt her hair tickling my pecs. I pulled the cover over us, and within moments, Cate was asleep.

Looked like we weren't going to have a repeat performance of last time.

chapter thirty

Catie

Disoriented.

   Surreal.

I must be dreaming.

I wasn't quite sure how to explain what it felt like waking up next to Blane, so I closed my eyes and willed myself back to my dorm room. When I reopened them, I was still there—in Blane's bed, my back to his hard front with his arm draped over me, and his breath hot on my neck.

I tried not squirm, but I couldn't help it. This was a first, waking up next to a guy.

Cupping my hand in front of my face, I surreptitiously tested my own breath and nearly gagged.

"Shit," I whispered, and Blane's arm tightened around me, drawing me even closer.

I sniffed. Oh boy, was that his?

"Hey," he mumbled from behind me. He pushed the mass of

tangled hair away from my neck and kissed a path to my ear before licking his way back down.

When I squirmed again, he said, "What?"

"My breath is really bad," I foolishly admitted.

"Yep, and so's mine." Blane flipped me over before I could respond and spread over me, making his way toward my mouth.

"No! Just no." I pushed on his chest, and he jumped out of bed.

"If I give you some mouthwash, will you not run out on me?"

I ducked my head, feeling heat steal over my face.

"Talk to me," he said.

Lifting one shoulder, I mumbled, "I've never done this before."

"Used mouthwash?"

Annoyed, I threw a pillow at him, and it wasn't until it dropped to the floor that I noticed the enormous bulge in his boxer briefs.

"Oh, you've never been with a dick this big before?" He winked at me before he picked the pillow up and lightly tossed it back.

I couldn't help but laugh nervously. "No, I haven't been with one. Or sleep over with one either." I ducked my face into the pillow, desperate to hide the red I could feel spreading over my cheeks, even though it probably wasn't too noticeable.

"Really?" Blane crawled next to me. "Huh, I'm pretty happy it was with me. I think it's cause for a little celebration, like breakfast in bed."

He ran his hand over my back, which I just realized was bare.

Oh. My. God.

"First, mouthwash."

I nodded quickly. "And a shirt."

"Definitely a shirt to go out to the bathroom. I have to share it, you know."

Blane hopped up and threw a large Hafton Athletic Department

T-shirt my way. I slipped it on before I stood, giggling a little when it draped to my knees and fell off my shoulder.

He took my hand and led me to the bathroom, where he gave me a few minutes of privacy to use the facilities, and then he came in and held us steady in front of the mirror.

"You're so stunning like this, all natural," he said to my reflection. He bent and ran his lips over the tattoo on my shoulder where the T-shirt had fallen again. "Love this." He flashed me a grin on his way up, and I pulled away to scurry back to his room.

I was curled up under the covers when he came back in and asked, "Bacon and eggs?"

"Yum," I murmured

He bent over me and gave me a closed-mouth kiss. As I watched, he pulled on low-hanging sweats. His large shoulder muscles were on display since he wasn't wearing a shirt, and my gaze lingered on the deep *V* his abdominal muscles formed.

My mouth watered, and it wasn't because of the bacon. *Definitely yummy.*

Blane went on the road with the team after our breakfast in bed, which included cinnamon rolls, the kind from the freezer section but incredible nonetheless. He dropped me at my place with kisses and promises before driving off in his truck.

Now it was Tuesday, and I sat like a fool glued to his game on TV. Blane looked awesome, his hair pinned back by his sweatband. I could see the sweat glistening on his body, even on the TV.

And to think I slept next to that very same body.

I shook my head, making sure I didn't get lost down the rabbit hole of the night I slept next to Blane, and focused back on the game. Ashton had just put up a three-pointer when my phone beeped.

Sarina: You okay?

Catie: Yep. I told Frank I needed some time after we spoke on Saturday.

Sarina: Good. You're a good person, Catie.

Catie: I don't know about that, but I'm making my own choices.

Sarina: We're still going to help you. The girls and I want to. Want to have a glass of wine tomorrow?

Catie: Yes.

Sarina: Usual time and place?

Catie: Yep. Goblet @ 9?

Sarina: See you then. Oh, and the girls are up for next weekend. Another "show and tell" session.

I sent her a thumbs-up emoji, and made it back to the TV in time to see Blane dunk. The crowd cheered, even the opposing team.

"Yes!" I said to the empty room, and pulled the blanket over my legs to settle in for the remainder of the action.

Several hours later, my phone beeped again, waking me up from a deep sleep.

Blane: Hey! You awake?

Catie: Now I am. Great game!

Blane: I'm pumped! Big party down the hall, but wanted to say hi to you.

Catie: Don't let me keep you.

Blane: Don't do that. I mean it.

Catie: OK.

Blane: Want to have breakfast in bed again when I get back?

Catie: Yes, that bacon was so good.

Blane: How about the chef?

Catie: Not bad either.

Blane: I'll tell him to step up his game. Maybe some croissants.

Catie: Go to your party.

Blane: Bye.

I snuggled under the covers and fell back to sleep with a smile, thinking about bacon. And the memory of hard muscle and an adorable shit-eating grin.

chapter thirty-one

Catie

Blane was back and texted on Wednesday morning. He wanted to go out that evening, but I had plans with Sarina. I couldn't cancel on her; her help was worth everything to me right now.

I went to my classes—statistics and Italian—and was heading home to my apartment when my phone beeped. Hoofing it to and from campus every day was apparently slimming; my jeans were loose and I had to keep stopping to tug them up. I ignored the phone and decided to wait to pull it out when I made it to Starbucks.

As I stepped into the store, with the scent of coffee tickling my nose and a sugar cookie calling to me, I felt myself being lifted in the air.

"Knew I'd find you here."

His stubble tickled my cheek as he lowered me, and I turned to see Blane with a decent five o'clock shadow.

I threw my hands up in the air. "A girl needs her afternoon coffee . . . and cookie."

He tugged on my hair. "You avoiding me? I texted you to see if you were coming here."

I shook my head. "Never. I just didn't want to answer my phone. It's cold out."

"Come on. I'll get you a coffee, and stomach another hot chocolate." He put his arm around me and escorted me to the counter.

"What's with the wannabe beard?" I asked when we'd made ourselves comfortable on the couches in the corner.

"We're winning on the road, undefeated this season, so I can't shave."

"A sweatband, a dirty one, and a beard. Any more superstitions I should know about?"

"Not for now, but you know our time together was sort of spectacular. I'm thinking it brought me luck on the road." He winked.

"I will take that under advisement."

"Hey, don't forget my parents are coming up this weekend. They're both coming to the home game on Saturday afternoon against Pitt. I got them tickets in separate sections, but maybe you could have breakfast with my mom on Sunday?"

I breathed a little faster at what he was asking, trying not to hyperventilate as I twirled my hair around my finger. The only thing missing from my '80s Valley Girl persona was some gum smacking.

"Are you sure?"

He leaned closer and growled, "Cate, stop it. Yes."

"Okay."

"Great, let's go. Between you and Ashton, I'm spending way too much time in these girlie coffee houses." He squeezed my leg and tilted my chin up. "I'm driving you home. I have some kisses to give you."

My phone beeped again, and I ignored it one more time because

I was still thrilling to Blane's words.

"Do you ever go to class?" I asked in the truck.

"I only have six credits, two classes, so not often. One's a gym elective—weight lifting, which Coach signs off on—and the other is civics something or other."

"Do you get to graduate with less credits than the rest of us?"

He barked out a laugh. "I wish! No, I've taken classes every summer because Coach makes us stay and work during his camp. It's quick and easy money, and it allows him to keep tabs on us."

"Oh."

"And you?"

"After being tossed out of women's studies, I'm down to being eligible for six credits too. Everything else needed prerequisites, and I was stripped of those last term. Plus, my major is undecided now. I'm like every other coed, living the dream and getting a bachelor of arts."

"Hey, if those women don't want you, their loss."

I shrugged. "I was thinking of transferring, somewhere closer to home. I don't know where, really. Somewhere better suited for me. I guess I'll see after this trimester, but I'm definitely going to be a few credits behind."

"You should do what you want, but don't run or hide, Cate." His voice was low and supportive. He didn't take pity on me; in fact, he seemed to actually get it.

"I'm not running, just finding a better place," I lied.

After he parked in front of my building, Blane, the perfect gentleman, ran around the car to open the door for me.

What the hell were they saying when they called him a womanizer?

Together, we raced up the stairs and out of the cold. When I fumbled trying to open the door, Blane wrapped his fingers around mine and helped twist the key.

"I'm going to kiss you now, okay?"

When I nodded, kind of liking the way he always asked me now, he pushed me up against the door and our mouths came together. He tasted like warm chocolate and mint, and my tongue wanted more. Blane held my weight up against the door, one hand behind my neck, the other on my ass as we tasted each other thoroughly.

When he released my lips, I took a deep breath. "Okay," I teased with a smile on my face.

Blane picked me up and carried me to the bed in the middle of my studio apartment and set us down together. Cuddled together, we began kissing again. His hand slipped behind my waistband and kneaded my butt, pulling me closer against his hardness.

"I want to get naked," he whispered in my ear. "It's all I thought about when I was gone, your body, your touch." He wove our free fingers together. "And your nipples." He leaned down, pulled my shirt away, and sucked on the top of my breast.

I nodded, and he lifted my shirt off and unhooked my bra. He splayed a hand over my boob, squeezing and plucking my nipple until it was hard and I was needy below.

His hand slid down my torso, lower and lower until he was way down south.

"Didn't I tell you I was a Southern boy?" His eyes practically twinkled, and the golden flecks that surrounded his pupils looked almost like fireworks.

I didn't have a chance to answer; he was already on his way down. He tapped my belly and I lifted my butt, allowing him to slip off my pants and boots, and then he knelt between my legs, gripping my love handles.

"Like these," he said, leaning over to kiss my hip and nibble the skin over my hipbone. I had lost control over that region, and my hips lifted and asked for more.

He gave it good, running his tongue along the crease where my thigh met my groin, inching closer to my heat. I should have been shy, but I wasn't. Good thing was after prepping for movies with Sarina, I was groomed there—

Ugh. I didn't want to think about that now. This was Blane, and that was something else.

His tongue found my clit and circled it lightly, teasing and tormenting me. As I threw my head back into the pillow, gasping and squirming, he picked up speed and slid his finger inside me. I ground down on his finger and sighed out a whimper. He didn't let up and continued to finger-fuck me, flicking my clit until I went off like a sparkler. Soft moans made their way up my throat and out my mouth, sounds I'd never really made before.

"This is happening a lot, with me naked and you fully dressed," I managed to say as he crawled back up my body.

"Do you want to do something about that? Anything but the sweatband."

I bit my lip to contain my laughter and ran my hands up his broad back, wondering why I deserved such sweet. *Dolce*, as my dad would say in Italian. I'd always been his sweet *bellisimo*.

And Blane was mine.

A shudder ran through me; we wouldn't always have sweet. But I had it now, and I intended to take every last bite.

With his shirt off and my hand trembling on its way to his jeans, he abruptly sat up and tugged the sweatband off.

"Fuck it," he said, and stood quickly to divest himself of his pants.

After falling back onto the bed in his boxers, he pulled me against him and kissed me hard. Our lips grazed each other softly, back and forth, before he nipped my lower lip and I opened up. As we tasted each other again, he rubbed his length against my stomach.

"Touch me," he murmured.

With trembling fingers, I found the waistband of his boxers and dipped inside. My hand barely wrapped around his girth, and I fisted him up and down like I watched him do the other night.

Blane leaned his forehead into mine and breathed out, "Oh God, yes." He shoved his pelvis back and forth, making his penis ride my palm, and I slid my thumb over his slit, using the pre-cum to wet his shaft.

"Feels so good," he choked out, panting.

When I tightened my grip and pace, he quickened his hips before bringing his hand down to still mine.

"I don't want to blow," he said, and took a few deep breaths. "I want to be inside you, but I don't want to rush you." His eyes were earnest as he gazed down at me, his desire darkening them to a deep green.

"I want that."

He ran his fingers over my landing strip and slipped back inside, coaxing the wetness out, and I allowed my fingers to graze his length. We played with each other for a few more beats until Blane removed his hand and reached down to his jeans on the floor. He pulled a condom from the pocket and stopped.

"You good?" he asked, his voice soft and polite.

Blane's insistence on asking first before proceeding filled me with a sense of power. And freedom.

"Yes."

He rolled the condom on and climbed over me, taking care not to crush me. Held up on one elbow, he reached down with his free hand and lined himself up with me. Circling me a few times, he teased me while covering himself in my wetness before pressing in. Slowly, he found his way deep inside me, filling me with an intense satisfaction. Together, we felt sweet.

He took his time, pumping slowly until I was clawing at his back and sweat had collected on his brow. I should have been afraid, there was over six feet of steel anchored over me, but instead I felt safe and secure. At least, at that very moment I did.

For the span of a few heartbeats, I allowed my mind to wander and think of the *what if's*. What if he found out? What if he found someone else? What if this was all because of some plan to get back at Sonny?

I pushed all the worries to the back of my mind because the *now* felt too good. Blane Steele was inside me, riding me with fervor.

Oh. My. God.

And that's exactly what I screamed when he swiveled his hips. So he did it again, harder, and in the other direction.

I came on a scream and Blane slid out, flipped me over, and grabbed me by the waist, pulling me up on all fours. With my knees and elbows sinking into the bed, he dived back in on one push and brought his hands to my hips. Gripping me firmly as his pelvis pumped against me, he brought himself to climax.

When we slumped down on the bed a ragged mess, Blane whispered in my ear, "Well, you worked off that cookie, sweetie."

I couldn't stop a big burble of laughter from rolling out of me. I'd just thought he was sweet, and he called me *sweetie*. An unfamiliar girlie part of my brain took over my thought process. I was all destiny, sweetness, and bliss.

Blane patted my butt, drawing me out of my Barbie-doll state, and went to dispose of the condom. I brought the blanket over my body when it dawned on me.

I just had some afternoon delight with Blane Steele.

Was he going to run out on me now? Did he still want me to go to breakfast with his mom? There was no such thing as destiny, so I didn't think breakfast was still on the table.

Moments before, I was consumed with *what if's*; now I was flooded with sheer *what the hell's*?

Blane came back to bed and curled up with me under the covers, our legs tangled and his hand running up my arm in soothing strokes.

"You sure you can't cancel your plans for tonight? I may even be able to find a funnel cake."

"I can't. I have to do this. It's the only way I can justify being thrown out of my program."

"But you can't tell me what?" His hand stilled on my forearm.

"Not yet."

"This isn't a fling," he said as his fingers picked up their stroking again.

"Either way, I can't say. Not now. Hopefully, soon."

I really needed to get my shit together. After a few more sessions with the women, I'd be able to bang out a first draft of what I wanted to write. It was my short foray into the industry I wanted to keep under wraps. I needed to ask Frank to pull the movies, but he'd already paid me and I'd spent the money. Would he do it?

Speaking of money, I needed some. Maybe Sonny would give me a quick shift or two, not as an intern, but he was bound to need help.

Ugh. Then I'd be back to kissing his ass.

"Earth to Cate," Blane said, tugging at one of my curls. "Was that good for you?"

I nodded into his chest, afraid to express my desires and wants, and then I remembered the power of choice.

"Really good. Want to do it again," I murmured against his skin, my finger tracing the tattoo by his pec.

It said my name. *Wow.*

"We can," he said, running his hand down my thigh and back up again.

"We can?"

He pressed his erection into my side. And we did.

Blane insisted on taking me to an early dinner at the diner before I went on my secret assignment, as he'd begun to refer to it. The diner was an institution on Hafton's campus, a greasy spoon specializing in breakfast and fried food, and they were always crowded. Pictures of all the winning sports teams lined the walls, and there was a special section devoted to Hafton alumni who went pro.

We sat right under Tiberius Jones's photo. He stood tall and proud in his Brooklyn Nets uniform, but wearing a Hafton hat. He'd inscribed the photo along the bottom.

> To the gang at the diner, where I took my lady
> on our first date. The ball was in my court.
> Tiberius Jones, Hafton Ball Proud

Blane's legs were stretched out under the table, mingling with my shorter ones.

"Hungry?" I asked as he studied the menu.

"Um, yeah. I worked up an appetite, Miss Oh-My-God."

I kicked his shin. "Shhh. Shit, everyone is going to hear you," I said through clenched teeth but with a smile. We really had worked up quite an appetite.

"Hi, Blane," the waitress said, leaning over the table so her boobs practically spilled out of her uniform.

"Hey, Cassie," he said without looking up.

"Who's this?" She pointed her pen at me. "Study partner? Tutor for Mr. Heading-to-the-NBA?"

"A friend," I said cheerfully. No need to go and give anything a label.

"More than a friend," Blane shot back.

She frowned. "Oh, is that why you haven't been in for weeks?"

"I didn't know you were keeping track," he said, still not looking up.

"Does Sonny know? I saw him last week, and all he does is run off at the mouth over you two and your antics." She flipped her hair to the side, revealing a Hafton *H* tattoo on her neck.

"Sonny isn't part of this." Blane didn't get a chance to finish because the bells over the door chimed and a loud, "Steele!" echoed through the diner.

"Yo, Mo," Blane called back, finally lifting his head out of the menu.

"I'll be back," Cassie said in defeat, and left. Not without shaking her ass, which Blane didn't notice because he was too busy staring down Mo, who had said, "Slide over," to me.

Mo rolled his eyes. "I'm practically hitched, Steele. Cool your dick. Sorry 'bout the language, missy."

"No problem. I use the word dick frequently," I said, unruffled. Swearing I could do.

"I love this one. She's a fucking firecracker." Mo tossed his arm around me and pulled me close. "You eating?" he asked Blane.

"That's why we're here."

"Good, me too. Saw your truck out front."

"Y'all always barge in on people's dates?" Blane eyed Mo, his green eyes narrowed and laser focused on his teammate.

"This ain't no date. The fuck, the diner?"

"He took me to Geno's the other night," I said.

"Did you now?" Mo asked Blane with a raised eyebrow.

"Look, it says right here that this is a date place." I pointed at the picture of Tiberius.

"Yeah, when you're Tiberius Jones and you got yourself hooked up with some slice of crazy." Mo jerked his chin toward the picture. "Nah, just kidding. Tingly's cool, but she was fucked up six ways to Sunday by her parents."

"How do you know?" I shifted in my seat so I could focus on Mo.

"My bro was roommates with Ty. Witnessed the whole crazy love affair. Now Trey works for the Nets, and Ty plays for them. Jamel too."

"Really?" I said. "I'm a Knicks fan."

"No shit? Your woman's a ball fan, Steele?"

"She is," Blane admitted. "Been sneaking in to watch us play."

"No way," Mo said. "I'm gonna get you some tickets."

Cassie and her boobs stopped at our table to interrupt. "You guys decide?"

Mo went first. "Protein breakfast with sausage, eggs over easy, and full stack of hotcakes, no whipped cream. And a large milk."

"Breakfast for dinner. Sounds good. Give me the same," Blane said without even glancing at Cassie.

"Um, can I have the pecan roll hotcakes?" I bit my lip, waiting for a reaction. It wasn't exactly what women ate on dates. At least, I assumed they didn't.

"Can I get a bite?" Mo asked me, nudging my shoulder with his. I nodded.

"You want a drink?" Cassie asked, giving me the evil eye.

"Coffee."

She turned and sashayed desperately as she walked away.

"So, what's up?" Mo looked at Blane and then me.

"What do you mean?" Blane's eyes remained evil slits.

"What's the deal-i-o with you two? On or off?"

"On." Blane's face finally relaxed as a smile formed.

I swallowed down my excitement—and regret—and raised my eyebrows.

"Definitely on," Blane repeated.

It was news to me. Not unwelcome, mind you, but it definitely deepened my regret about my actions over the last few weeks.

I didn't have long to dwell on it because Mo slapped my shoulder and said, "Well, thank you. He's been in a better mood. He wasn't good with all that . . . stuff . . . backed up."

"Maurice," Blane growled.

"I'm just kidding, bro. So tell me, darling Catie, why aren't you on the air anymore?"

"Um, I sort of lost my way and I was pissed at Sonny, but I'm rethinking it."

He nodded. "Good girl."

"And how's your girlfriend?" I asked.

"Angie's good. She's starting to show, so I guess I'm having a kid."

"Ya think?" Blane leaned forward.

"Shit, man, this is not real. Me a dad, but it is."

"You seem like a good guy," I told Mo.

"Why, thank you, Catie."

Our food arriving at the table interrupted our conversation, and the guys dug in. Mo made good on his wanting a bite of pancakes.

When the check came, Mo snatched it.

"Hey, it's the least I can do after crashing your date and all." He pushed Blane's hand away and got up to pay.

Blane stood and helped me put my coat on, and then draped his arm around me.

"I didn't know we were a thing," I whispered in his ear.

He tugged me tight and said, "Oh yeah, we are, and I'm not sharing you with anyone."

I gulped down the lump lodged in my throat and snuggled a little closer into Blane's embrace, committing the feeling to memory before I went home to get ready to meet Sarina and the gang.

Every single encounter with the ladies further jeopardized Blane's career, and yet I couldn't stop myself from seeing them.

Or him.

chapter thirty-two

Blane

"Turn it up," I yelled to Ashton after a grueling practice on Thursday.

Coach had us going hard at the hoop in preparation for the upcoming game, and we were all taking our time in the locker room. I'd come out of the ice bath when I heard her.

"Hi there, Hafton. Catie P. here, back on the air at 96.9. Have you missed me?"

A grumble came over the air, and then a bang.

"Haftees, it's Sonny B. I had to grab the mic for a hot second. There was no not allowing this little missy back. Plus, that other dude was junk, and of course, Catie begged. Give my girl Cute Catie a big hello, and tell her to turn up the heat."

With a towel wrapped around my waist, I sank onto the bench and listened as if it were a post-game interview.

"Thanks for allowing me to have the mic back, *Sebastian*, but this is my show so you may exit the booth, *mister*."

Zing. Good girl.

"So, let's see," she said. "I took a little break and missed you all. Not Sonny, but don't tell him that. Today, I'm going to play some music and, of course, take some calls. Not dating advice, though. How about this . . . Have you ever felt pressured by a professor to do what they wanted? Write what they wanted? Call me. Don't use your name, just fill us in. While we wait, here's a new one by the Dirty Souls. Remember how good they were at the music fest?"

Mo slapped my back with a towel. "Aw, shit, that girl likes to poke the bear."

"Christ, Steele, when you decided to snatch one," Alex teased, "you picked one that's a handful. The bitch is ready to take on the whole school."

"Fuck off, White, and don't use bitch when you're talking about women," I shot back, but agreed she was going to get into some shit.

He gave me the finger and walked toward the steam room.

I dressed quickly while the song played and plopped down on the couch for the rest of the show. Holy shit, were there a lot of discontented people.

"Hi, Catie. Thanks for having this discussion. By the way, are you getting back on Twitter?"

Cate laughed into the mic. "Go on."

"So, my professor asked me to redo a paper, taking a different stance, one that was more in line with their thinking. It was a big part of the final grade, so I did it."

"Did they now?" Cate asked, and the caller went into all kinds of detail without revealing names, but it was pretty obvious. It sounded like she was some type of business major, and the prof didn't agree with her business plan.

Finally, Cate said, "Listen, all you have are your convictions, darling, so I say stick by what you wrote and see the head of your department. But don't tell them I sent you."

"Thank you, Catie. I feel better with that off my chest."

Then she played some more crap alternative music and took a few more calls before signing off.

I stood in a hurry and thought if I hoofed it, I could meet her by the station. After grabbing my bag and coat, I headed for the exit. Of course, Coach stopped me outside the office, wanting to check in on how I was feeling. I tried to make it quick, but it was no use. Conley was on a tear.

We needed to beat the crap out of Pitt, he said, ". . . make them never want to come back." Rumor was he wanted a job there and they turned him down. I guessed it was true.

I kept nodding and agreeing all through his speech, but by the time he shut his trap, I was pretty sure I'd missed Cate.

Just in case, I drove to the studio and double-parked in the lot. Sonny was sitting in his cubicle when I rounded the back of the studio.

He looked up and slammed his laptop closed. "Steele? What do you need?"

"I was looking for Cate. How you doing, man?"

"I'm good. In fact, I was looking for her too. She came and asked for her gig back, and I let her have it right away. Now, I'm not so sure."

"What the fuck, man? Don't be a prick," I yelled at him as I ran back toward the exit.

I faintly heard him yell, "Me? A prick?"

"Yeah, you," I tossed back.

I jumped in my truck and headed toward her apartment. When I found Cate waiting by the bus stop, I pulled over to the curb.

Rolling down the window, I called, "Hop in!"

She jumped into the truck, her hair tucked into a beret and a coffee in her hand.

"Hey, you were good," I told her as I checked over my shoulder. "How come you didn't text me and let me know you were going on?"

"I had to make sure I didn't bomb."

"You were great," I said, pulling out into traffic.

"You going home?"

"Yeah. I'm done for the day."

"Wanna grab lunch?"

"I have to be back by three. Does that work?"

"It's twelve thirty, so I'm pretty sure we're good. We can have dessert too," I said with a wink.

We would definitely be having dessert, just not the kind she thought. Well, we could have that too. My girl loved her sweets.

"What kind of dessert?"

When she interrupted my naughty train of thought, I dog-eared the sweet fantasies I was having. "That's for me to know and you to find out."

I drove to Chantilly, which was a big buffet located on the edge of campus. The normal meal plan didn't include it, but athletes could go whenever they wanted. *Of course.*

"I've never been here. Or heard of it." Cate got out of the truck, taking in the red brick building.

"It's a perk of ours; we can come anytime. It's good." I stole her hand and walked toward the entrance.

We walked through the big glass revolving door and shrugged off our coats. I tossed them in a heap on a table by the window.

"Come on." I took her hand and led her toward the line. "Cathy, I have a guest today," I told the lunch lady.

"Hey, Blane, sounds good. We have omelets today." She pointed toward the back.

The buffet wound its way around the perimeter, with a large crystal chandelier hanging in the center of the room above the beverage station.

"Wow," Cate said. "This place is insane. How much is it? I should pay you back."

"Like I said, we get to come anytime, as many times as we want. A fringe benefit of dating me."

She punched my arm and said, "Fuck."

"Not here, babe." I winked and gave her hand a little tug.

She punched my arm a little harder.

"Hey, that's my shooting arm."

"Well, we wouldn't want to hurt that. Then we couldn't eat here."

I handed her a plate. "Hush and go get some food."

I wandered over to the omelet station first. "Y'all got shrimp today, Murray?"

"As a matter of fact, we do, Southern boy," he called back.

I piled my plate high with creamed spinach—hey, I needed my strength—and fresh rolls while waiting for my double omelet.

"Thanks, Yankee," I called to my friend in the chef's hat.

If I were honest, I didn't want to leave this place. I could have last year, but a small part of me was scared to go out in the real world. Hafton was good to me; pampered me, even. Would the real world be as nice?

Cate stepped up next to me carrying a tray with a big salad piled high with fried chicken strips and loads of french fries on the side. The girl destroyed any worries I might have had, always making me feel like everything would work out. She was strong in a way I wasn't. Look at how she'd lost her major and was finding new purpose.

"Nice! You're going to need that strength for dessert," I told her and she smiled like a devil. I'm surprised she didn't grow horns, her grin was such a naughty smirk.

"You mean I'm not going to get dessert here? Look at that cheesecake."

She got my drift earlier? Good girl.

I patted her ass. "It's a double-dessert kind of day. If you're sweet enough."

We sat next to the window, eating and chatting as if we'd been doing this forever.

"My mom gets here tomorrow around noon, and she'll probably burst into the locker room and pester all the guys," I admitted. "She's a bit of a flirt; she ogles the whole team."

Cate shifted in her seat. "I'm a little nervous to meet her. She sounds all sexy, like some seductress."

"She'll love you because you're real people. She hates all the plastic ball babies."

I nabbed one of Cate's fries, dipped it in ketchup, and fed it to her. Her lips folded around the fry and, yes sir, my cock got immediately jealous.

"So, is that why you're keeping me around? To ward your mom off the ball babies?"

I leaned over and kissed her nose. "I'm keeping you around because I like you, Cate."

"Oh." Her mouth made a small pout.

I ran my finger over her pursed lips. "I do. A lot."

"Blane, I think—"

"Steele! Get your ass over here. They say you ate all the shrimp," Alex called from across the room, interrupting Cate.

I flipped him off. He didn't take the hint and walked over, turned a chair, and straddled it.

"Seriously, you dudes have the worst timing," I said, eyeing him up.

Alex ignored me and addressed my lady. "How ya doing, Ms. Catie?"

"This place is awesome. Want a fry?"

Of course, the ass took it.

"You know what? We're taking some cheesecake to go," I said.

"Now?"

Cate looked at me with half-lidded eyes, and I didn't care if it was the cheesecake or me putting that sexy look on her face. I wanted that face under me and turning around, looking at me when I was behind her. Now.

"Peace, White. Sorry about the shrimp. Try the ham." I bumped his fist and grabbed Cate's hand, dragging her out of the place.

Catie

Blane dragged me out of Chantilly, but not before slapping half of a cheesecake on a paper plate. I was certain if he hadn't had the cake in his hands, he would have thrown me over his shoulder. And I couldn't say I would have minded.

My hormones were raging and my heart thumping. For the first time in forever, it wasn't over hand-cut french fries or New York cheesecake. It was because of a man.

"Let's roll," he said, his voice all rumbly once we were in the truck with the cake on my lap and his eyes narrowed on the road ahead.

I smiled and caught Blane watching me out of the corner of

his eye. We clearly didn't need any words. Only smiles and dessert innuendo.

A small part of me felt guilty. I wanted to tell him about my project, to clear the air. I felt I owed him that, but we were interrupted. And then he got that look. The *sexy-sexy* one, and I couldn't see straight.

I was turning into a trollop.

Scratch that; I actually was one.

Ariel might have been my alter ego, but her existence stood to burn me forever. My hand actually shook at my side, and I slid it under my leg to quiet the tremor.

When we pulled up in front of my building, Blane jumped out and ran around to my door. He opened it before I could even move. Swiping his finger across the top of the cake, he ran some cherry topping over my lips. My tongue darted out to lick it off, and his mouth joined mine.

"I wasn't sure if I liked cheesecake, but I definitely do. Come on." He grabbed the cake and my hand.

All thoughts of Ariel flitted from my head as we hurried inside my building. Avoiding the elevator, we took the stairs and ran to the privacy of my apartment.

Blane walked inside calmly, but as soon as he kicked the door closed with one boot and set the cake down, he was a madman. He tossed his leather jacket aside and ripped his shirt over his head, taking his sweatband with it. His hair was a wild mess and he pushed his fingers through it, shoving the thick waves out of his face. Then he kicked his boots off and approached with a determined glimmer in his eyes.

The tattoo with my name on display made my mouth water. I swallowed my lust and breathed faster as he stalked me. Highlights of that first porno we watched with Stanwick flickered in my mind. It was hot, but nowhere near as hot as this.

"Wait a sec, I'm going to get you naked," Blane said while shoving off his pants, leaving him in nothing but dark green boxer briefs.

"I like your underwear. Way to show your team spirit," I joked.

"Those are my lucky underwear, I'll have you know. And right about now, I think they're extra lucky."

He pounced on me, cupping my face and kissing me as he walked me backward to the bed and sat me down. It was a seamless transition. I perched on the edge of the bed as Blane pushed my coat off and lifted my shirt, tugging it over my head before he unsnapped my bra. Dropping to his knees, he shimmied down my leggings and slid my boots off. My pants and undies joined our other clothing in a messy heap on the floor.

He crawled back up, kissing a path from my ankle to my knee, stopping to slide next to me on the bed. He took my face in his hands and kissed me with urgency. We kissed like savages, taking each other's mouths, knocking teeth and bruising our lips. It was nothing like the sex portrayed in pornos. It was pure, unadulterated passion.

"Taste so good," Blane mumbled. "But it's gonna be sweeter."

He stood and motioned one sec, and went to the kitchenette. With the plate of cake in hand, he made his way back to the bed. Grinning, he set it next to me and swiped off a bit with his finger. Then he painted it across my abdomen and proceeded to eat it off, licking and sucking until he reached my bare skin.

Not satisfied, he fed me a small bite off his index finger and I licked it clean. Another piece he smeared around my nipples and took his time eating it off, which drove me insane. My nipples were as hard as his dick when he was done.

I'd never liked dessert this much. The room smelled like cherries, sugar, and impending sex. I pressed my thighs together, soaking wet between them.

Blane found my nub and rubbed me to a quick orgasm, swiping his finger back and forth over my most sensitive spot while fucking me with another few fingers. On a scream, my body fragmented in a million pieces, my senses on overload from the kisses, the food, and the orgasm.

As he reached for his jeans, I whispered, "Wait."

He stilled, and I knocked him flat on his back. With my right hand, I grabbed some cheesecake and moved down his body to smear it around his navel. I took the tip of my tongue and cleaned him up, and when I was done, I grabbed another piece. This time I painted his inner thigh, taking my time to nip along that sensitive spot between hip and groin while devouring my new most favorite dessert.

When I was done, I wrapped my free hand around him and pumped his length.

"I'm not going to last like this, I'm too hot," he said.

No problem. I bent down and took him in my mouth, taking leisurely trips up and down his length, and stopping to pay attention to the slit. I had been studying up on this, and judging by Blane's moans, I was doing better than I'd done in women's studies. I tickled his balls with my sticky fingers and used my other hand to pump him while I sucked hard.

"Christ, I'm going to come," Blane roared.

I didn't back off but stayed the course, my inner thighs totally drenched by the time he exploded into my mouth.

Collapsed in my bed in a sticky heap, I shut my eyes and dreaded getting up, but we did. I had to be ready at three, and Blane needed to watch tape.

With promises of finishing later, we parted ways.

chapter
thirty-three

Catie

"Heya, girl."

Chantae pinched my cheek and headed straight for the kitchenette, wearing a ruby-red scarf over her wild curls. I had coffee ready to go, and she helped herself to a huge mug.

"Mich is sick," Tish said as she came through the front door, wearing stiletto boots paired with skinny jeans.

Brittany was right behind her, looking like an average coed today in leggings and a sweatshirt with little makeup and cold-pinked cheeks. *Like me.*

"Hope she feels better," I said.

While the others grabbed a coffee, I surreptitiously sniffed around my apartment, wanting to be sure it didn't smell like Blane and I had just got it on. Which we had—exchanging orgasms with our fingers and mouths, and eating cheesecake off each other. A tingle ran through me at the thought of what might come later.

"Hey," Sarina said, the last through the door.

"What's up?"

"I'm good. My son's sick, so I had to scramble to make sure his sitter was all prepped."

I ran my hand down her back. "You have to go?"

Her situation made me firm in my resolve to see this project through. If Sarina worked in a bank or a school, she would have sick days. As it was, she didn't get time off in the movie-making biz she called her career.

She shook her head. "I'm going to shoot a few extra clips for Frank tonight when I leave here, and then I may take tomorrow off." She ran her red-tipped nails through her straight hair, tucking it behind an ear as she let out a long sigh. Pulling me into a hug, she said, "I appreciate what you're trying to do, help us justify our choice to the rest of the world."

"Hey, don't get all sappy on me." I squeezed her tight.

She laughed and we parted, both of us grabbing coffee and joining the other girls.

We sat around for an hour discussing where the women saw themselves going in the long term.

"I'm just paying my way through school, but part of me wants to be discovered. I kind of like it," Brittany quietly admitted. "I feel like I'm in charge of my destiny, self-sufficient."

"What's your degree in? Journalism?" I lifted my mug of coffee to my lips.

She nodded. "Yep. In fact, I think I'll look for an internship at *Playboy* or *Esquire*, somewhere like that."

I felt a weird sense of pride at her courage to make her own choices, choose her own destiny.

"Me, I'm gonna bank as much money as I can and open a little boutique," Chantae said. "Scarves like this and hair ornaments.

Probably African jewelry and maybe some art."

"Where? Here?" Sarina asked, a worried look on her face.

"I'm not leaving you, babe." Chantae winked at her.

"You're my family," Sarina admitted. "All of you. This little gang. If you go, what will I do?"

There was something else to consider when writing all this up. The network these women had formed gave them bonds stronger than most I had ever experienced. They not only were a support system of friends, but were also sisters, caregivers, and protectors.

"Mich and I are going to try to start our own web TV thing," Tish said. "We're going to do something with gay men, I think."

"Get out!" I blushed at the idea, but since I'd been so affected by porn, maybe gay men were too.

Hmmm? I would google that.

We laughed for the last half hour, the girls teasing me about Blane.

"Our girl's got her a good one," they joked.

At four thirty, they all filed out to do what they needed, and I texted Blane.

Catie: You still watching tape? I'm going to make dinner.

I wasn't sure, but it seemed like that's what couples did, touched base on the minutia of their day.

A tendril of anxiety curled around my heart while I waited to hear back from him. When I got no response, which wasn't like Blane, I told myself he was busy with the team, and tried not to make it into something bigger than it was.

A lonely package of mac and cheese called to me from the cabinet, so I scrapped any plans I had to do something fancier. Nothing better than processed cheese on a winter's night.

With my belly full of pasta, a while later I sat down at my laptop and banged out about twenty-five pages of what I had learned. So far, I had close to a hundred pages of the book I planned to either shop around to a publisher or self-publish. The title was *Feminist Choice or Choice of Feminism.*

I'd considered using a pen name, maybe Ariel Something, but tossed that idea out. This mission was mine, and I decided to tie my real name to the whole wagon. I'd also sent out some feelers regarding transferring to another school. It was time. I was doing this, raising my flag as the ambassador of adult-movie stars.

And if Blane's silence wasn't enough of a reminder, my lack of a major was.

I had an abundance of choice, right? With several dozen credits toward my degree, some money in the bank, and a promising part-time career as a barista, I had more choice than most women with only a GED or high school diploma. Although there was no escaping the fact that my savings was from filming porn. Even with all my choices, I needed the industry to get ahead . . . so there was that little fact.

At midnight, my phone pinged.

Blane: Sorry I can't make it. I just finished with the team.

That's all he wrote. No promise of a rain check or confirmation of meeting his mom this weekend.

I crawled into bed and closed my eyes. My phone pinged with an e-mail a few minutes later, but I ignored it. With my mind unsettled, I drifted off to a fitful sleep.

chapter thirty-four

Blane

My cock was semi-hard and ready to go again when I arrived at the field house for our team meeting. Damn, Cate could give a blow job; the way she grabbed my balls had me so revved up.

Honestly, I'd meant to spend more time with her at Chantilly, but Alex had ruined that idea. Maybe not entirely, I thought, because look what happened after stealing that cake and getting the hell out of Dodge. *Christ, that cake came in handy.*

I was looking forward to hurrying back to Cate's place when I entered the locker room.

"Put it away," someone said, and a loud, "Shut it off," came next. The guys were huddled on the couch, all eyes on me.

"What the fuck?" I joked, trying not to be unnerved by the intensity of their stares. "Do I have something stuck in my teeth?"

Ashton shook his head and stood up.

"What the hell?" I said as I took off my coat and tossed it on the bench. "Are you guys having some gay combine or what? I'm not a homophobe, but seriously, can we stop canoodling and get this meeting over with?"

"Steele, I don't want to be the one to show this to you, but someone is going to," Alex said from the couch as he opened the laptop.

Mo punched him. "Dude, I thought we agreed to let it go until after the game tomorrow."

"Come here," D said, sighing as he beckoned me over.

Trying to make fun of their seriousness, I walked over to the couch and perched on the arm of it. "You guys are whacked."

Alex gave me a sad look. "You know how someone said they'd seen a porn star at our games?" His voice was strange, all slow and calm as if he were talking to a mental patient.

"No." I shrugged. "Where? When? Who?"

"On Twitter," Ashton said. "Her name's Ariel Stone; she's new. She doesn't get all raunchy, but she's sexy as all get-out. Curvy and shit. Big tits—"

Mo punched Ashton in the arm, interrupting him.

"Get to the point," I said abruptly, losing patience with this shit. "What does this have to do with me?"

Ash averted his eyes. "She's made a name for herself for letting men come all over her chest."

"Great, and she's a fan?"

"Yes. She's a fan, and a bit more," D said.

"Gimme that." I grabbed the laptop from Ashton and set it on my lap.

There was a video paused, so I hit Play and a cheesy music track came on, something that was supposed to be sexy. A man leaned over a couch, a side view that showed his naked ass pumping back and forth as he jacked himself off on a woman.

The room around me went totally silent as I watched the camera pan over the woman's tits and across her jawline toward her eyes. She looked familiar. Her skin was flawless, her tits plump, and her face was somewhat obscured under big auburn waves . . . but the eyes were the same ones that had stared up at me earlier today.

I shut my eyes and reopened them, hoping it would be a prank, but there was Cate dressed up as some Ariel chick, moaning as a dude whacked off all over her chest.

Stunned, I looked at up and realized everyone had abandoned the couch. The guys stood huddled by the lockers, shifting nervously in place as they watched me.

I jumped to my feet and tossed the computer to the floor. It clattered and spun against the table before landing on the carpet. "Who showed you this?"

They stood there silently, not a fucking peep out of a one of them.

"What the fuck? Someone answer," I yelled.

"Sonny called me," Ashton finally said, lines of regret creasing his face.

Confused, I reached for my sweatband and ripped it off, grimacing as strands of my hair came with it. "Why? What's it to him?"

"Well, he was dating someone and now he's not, and every dude kept calling in about this chick, so he decided to google her," Ashton explained. He was leaning against his locker, looking loose and relaxed, but I knew he was waiting to pounce on me if I went to hit him.

"Why did he call you? Why did he have to ruin the one good thing I have? I like her . . ." Devastated, I sat back down on the couch, and dropped my head into my hands.

"Let's go!" Conley's voice bellowed through the locker room.

Mo put a hand on my shoulder. "We've got to go to the meeting. You don't want him to find out about this."

I stood on weak legs, swaying for a second before I followed him. I might as well have had spent the day doing weighted squats. But I sat through the meeting, going through the motions, nodding my head at the right times as I watched the tape, but I didn't really see it. My mind was on overdrive.

I guessed Cate didn't need to explain her secret project anymore. Part of me wondered why she was doing it, and the other half didn't give a fuck. If Sonny knew this shit, I gave him a day to keep it to himself. Soon it would be everywhere, and the whole fucking world would be watching my girl get her titties fucked.

Coach dismissed us, and I walked in a daze back to the couch in the locker room.

"Dude, best to learn this now and cut ties up front," D said. "League is coming for you, and you can't be linked to the campus porn star."

Sad thing was, I didn't care what the league thought. I cared about sharing Cate with every other man in America.

She was supposed to be mine.

chapter thirty-five

Catie

B lane didn't touch base on Friday, and I couldn't help but feel used and spit out. He must have been busy with game-day preparations and grabbing his mom from the airport, but something didn't feel right. Had he used me?

Sonny called and asked me to cover a few hours at the station, and I accepted. I thought it was odd, but if he needed help, I'd take the shift. I needed a distraction, so I grabbed a coffee and took the bus over to campus.

When I arrived at the station, Sonny was laughing into the mic, discussing romantic Valentine's Day dates with a caller. Michael Jackson's "PYT" played softly in the background, and Sonny laughed like a hyena when the caller said pizza and a movie rental was romantic.

"Dude, you need to go to the bookstore right now and buy *Dating for Dummies*," Sonny was saying into the mic as I entered the booth. "Look who just showed up—my old intern, Catie P. She might have some movie recs for you. Hmmm, one sec, let me show her this quick clip and I'll be back with her suggestions." He turned the volume up slightly on the music and hit Play on the laptop in front of him.

There I was on the screen, Rick coming all over my cleavage and rubbing it into my skin. I stared at it like it was a bad hallucination, a figment of my imagination and a horrendous mistake. It was someone else, Sonny had to be mistaken.

Sadly, he wasn't.

Embarrassment swept over me, sending heat over my entire body. Ready to run away, I turned to find Sonny glaring at me.

I'm gonna get you for this, he mouthed before he grabbed the mic.

"Turns out Catie has so many recs, she's going to make a list right now. While she does, I'm going to play some tunes. How about a little Macklemore? 'Downtown,' you like to go there? Don't you? Down? Get it?"

Sonny smacked the button, turning off the mic, and swiveled toward me. I was trapped in the booth; he'd slid his chair in front of the door, eliminating my escape route.

"Why are you doing this?" I demanded.

"Me?" He pointed at his chest with his thumb, as if surprised I would question his motives.

Narrowing his eyes, he laid into me. "I took you back here as an employee, and now I find out you're fucking any dick . . . on camera. Fuck, I'm sure you've violated a million different school policies, but fucking Christ, I can't whack off to my intern, Blane's lady. Whole fucking school is talking about Ariel Stone and her tits of wonder, so I chanced a look. Nearly poked my eyes out when I realized it was you."

All at once, Blane's absence and my niggling worry clicked.

I gaped at Sonny. "You told him?"

It wasn't even a question. Blane's silence spoke volumes. He knew. Sonny was the one who told him.

Not waiting for an answer, I ran from the booth, straight through the building and out the door as tears threatened to break free. They fell as I burst through the exit and hit the cold winter air, burning as they froze on my cheeks. My vision blurry, I searched desperately for a corner where I could hide. I spun in a circle, wetness covering my face.

I knew it would happen eventually, that Blane would find out. I'd just hoped it would be after I transferred and he had won the championship.

"Catie, is that you?" a voice called from behind me.

I froze in place for a second, wanting to escape, to disappear, but I turned around.

"Shelby, it's not a good time." Frowning, I brushed the back of my hand over my face and sniffed back snot. I probably looked like a mental patient.

She gave me a concerned look. "What's going on? I haven't seen you in forever. Tess said you texted that you were working on a paper and busy dating the basketball player. Did he hurt you?"

"Shelby, really, I'm fine, but I have to get out of here." I straightened my posture and attempted to look like I had my shit together.

I'm anything but that. And what's it to her, anyway?

"Can we chat later?" I asked, pleading with my eyes as well.

Shelby wasn't taking the hint. Wrapping her arm around me, she said, "Why don't you come back to my room?" She steered us toward the dorms, whispering something about hot cocoa, and we both startled when a car pulled up to a screeching stop just ahead of us.

Not a car, but a truck. Blane's pickup.

"Cate, wait. I'm sorry I blew you off. I needed time to process," he yelled, jumping out of the truck and running back toward us.

"Leave me alone," I spat back. "Please don't make a scene."

Out of breath, Blane skidded to a halt in front of me. "Sonny texted me and told me it was minutes away from spreading all through campus. He's sending it viral. I had to find you."

"What's going on?" Shelby stood next to me, holding my arm protectively as Blane and I squared off.

"You could have come to me," I muttered, "had the decency to say you saw it to my face."

"I didn't know what to say," he said, his voice contrite. "And I was mad."

"I had my reasons for doing it, and this is exactly why I didn't want to reunite with you. Or whatever we're doing." I sounded like an idiot, blubbering and using words that didn't even work with the context. *Reunite?*

"Cate, I realized you must've had your reasons, and I want to hear them."

He reached for my hand as he approached slowly but I backed up, taking Shelby with me.

"Let's go," she whispered in my hair. It was blowing wildly in the wind, reflecting my manic mood. "We're making a scene."

"Let me take her," Blane insisted to Shelby, coming closer.

I shook my head. "The jig is up. We're done. Go do what you need to do. Buy your mom a house, sign a deal, forget me."

I tugged on Shelby's coat sleeve and forced her to walk away with me. Her arm wrapped around my shoulders, and she glared back at Blane before tightening her grip on me.

Once we got back to her dorm, I spilled it all. What I had been up to and why, my plans to write a tell-all, and how Sarina had taken me under her wing to help me.

Shelby held true to her promise and made cocoa, rubbing my back while I took sips and defended my position. Once I was done, she shook her head.

"To me," she said, "it sounds like you gave up your personal happiness to prove these women's plight."

I cocked my head and stared her down. *Really?* She was going to go there?

"I don't know. Sounds pretty selfless, babe, a sign of a true feminist. Putting other women's rights and needs first," Shelby said, finishing her thought.

"Yeah?" I asked through tears. I seemed to have an endless supply of them.

"Yeah." She gave me a small smile as she swiped a thumb over my cheek, and then ran her finger over my shoulder where she knew my tattoo rested. "Why are you shutting out Steele?"

I shrugged, looking away. "He doesn't need this, and you saw his face. He's disgusted with me."

"It looked more like disappointment from where I was standing. Maybe he genuinely cares?"

Shelby lay back on the bed and pulled me into her arms, running a soothing hand over my back as if I were a small child. If one good thing came out of this whole debacle, it was that I'd developed a sisterhood.

"He's going to play professional basketball," I mumbled. "He doesn't need to have his reputation tarnished by a girlfriend who made a few pornos. I know I had to do it. It makes my stance stronger, but still. He needs to move on, and really . . . what were we? Friends who messed around a few times?"

"Is that all you were?"

I sighed. "We made each other laugh, and he was so sweet despite that rep he has. I don't know, we'd become very good friends, I guess."

She smoothed my hair behind my ear. "That's it?"

"There was a definite attraction." My throat tightened. "But that was all before he knew. Why would he want to touch me now?"

"Maybe we should call him and hear him out. It's private here."

I shook my head. "No, one day when the tears stop, I'll look back on this year and say, 'That was the year I loved a basketball player.' But now it's over, and I need to do what I set out to do."

This made me think of Sarina. I pulled my phone from my pocket and found a text waiting from her. It said *Call me*, and so I did.

"Ri," I said when she picked up the phone.

"Oh, honey . . ."

"Tell me what's happening." I spoke into the receiver with my head resting on Shelby's chest.

Apparently, rumors about my story had broken on the evening news.

"The news said it was an anonymous source, and they were pretty vague about your identity. They only said, *Hafton student believed to be moonlighting as porn star Ariel Stone.*"

She explained that Frank had shut the studio down for the night as a precaution. "Lots of people fishing around for details but not finding much."

I sighed. There were no words.

"Frank saw it first and called me. I looked it up on the web, and he saw it correctly. There was no mention of your real name, but Brittany is crazed right now. She's ready to start a whole movement. She wants justice for all the women who pay their bills doing this," Sarina went on. "She's not going to let this go."

"Well, I'm going to finish the project and self-pub the exposé, but first I have to go back to my place and try to make my transfer happen."

"Aw, babe, I don't want you to leave."

"The sooner I get the hell out of here, the better. I can't show my face around Hafton now that I'm outed, and after I publish my research, the program will never let me back in. This small town may as well be dead to me. I gotta go now, but I'll call you in the morning," I told her.

I disconnected the call and then rolled over to kiss Shelby on the cheek, telling her I had to go.

It was dark as I slipped out the back door into the night. I took an unmarked service road to the edge of College Avenue and walked all the way home with my beret pulled low and my coat collar pulled high. Inside my apartment, I undressed and slipped on big sweats and a Hafton T-shirt, and then turned on my laptop with the intention of googling Ariel Stone to see just how bad it was.

But first, I looked up the score of the Hafton game. We were down ten at the half.

I glared up at the ceiling of my empty apartment. This was all on me.

"Fuck," I screamed at the walls, fisting my hand and punching the mattress.

Their loss, Blane's pain, Sarina's inability to work tonight . . . all on me.

After reading speculation in articles and blog posts with titles like "Who really is Ariel Stone?" and "Why would a college student do this?" and "It's Cute Catie," I curled up into a ball and cried myself to sleep, tangled up in sheets that smelled like Blane.

The revelation of my identity came from Johnny, Sonny's intern who followed me. Apparently, he had an informant at the station as well as an ax to grind with both Sonny and me. When he found out

Sonny uncovered something salacious, he went to work to steal his thunder.

It didn't matter now. It was all out there, and I was ruined.

Over the next few days, I kept a low profile. *Very low*. The school told me to take a few days off from my classes, so they could deal with the media storm raining down on campus. My Italian professor called to see if I was okay, and asked if she could bring me a cappuccino or scone. She seemed almost empathetic to my plight, but I turned her down.

I'd involved enough people who didn't deserve this. She definitely did not.

On Saturday, Sarina sneaked in via the fire escape of my building wearing one of Chantae's scarves and carrying food from the diner. I could barely swallow the soup; the diner's label on the lid was a painful reminder of Blane.

I shouldn't complain. I'd had a few months of fun, a few moments of extreme bliss, and certainly enough memories to die happy. Not everyone lived out every second of his or her lives smothered in happiness. Why should I believe I would?

On Monday, Mo called me; apparently he'd stolen my digits from Blane's phone.

"Seriously, you got to talk to my boy," he pleaded with me.

"You're winning, and he doesn't need me," I said.

"See? You still care."

"Mo, thanks for calling. I have to go."

After I hung up, I changed my phone number for the second time this trimester, which meant I didn't receive Blane's texts anymore. He'd been sending them consistently. Mostly they said, "Can we talk?" or "The ball is in your court, you have the power here. But come on, Cate." Another one said, "Please? Let's talk. I miss you."

Now his name didn't flash across my screen anymore, and all that was left was the memory of his touch, the burn of his name tattooed on my skin, and the scent of him that I believed lingered in my apartment.

I cried over the missing texts, at the thought of not ever knowing if Mo's girlfriend had had his baby yet. I wouldn't know if he had a girl or boy, or what they named the baby.

Tears came and went hourly.

Sarina came back and held me daily.

Brittany became a fixture at my place, ranting and raving, listening to rough draft after rough draft of my book without complaint, and making turkey sandwiches.

One night after she'd done a shift with Frank, she popped over to my place with pillow and homework in hand. We lay side by side in my bed while Britt stroked my hair, curling it behind my ear as we talked about our dreams.

"Frank says he got every last frame of you off the Internet. Cost him a mint, but worth it, 'cause he knows what you're doing for us."

"It's just a book," I said. "One book."

"Babe, you're leaving this school and this state with a scarlet letter on you because of us. I know what you're going to do at the next stop—more of this do-gooder shit for the porn stars. You got that dreamy look in your eyes. I can see it; you're not done."

When I said her name, it came out on a choke and a sob.

Brittany let out a little huff. "Don't get all pansy on me. I'm gonna do my movies and graduate with honors. Go to law school, and take on civil liberties and crap. Your girl Shelby has me all kinds of wound up now. We may go to law school together. And then you and me are going to do some big project together. You'll interview me on TV."

I kissed her cheek and snuggled against her chest. We fell asleep like I'd dreamed about sleeping with my blood sisters for years.

chapter
thirty-six

Catie

Over the next few weeks, the only times I ventured in or out of my building, I had to force my way through a barrage of media people camped outside. "No comment," were about the only words I muttered as I gathered the rest of the research I needed, and the media's reaction was now a crucial part of the package.

After the phone change, I'd had zero contact with Blane or anyone on the team. Begrudgingly, I gave my mom and sisters my new number, but they only used it to berate me or rub my nose in shit.

"Told you, you'd make a mess," Clara had said, her tone condescending and indignant.

And if my mom could spit through the phone, she would have.

My dad—my rock—had taken a gentle approach. He told me to call when I was ready or needed him.

The school allowed me to finish up the credits I'd paid for, but I did appear before a judicial board, who decided this would be my last trimester at Hafton. Apparently my conduct had broken some type of ethics clause, but not because it was pornography. I'd argued freedom of speech and expression, and they had conceded on that issue.

No, I was being tossed out on my butt because they believed I'd done pornos with "malicious intent" and to "deceive the women's studies program." The judicial board didn't take too kindly to my "personal crusade to go against Professor Stanwick."

Fuck 'em.

Coach Conley made a statement to the school paper. "Yes, Ms. Presto is a fan of the team and was friends with several members, but we had no prior knowledge of her illicit activities."

Professor Stanwick commented in an article in *USA TODAY*. "She was a student in our program, but not of the caliber we've come to expect at Hafton. She was released when she went on this rogue and illicit mission."

Shelby was quoted in the local paper as a character witness. "I was with Caterina when the news broke. She's a good woman who wants to defend the rights and actions of other women."

As the season rolled on, Hafton continued to win. But Blane was questioned at almost every press conference about the nature of our relationship. The questions always went something like this:

"Mr. Steele, what do you think of the illicit actions of Caterina Presto, a.k.a. Ariel Stone? You were seen with her several times before it broke. Did you know? Were you a part of that world?"

There was one word synonymous with my name these days. *Illicit.* My actions and I were illicit, dubious, dirty, and disgusting.

I didn't dare show my face inside the field house, even sneaking around. My phone pinged with an alarm every time the guys stormed the court, and I caught every game on the Internet. I was lucky Hafton streamed the games for students who weren't lucky enough to get seats in the student section.

Toward the end of February, I sat alone in my studio apartment and watched the team clinch the conference title on national TV. They'd been favored, going into the game with a twenty-five and three record. It was the best record in Hafton history, even better than when Tiberius Jones and Jamel Lincoln were on the team.

I knew because I'd looked those guys up during one of my sad-sack pity fests.

Blane was at the top of his game after that one dreadful loss, constantly moving the ball down the court toward the basket, his sweatband atop his head and his steps sure, like a lion chasing its prey. The other two losses came after Mo and Demetri found themselves in foul trouble and were seated on the bench.

But nothing stopped them tonight as they conquered the conference, not even my tarnished reputation. As I watched Blane sink a three and run back on defense, high-fiving his teammate, I knew—just knew—I'd done the right thing.

Blane

After we won the nationally televised conference on the road in front of our biggest audience ever, Conley gave up on quieting us down and hustled us out of the gymnasium. ESPN was waiting in the locker room when we filed in, so we gave TV interviews for what felt like hours.

When the reporters left, we slapped each other on the back and celebrated.

"Your dunk, my man, is sure to be top ten tomorrow," Mo screamed in my ear. "That shit was insane, the way you went over that dick's head!"

I managed a smile. Okay, more than a smile; I was damn fucking proud. We were over halfway to my dream . . . all of our dreams. The championship was staring us in the face. The league was going to come hard for me, and then I'd be able to buy my mom a house like I'd always wanted. I'd be living my life the way Cate had predicted. It was all fucking coming true, just like she'd wished for me when she set me free.

"That alley-oop was no joke either, brother," I hollered back to my roommate. "Wouldn't be surprised if your move beat me out on the list, Ash."

He deserved the good juju after living with me for the last few weeks. To say I'd been a prick was putting it mildly.

Yeah, I was more driven than ever to win this fucking title, but not because I wanted the fame and fortune. I wanted to control my fucking destiny and go get my girl. Yeah, she'd cut ties and thought I'd easily accept all that. Little did she know, I was letting her have her way and watching her do her thing from afar.

She was demolishing common thought around here, and I smiled just thinking about it. I laughed to myself. She'd thought she was so cunning and smart, breaking free. We'd only been intimate a handful of times, but Cate and I were friends. Maybe even the best of friends, before the sex.

She'd grown on me quickly with her sassy mouth and cute ass. I missed our banter the most, and I had a few tricks up my sleeve. The shrimp thought she'd outsmarted me.

Nope. Not even close.

The guys made on like I was ridiculous not to use the "hall pass"

Cate had given me. Alex moaned about it all the time. I didn't know why he was so worried about my sex life; he wasn't attached and could have as many ball babies as he wanted.

Mo whined that he wanted one pass before becoming a dad, and then he'd whisper in my ear he was lying. "On my soul, Steele, this baby, that woman, best thing ever. But I got to keep my rep," he'd murmur.

"Fucking did it, yes!" Mo shouted, bringing me out of my stupor and back to the present.

"Where's the party when we get back?" Alex called through the locker room as he pulled on his boots.

"Heard Sonny wants in," Ashton said.

"No," I said, raising my voice over the din.

It was one word, but firm. The guys knew one thing to be true—Sonny was dead to me. He could have controlled some of the burn, corralled his urge to spread the gossip. He could have stopped the dumb fucking intern, but he didn't.

"We know, bro," Ashton said. "No Sonny. Party's at Alex's, and D got some heavy hitters to make sure he doesn't make his way in."

Coach walked in and raised his hands to stop the chitchat. "Enough party talk, gentlemen. We now have a tournament to win. So get your heads outta your asses and get on the bus."

We all nodded but grinned as we shuffled out to the bus in the dark night. There was no way we weren't having a party.

Then we were going to win the whole fucking shebang, and I was going after my lady. After all, I wore her name on my body and she wore mine. As far as I was concerned, she was ruined for any other man.

chapter thirty-seven

The game was over and my hands still shook. Adrenaline and pride flowed through my veins, making my whole body tingle.

Hafton won the championship!

I'd only been a part of it for a short while, on the far periphery of the world these guys lived in, yet I couldn't help but cherish the moment. *My guys did it.*

The New York-based arena was a sea of dark green and white. Fans swarmed onto the court afterward, cheering for the players hefting a trophy over their heads. I'd watched from the nosebleed section, staring down at the hardwood from so far up, my guys in green had looked like tiny action figures moving the ball up and down the court.

Stupidly, I'd traveled home to New Jersey the day before, licking my wounds and under the guise of wanting to check on my dad—when I only wanted a hug from him—before heading to my new school. I should have gone straight there as soon as the trimester ended but I didn't, making all kinds of stupid excuses.

I could lie to myself all I wanted, but the truth was I still liked Blane. I wanted to see him happy and successful. It couldn't be with me, but maybe I'd catch him making out with a ball baby. Perhaps seeing him move on with my own eyes would finally shut my fucking head up.

Earlier this morning, fully ashamed with myself for making excuses, I boarded the train to New York City. As I'd walked to the subway and then the thirteen blocks to the Garden, anticipation had begun to pump through my veins.

My guys were going to do this.

Filing into the arena, deep in thought as usual, I'd bumped into the guy in front of me and prayed he didn't turn around. Muttering, "Sorry," I pushed forward with my head down.

I tried not to catch anyone's eye as thousands of us filed in, opened our bags for inspection, and showed our tickets. I hoped my few moments of fame in the Midwest were sandwiched between more salacious news back east. Just in case, I had a baseball cap pulled low over my forehead, my eyes painted a smoky gray, sheer pink lipstick glossing my lips, and a nondescript dark green shirt covering my tattoo.

Like I expected, my team had done it. Now they were celebrating down below, and I was a lone bystander in the distance. They weren't *my guys* anymore. I'd done a bang-up job of making sure of that.

It had been all on me, a phrase I'd become all too familiar with.

But I'd owed Sarina, and I still did. She and the other girls had put their lives on hold for me, shared their secrets with me knowing I was using them for my own personal redemption, and had my back when shit went down. While my personal life crumbled and I lost any chance with the first guy who called us a *thing*, those ladies held my hand and rubbed my back. Shelby and Tess too.

I would miss them . . . a lot. Despite their pleas for me to stay in Hafton, I was leaving. I'd been asked to join two other women's studies programs. One offer was from a school with a strong communications department where I could double major.

My dream career was right there, swimming in front of my eyes like a mirage in the desert. I had to take it and leave the women I'd started to call family. They were part of the reason I so quickly accepted; they needed to be rid of me.

Fuck, I need to be rid of me.

Now—just like that—all the waiting was over. Blane had led the team to a national championship and was on his way to the league; I was sure of it. Agents would be waiting for him outside the locker room and calling his phone nonstop. Coach Conley had kept slapping him on the back after the game and whispering in his ear—at least from what I could make out through squinty eyes.

I was certain they were off to party, and I was ready to go home. Alone.

I couldn't bring myself to leave the stadium until I saw every last person file off the court. I watched the maintenance staff run a wide soft-cloth broom over the glossy pine, scraping off confetti and streamers. One bent to pick up a few sweaty towels and folded up the chairs along the bench. I envisioned Blane, Mo, and Alex hooting in the locker room, celebrating, showering . . .

Wait, not showering. That was a definite no-no—thinking about Blane in the shower.

When silence finally fell on the arena, I walked slowly down the stairs to the exit, running my hand along the handrail, taking in the last few minutes and trying to soak in the win. I followed the narrow tunnel leading out to the concession area and found the escalator to the exit. The halls were mostly empty, other than a couple of stragglers sucking down the last of their beer.

At the bottom, I looked left and then right, wondering which way led out toward the subway. I chose right, winding my way through the desolate concrete jungle until I hit a dead end. Realizing I should have chosen left, I turned back the way I came.

"Catie?"

Someone called my name from behind me, but I ignored it. I knew the voice.

"Catie, stop!"

I picked up the pace, forcing my legs to work overtime.

"I'm faster than you," Alex called out, his voice echoing off the concrete walls. And he was.

He caught me, his arm coming around my body, stilling me.

"If it isn't the big bad wolf," I sputtered into his face.

"What are you doing here, Goldilocks?"

"None of your business."

His eyes narrowed, boring down into me, searching my soul, and I gave in.

"I wanted to see you win, all right? All of you, Alex."

"Why didn't you let him know you were coming?"

There was no point in pretending I didn't know who *him* was.

"He doesn't need to know I was here," I said, bringing my hand to my hip.

"He's not mad about what you did. When word got out you were defending your stance against some professor, he was happy. Proud or some shit. It's nothing like how you're making it out to be."

"It doesn't matter." It was a whisper, my lips lying for my heart's benefit.

"It does. He was hurt you did that . . . with other dudes. His pride hurt. But seriously, you should go see him." Alex's eyes pleaded with me.

I shook my head. "I have to go. Congrats, Alex." I pulled away and took off toward the exit, and he let me.

I took the train straight back to Jersey, hugged and kissed my dad, and then called a cab to the airport. I didn't bother with my mom and sisters. They'd become close to slaying me to the media themselves. In fact, my dad had to threaten them with taking them out of his will if they didn't cut that shit out. Seriously.

It was time for me to make a fresh start, someplace where I was wanted. Professionally, anyway.

I was pretty sure I'd burned my one chance at being wanted *personally*.

chapter
thirty-eight

Catie

Early July

I walked reluctantly through the revolving door into Florida's muggy, oppressive heat. Knowing the humidity would instantly curl my hair, I stopped outside the exit to fasten my unruly curls on top of my head in a messy bun. My T-shirt was stuck to my stomach and I lifted it, fanning it for a moment.

When I'd left Hafton right after the winter term, I welcomed the change in climate. April and May were much better in sunny Florida than rainy Ohio, although July was turning out to be a challenge, what with the heat and humidity.

I was thrilled when the University of Central Florida welcomed me into their women's studies program. There I'd finish my degree with my major in women's studies and a minor in mass communications. I'd even qualified for on-campus housing, which was good because my dad could only afford so much. The tuition was more expensive in Florida, but I'd earned a sizable student-aid package complete with a paid internship at the student TV station.

I was going to be on television!

"We love your fresh, no-holds-barred approach and sassy demeanor," the dean of the communications department had told me.

Take that, Sonny. Speaking of Sonny, I'd laughed when I learned he was tossed out of Hafton for inappropriate behavior, three credits shy of a diploma. I hoped to hell he was stuck in some Midwest bullshit radio station fetching coffee for the talent.

When I'd first told my sister Grace I got the TV gig, she practically slammed down the phone in a fit of jealousy. Or maybe she was just in a hurry to sell my story to the media, but who cared? Thanks to my dad, she was leaving me alone.

This summer term, I was busy doing research for the student news program, but I'd been promised my own segment in the fall—a segment dedicated to young women's issues. Apparently, I was free to explore whatever I wanted as long as I backed up my statements with data and research.

They knew I could do that based on my self-published book, which had been solid in the Top Ten on Amazon for the last month. It was a tell-all, not well-edited, but according to reviews, I "laid it all bare" and "put it all on the table why some women's best choice is pornography."

The best news about my transfer was my schedule. I was one hundred percent busy with my classes, the internship, and working part-time at a coffee shop. I stayed away from sports television and anything that might have to do with Blane. He was too nice for me. All I'd done was taint him, and he needed to make a go of ball.

The draft had been last week, and I'd avoided coverage of it like the plague. I knew he went as one of the top picks—to New York— and I wished him success. He would be one of many other Hafton guys who played or coached there.

Maybe come fall, I'll try to watch?

With my hair securely tied up and my backpack firmly on my shoulders, I drudged through the thick air toward the main drag of campus to catch the bus. It wasn't a huge campus, but it wasn't right in town like Hafton, so they provided buses to the small community outside the university gates.

As I took a shortcut through the visitor parking lot, small rivulets of sweat worked their way down my back under my T-shirt. Tanks weren't possible with the tattoo. I didn't dare flaunt his nickname out in the open, yet I couldn't bear to think about removing it. I'd heard it's painful, so I blamed the pain. *Sue me.*

I snatched my water bottle from the side of my bag and took a chug before pressing on, not wanting to be late for my shift at the coffee shop. There was a commotion to my left, which I ignored because I didn't want to be late.

"Hey, you," someone called from that direction. "Hey, girlie in the gray T-shirt!"

Did he mean me? Half of the coed population wore gray.

Some guy, shirtless and wearing athletic shorts, ran over to me and poked me on the shoulder. "Hey, didn't you hear me yelling?"

I stopped and let out a huff. "What?"

"Aren't you the girl we saw on the news a while back?"

"Yeah. Freak show's over, buddy." I turned away and started to walk again.

"No, it's not that, but wow." Looking a little uncomfortable, he said, "Um, we need you."

Rolling my eyes, I said, "I know; everyone says that."

I'd become a little jaded, hardened to the propositions that came with the fame and notoriety. Not all of it was as good as my new placement.

"Seriously, I'm not trying to harass you." He jerked his head toward the left. "That dude over there says he's here for you."

I squinted toward where he gestured, noticing there was a sizable crowd.

"He said he would take some pictures and sign shit if I came over and grabbed you. I didn't even know who you were when he said it."

I didn't respond; I couldn't. It was like I'd been turned to stone, and even my chest was frozen, unable to draw the smallest of breaths. My feet planted to the asphalt, as if glued there. With my heart pounding so hard I could hear it whoosh in my ears, I simply stared.

There was a man at the center of the commotion, surrounded by students trying to get his attention. He was very tall with wild blond hair, leaning against what appeared to be a black pickup truck. A really big, shiny one.

"Are you coming?" The shirtless guy poked me again.

I shook my head. "I need a second."

"Are you okay? You know who he is, right?"

This time I nodded, still staring.

"I don't think you should make him wait."

"I just need a few moments," I muttered, and my voice came out croaky.

Blane Steele was standing in the parking lot of the school I now attended.

Blane

Cate stood there staring at me, the sight of her a tasty snack for my starving heart. She looked like she'd filled out a bit again in her gray T-shirt and jean shorts, dark green Chucks on her feet, and her hair piled in a messy bun on her head.

She didn't move and neither did I. Actually, I couldn't because I'd promised a few photos and autographs.

I glanced at the students swarming around me. "Hey, I know y'all want to hang, but I have to go see that girl over there. How 'bout a big group shot? If you e-mail me your addresses, I can send y'all something autographed. It's Blaneassistant at Gmail, okay? Now, let's pose."

I had to wince a little at the sound of myself. My Southern accent was heavy, even after only being back home for two days.

We posed and they took a million selfies, holding me back from the one person I wanted to be with, but I had to play nice. Especially down in Florida. *Now.*

"I'm going to send y'all something awesome," I said over my shoulder as I made my way toward her.

She stood stock-still, not moving, not making a sound. I stopped when I got close, not touching like I wanted to, but close enough so no one else could hear me.

When I breathed out her name, she said, "What are you doing here, Steele?" She tilted her head back to look up at me, ready to throw down—as usual.

"I came to get my girl back."

"Stop. Just stop," she said, turning to walk away.

Gently, I grabbed her wrist and turned her back toward me. "I'm always saying *don't do that* to you, but this is the last time I'm saying that shit because I'm here for you. And I'm not letting you go."

"Blane . . ."

"Cate, see this?" I pulled up my shirt and exposed the tattoo of her name.

"Put that down," she said through clenched teeth. "You're making a scene."

"Afraid that's sort of par for the course these days, but you need to listen to me."

From the corner of my eye, I could see smartphones lifted in the air, pointed our way. Yep, we were making Internet fodder as we spoke.

"I have to get to work, Blane."

That was her excuse?

"I can drive you and we can talk along the way. We can get out of the public eye."

I really wanted to suggest she quit the damn job—she wouldn't need it now. But I could see her feminist tendencies swirling around, ready to lash out and beat the ever-loving shit out of me.

"I swear, just a car ride and a chat." I put my hand up in the air. "Scout's honor."

"Okay, only because I can't deal with this." She gestured toward the crowd that lingered. "With everyone watching us."

She was going to have to get used to it, but it wasn't time to tell her that.

"They're snapping pics, and there's going to be more of that when we get in the car. I'm warning you, keep your head down." I threw my arm around her, tucking her close against me as I walked her toward the truck.

"Shit," she mumbled under her breath.

"The novelty passes."

"I don't know about that, Steele."

"Hey, guys. Can you step aside? I got to drive my lady to work," I called out when we neared the parking space.

They were probably all tweeting and snapchatting my vehicle, complete with the license plate. I'd have to text my assistant and get a new one.

"We didn't know your girl went here, Steele," someone from the crowd called out.

I opened the door and shoved Cate in. I knew what was coming next, and I didn't want to show my true feelings in front of these pricks.

And one, two, three . . . there it was.

"Is that why you wanted to be traded?"

Yep.

I hustled over to the driver's side and said, "See you all at a game hopefully," and jumped in the cab.

"What are you doing here?" Cate's gaze roamed my profile as I turned the key.

I ignored her question. "Where were you going?"

"Corner of Fifty-First and Pelican. There's a small place called Steamers."

"Oysters?" I asked, raising my eyebrow and throwing the truck in drive.

"Coffee. Now answer me."

"I'm here for you."

"Blane, I'm making a new life here, getting a degree. I'm going to be on TV, something I never thought I'd do. You're going to be in New York, and you can have anyone you want. I don't want to be some story or shit from your past."

I pressed the gas pedal and pushed forward when all I wanted to do was brake hard and shake her.

"I got traded and I'm here. With the Magic. Not because I want you to be some goofy story of my past, but because I need to be near you while *you* conquer the world."

"Stop the car!" she shrieked.

"Why? I'm not letting you run," I said evenly, despite feeling anything but calm.

She tried to grab the wheel. Seriously, her short arm came across the center console, grabbing for it.

Fucking Cate. I forgot how pig-headed she could be. Although I wasn't sure how—we'd just spent the last five months separated because of her stubbornness.

I veered over and pulled up to the curb as campus buses and cars whizzed by, honking at my abrupt maneuver.

"What do you mean? You were traded?" She turned to face me, her brown eyes dark with fury, her mouth tight and her arms crossed over her chest.

I ran my hand over her shoulder, sliding her shirt to the side to expose the tattoo on her shoulder. "I'm here for you. See that, the Stealer? You're mine; that even says so." I traced the outline of my nickname, causing her skin to prickle with goose bumps under my touch.

"You can't do that," she said, shaking her head. "Move here."

"Don't you care about me anymore?"

"This isn't about whether I care for you or not."

"That's exactly what it's about, Cate. So, you don't?"

"No. Yes." She shook her head again, frustrated. "Yes, I'll always care for you, but this can't be. We were friends. Had a few moments, but—"

"Cate, you're right." I grabbed her hand and held it tight in mine.

"We were friends, and then more than friends. For more than a minute, if I remember correctly. And then we were nothing."

She looked up at me, her eyes filled with unshed tears. "But what about what I did, what I'm doing?" she whispered, and dropped her gaze to the console.

I had to tread carefully. Somewhere along the line, she'd slipped into a protector role when it came to me. She was guarding my heart, but this was a team sport and we needed to share it.

In my mind, I conjured up the X's and O's of what I wanted to say and how to say it in a carefully constructed way so she didn't open the door and run into oncoming traffic.

"I didn't like what you did. Not because I thought there was anything wrong with it. Yeah, at first I was pissed and then jealous and then mad. But then I had to hear from someone else why you were doing it."

"What?" She lifted her head as I squeezed her hand, making her dark curls fall over her furrowed brow, framing her face.

"Your friend Sarina came to talk with me."

"What?" she shrieked.

"She did. She also knew you'd be mad when you found out, but she explained how you two met and what you were doing for her and the others."

"Did she say how easily I'd been lured into making one?"

I dared to run my free fingers through the loose tips of her hair, and she didn't pushed me away.

Breathing a small sigh of relief, I said, "Cate, honey, she explained how tormented you were over making them, but the money was what you needed. You were also smart enough to know you'd have to speak with some experience to give you authority when you wrote your book. She adores you, you know."

Cate nodded.

"Sarina knew you wouldn't explain this all to me yourself, so she told me."

"I can't believe it," she murmured and absently ran her thumb along the inside of my palm. She probably didn't even realize she was doing it, and I wasn't going to clue her in.

"I would have come to you sooner, but you needed time to finish what you were doing—"

"And you had to win a championship. Oh my God, this whole time, I never said congratulations." A smile lit up her face, transforming it.

"I know you were there."

"Alex?"

"Bingo."

Now came the part where I had to be ultra-smooth for my plan to work.

"Cate, I came to love you as a friend."

Her smile flitted away, leaving a gutted expression.

"And as more."

She swallowed as she took in my words. "As more?"

I nodded and ran my finger under her chin, urging her closer over the center console. "As more," I whispered, and then kissed her.

It was a closed-mouth kiss, slow and sensual, and on the side of the road in Bumfuck, Florida. My only worry was that she wouldn't kiss me back.

But she did.

"I really missed you," she murmured into my mouth.

"I'm here now," I mumbled back. "Well, not here exactly, but nearby. We can discuss details later."

Then I pulled her tighter for a deeper kiss. I nipped at her lower lip, and she opened for my tongue. Her breath came faster, and her soft moan zinged all the way to my cock.

Suddenly she pulled back. "Shit," she said, pulling out her phone to check the time. "I'm late for work."

"Can you take the night off? We still have more to discuss, like if you can live with me."

"Blane, stop. Don't push. I have to go to my job and figure this all out. You can't swoop in and rescue me like I'm some damsel in distress."

Our hands were still connected, and I ran my finger along her palm, tickling her.

"I have cheesecake," I said, and that got me a big smile.

"Maybe. Let me see."

chapter thirty-nine

Catie

I wanted to go all robo-feminist, but the bottom line was that I was already forty-five minutes late for my shift. And Blane had cheesecake. I wondered if it would be rude of me to ask what flavor, but then again, I didn't really care.

Blane Steele loved me *as more*. Within seconds, I'd been reduced to nothing more than a girl smitten with a guy.

But who cares?

It was another step outside the mold I'd created for myself. I did it once with Sarina, and look what that had done for me. All my career dreams were coming true, and now Blane . . .

I banged on my phone, typing a quick text to my manager to let him know I'd be late.

Ralph replied right away that it already was all over Twitter, and he assumed I was never coming back.

"Oh God."

"What?" Blane asked, a deliciously evil grin on his face.

"Apparently, we're all over Twitter."

His grin broadened as he whipped out his phone and touched the app icon with the blue bird on it. When his feed came up, it was filled with pictures and video of the two of us squaring off, facing each other down in the school parking lot.

Blane started to read some of the tweets out loud.

> @GoGoFloridaTeams:
> Rumor has it @BallerSteele just picked up "his lady" at a local Florida school - looks like he had a reason to trade here #justsayin

> @SonnyB_KnocknBoots:
> My man, @BallerSteele: Remember, I made it all happen

> @Hafton101:
> STFU @SonnyB_KnocknBoots—you almost ruined the whole season. Do your thing, @BallerSteele #Haftonalumniruletheworld

"Can you believe him? Can he let it go?"

I peered over Blane's shoulder and tried to grab the phone from him. "Lemme see," I demanded.

> @BallBaby100:
> What's up with @BallerSteele—he was supposed to be mine? #allthegoodonesaretaken

"I've had enough," I said, grabbing the phone and tossing it in the cup holder.

"What are we going to do now? I was basically told not to come into work on the assumption that I don't need a minimum-wage job anymore."

"How about we go get some food and take it back to my place?" Blane brought me in for another quick kiss full of promise.

"Where's your place?"

"Not far."

"What about your mom? Did you buy a place big enough for the both of you?"

"No, I bought a condo for my mom in a sweet building that allows dogs and has a pool, but I made her promise that she would move on and make a life. Then I bought a house big enough for the two of us. You and me, I mean."

I punched his arm, trying to play it off. He couldn't be serious. "Don't be ridiculous; I can't do that. I'm hungry, so let's go."

I couldn't live with Blane.

Or can I?

Blane pulled out into traffic and I rummaged through my bag for my sunglasses. Not because of the brightness, but him. I was getting all puppy-love weepy, dealing with some emotion I'd never felt before sweeping through me. It fucking left me teary-eyed and emotionally spent.

"We can call out for pizza?" Blane suggested, glancing my way.

I nodded. "Sounds good. Or we could skip right to dessert," I suggested, letting my inner hussy come out to play.

He smirked. "Nah. No rushing. I'm here; you're here. I'm not going anywhere, and you don't have any more secret projects. Right?"

"Of course not."

"Great, then no rushing needed. I plan to take my time with my dessert, savoring each lick."

I squeezed my knees together, desperately trying to stop the reaction his words evoked that was sure to ruin my panties. *Savor each lick.*

"That's right, Cate. I hope you don't have plans for tomorrow because I do, and it involves all your favorites. Cheesecake, scones, muffins, and me." He turned and winked at me before quickly refocusing on the road.

Between my muddled thinking and my vagina throbbing like a marching band in the homecoming parade, I couldn't even pay attention to where we were heading. All of a sudden, we were speeding down a palm-tree-lined highway with blue skies overhead. I shivered, and Blane turned the air off. It wasn't because of that, but I didn't say anything.

We got off at an exit, and I tried to focus as Blane made a few turns. Eventually he slowed and turned into an enormous golf course community. We drove past houses that got larger and larger, until toward the end of the course, we turned right into a gated housing community. Monstrous mansions sat far apart from each other, and lush green grass—the ultimate luxury in the Florida heat—separated each property.

The few cars we saw on the neighborhood roads were mostly Cadillacs and Mercedes; since the houses all had three- or four-car garages, the driveways were empty. I smiled at the sight of a couple of kids speeding down the sidewalk in those little mini versions of Escalades. Through breaks between the houses, I caught glimpses of the course. A few golfers zipped along in electric carts, braving the heat as they headed to the green.

Blane gave me a curious glance. "Like it?"

I nodded, mostly because I was speechless. "When did you do this?"

"Put in a bid a couple of weeks ago when talk of the trade began, and closed a few days ago."

I turned to face him, raising an eyebrow. "Cocky much?"

"Hopeful." Of course he had a comeback.

Finally, he turned into a driveway. The house was the last one on the road, bordered on the right with a man-made lagoon, complete with a fountain, and separated by heavy landscaping from his neighbor on the left.

Blane gunned it down the drive and threw the car in Park in front of a three-car garage.

"The place is new, bought the last unit available," he explained as he unlocked the car doors.

I hopped out of my side and took in Blane standing next to me in the driveway, looking at his house.

"So, what do you think?" he asked.

Then it dawned on me. This was a guy who grew up in a trailer park; his dad drove a truck for a living, and his mother worked as a waitress. He'd never owned a house, and this was his first one. I figured it could have been a ramshackle fixer-upper, and he would still want to know what I thought.

"It's spectacular. Almost like a dream."

And it was.

It wasn't one of those single-story stucco villas common in Florida. Instead, it was a two-story all-brick home, and the grounds around it were landscaped to show off the house.

"See that?" Blane pointed to the house's facade. "The front reminded me of the barn in Ohio."

It did.

I didn't have any words.

"See the way the wooden slats crisscross on the door? It's just like the big barn door where I took you."

I swallowed, my emotions getting stuck in my windpipe. "That's not why you bought this?"

"Yep." He took my hand and walked me toward the front door.

"You can't do that, buy a house because it looks like the barn."

"Well, I did. Never had a house before, Cate, and I wanted this one. It made me think of you, and then I found out it was all new, never been lived in by anyone else. It didn't have any memories. It's all ours."

My eyes welled up with tears, and I groped at my face to be sure I was still wearing my sunglasses.

"I wanted a place where I could make a life with you."

I couldn't speak. There was nothing I could say, no words at all. No objections or arguments could be made against this, because what he just said touched the deepest, most inner part of my being.

And I wanted that too. *A life with him.*

Squeezing his hand, I brought Blane to a stop and stood on tiptoe so I could take his face between my hands.

"I don't have an answer," I said softly. "I just know that whatever you said makes my heart beat at a frantic pace, and I like it."

"Thank fucking God," Blane said on an exhale before he bent and kissed me.

It wasn't a slow kiss, or a simple press of his lips against mine. No, it was hungry and passionate, involving tongue and moans.

I stood up higher on the balls of my feet, and he lifted me in the air so we didn't have to stop. There was no one around to see us kissing passionately in the driveway, the humid Florida air swirling around our already hot bodies, the only sound the fountain in the yard next door.

"Come on." He finally broke free and led me through the front door.

As he toured me through the house, he exclaimed over everything like it was Christmas morning. "How about this?" he said when he showed me the jaw-dropping view of the golf course from the floor-to-ceiling windows in his huge living room. "Look at that!" he said when we walked into the master bathroom with its Jacuzzi tub and shower large enough for four people.

And in the whole house, there was no furniture other than an enormous king-sized bed in the master bedroom.

Finally, we ended up in the kitchen, one any chef would drool over, where he picked me up and plopped me on the kitchen island. "I want you to live here with me."

"Blane." I tried to shove the rock-hard wall of his chest.

"Seriously."

Overwhelmed, I ran my hand down his cheek and pushed his unruly hair behind his ear. "Can I think about it? This is a lot to take in."

He nodded and leaned in for another kiss. We took our time exploring each other's mouths, but were interrupted by the incessant ringing of Blane's cell.

"What?" he barked into the phone after swiping his finger angrily over its screen. "Yeah, Mo, we did. Worked it all out, so can you let me go now, bro?"

As I gave him a dirty look for trying to rush, he held up a finger for me to wait, and his expression gentled at what Mo was saying.

"How's the baby?" He listened intently. "Well, I'd say right about now, you're lucky to be having those sleepless nights, my man."

He nodded a few times, and then said, "Yeah, I will. Say hello to Angie, and text me a picture. Talk soon."

Blane powered off the phone and tossed it on the counter.

Standing between my thighs, his heat touching mine, he said, "That was Mo. Apparently we're a Twitter sensation."

"They had the baby?" I didn't care about Twitter right now.

"A few days ago, a little boy. Named him Maurice Demetri. He was a little late and jaundiced, but he's cool now."

"Wow," I muttered.

"We can go see them. Mo's in New York near your family."

"I want to see the baby, but there's no one in my family I want to see except for my dad."

"You want to talk about it?"

I shook my head. "No, I want some dessert."

Blane smirked and stepped over to the fridge, where he pulled out a caramel cheesecake.

"With extra caramel," he said. He opened the sauce container, and I quickly swiped my finger through it.

"Mmm." I licked my finger, but didn't get it all off because he swooped in and captured it in his mouth.

"Mmm is right."

He gently nudged me to lie down on the cold, granite-topped island and tugged my shirt over my head. His mouth found my nipple instantly, sucking my breasts through my bra for moment before he unhooked it and dropped it to the floor. Then he dribbled caramel on my breasts, and climbed up on the island to straddle me. Bent over, he put his tongue to work, lapping over every sticky inch.

I was hot on the inside and chilled everywhere his touch abandoned me. Needing to feel his skin on mine, I grabbed fistfuls of his shirt. Now that I looked more closely, I could see it was an Orlando Magic T-shirt. *I should have known.*

Blane didn't wait for me to do the honors. He whipped it over his head and bent lower, touching chest to chest as he made love to my mouth.

"We need more room," he said, and jumped down to lift me onto his hip, and carried the cake and me upstairs.

Setting the cake on the pillow, he placed me on the bed and shimmied my shoes and shorts off in seconds. I watched as he shoved his basketball shorts down, revealing dark green boxer briefs.

"Wore my lucky underwear today," he said with a wink.

"Are they working?"

"Oh yeah," he breathed out, and then he was on me. He dunked his finger in the cake and placed some on my tongue. I lapped it up. He went back for more, but ended up knocking the cake on the floor.

My eyes grew wide and we both leaned over the side of the bed to see the cheesecake smashed onto the hardwood floor. When our gazes met, we laughed.

"Fuck it," he said. "I'd rather have your sweet any day."

Sliding down my body, he sent his tongue on a path to my heat. With the tip of it, he traced my folds, finally landing on my clit. I moaned loud and long.

"Hurry," I urged him, but he didn't.

He took his own sweet time on me, wringing two orgasms out of me before crawling back up my body.

"Want you," he whispered in my ear.

"I need you to roll on your back first."

He grinned at me. "Do you now?"

"Yes."

He did as I asked and I moved down his chest, my hand roaming the hard planes and my finger swirling his flat nipples. He lifted his hips so I could slide off his lucky briefs, giving me a glimpse of what I wanted.

His dick bobbed as pre-cum dripped, and I wrapped my hand

around it and jacked him up and down. I watched his head loll back on the pillow and his mouth open on a moan before I lowered my own head. My mouth found him, and I sucked gently on his length before picking up the pace. When his hips lifted toward my mouth, I pulled stronger on the tip with my lips, sucking and now jacking harder with my hand.

It was sensual and hot and beautiful all at the same time, not the least bit raunchy or distasteful. I felt sexy and wanted as he continued to pump into my mouth.

"Cate, this isn't how I want it to end right now, honey," Blane mumbled. He grabbed my shoulders and hoisted me back up his body, his mouth meeting mine.

I brought my knees up and straddled him until his tip hit my clit, and a loud groan escaped me at the skin-on-skin contact there.

Catching his eye, I breathed out, "I'm on the pill."

"I'm clean."

He brought his hand down to where we almost met and positioned himself. I slowly lowered on him, taking my time, and he grabbed my ass and held me in place. We stilled for a moment, both of us savoring the feel of being bareback for the first time.

"Ecstasy," he muttered. "Better than the 'ship."

"Oh, please," I said on a smile.

I started to move, riding him with abandon, our mouths fused until we broke the kiss and I moved faster. His hand rested on my hip, guiding my pace, his hips lifted off the bed and meeting my thrusts until he said, "I'm close."

His hands roamed my body, scorching my side cleavage and finding purchase on my breasts. He held them, grazing the nipples with his thumbs as he stared directly into my eyes. His focus said it all.

He was all mine.

The thought of him coming inside me with no condom, a first for me, set me off. My whole body sparked and tingled as Blane finished inside me, pumping until he was completely spent. Slumped over him, I didn't want to get up, but I was dripping.

"Let me clean you up," Blane murmured. "Then we'll cuddle a while until I recover."

"What about the scones?" I scooched up on the pillow while he walked toward the bathroom.

"They're not going anywhere. Like you," he said over his shoulder.

epilogue

Blane

L ate June, *nearly a year later*

"Blane Steele, your team just won the NBA finals. Where are you going now?"

I was leaning against the guest lockers in the Phoenix arena; we were on the road and had just clinched the national title in game five. I hadn't showered yet, and my sweatband was still stuck to my matted hair. I could smell myself and it wasn't pretty, which made it hard to believe this idiot actually wanted to stand near me.

Excitement and nervous energy swam through my veins. I wanted to get home and wasn't in the mood for the interview. I'd hated being interviewed ever since Sonny and his dare—although that had ended well for me.

Fucking around with the guy, I asked, "Why do you ask?"

His brows drew together. "Well, you live near, you know . . . the place," he prompted, encouraging me to say the words he wanted to hear so we could both get paid.

Truth was, I was going to Disney.

I gazed upward and snapped my fingers. "You know, that place with the guy with the big ears. What's it called?"

"You don't know? You live in the same city." He raised his eyebrows at me.

"Disney! That's it, that's where I'm going."

Mark, the reporter, gulped, relieved I'd come through. Disney was probably paying for his trip here.

"Seriously, dude, I'm going to Disney World . . . I live in Orlando. We all are; the victory parade will be there later this week. Wait, one second." I grabbed his mic and looked straight at the camera. "Cate, honey, meet me at the castle," I finished with a wink. She'd know what I meant.

I handed Mark back his mic. "Okay, you want to talk about the game? I have a plane to catch."

"What do you attribute your success on the road to? You've had a tremendous season on the road."

"We're all very serious right now about ball. I wish I could say more, other than we're hungry for it and go after what we want."

My hair dripped sweat down my forehead, and I pushed my sweatband up. I was going to have to frame this bad boy; it had brought me a lot of luck.

As for being hungry, we were. As the resident loudmouth, I kept the team on track, spouting shit all the time about staying healthy and being ready to win.

Yes, I'd gone out and bought a big mansion and spent a ton of cash doing a few things—like buying my mom a condo, paying in advance for Cate's tuition, building other crap, traveling and eating at the best places—but I knew what the other side of the coin looked like. I wasn't going back there. I needed a job, and that was playing ball. To do that, I had to be on top of my game.

Pun intended.

Mark was rambling on and on about a certain pass of mine to a teammate for a dunk, and how many times I'd gone to the line. I kept nodding and smiling. I hadn't loved the media after what they had done to Cate and me in college, which was ironic considering she was part of the media now. At some point, I'd have to make my peace with the mic.

My girl had just graduated early and scored a gig on cable TV. HBO—*no shit*—had hired her to do a series on women. It would mean travel for her and me, which would require extra planning on both our parts.

Mostly, I had to get back to Orlando right now. I needed to do something and fast.

I wrapped up the interview, hit the shower, dressed in my suit, and tried not fidget through the press conference. Then I rushed to the plane.

With the time change and the long flight, it was morning by the time we touched down in Orlando, and I knew Cate would be drinking her coffee and waiting for my text. She couldn't travel to the game for a good reason, but I had to hurry up with my current plan. When the team landed at the airport, we were swept up in Lincoln Navigator limousines and shuttled to the arena where our personal cars waited.

I fiddled with my pocket the whole ride, my knee bouncing and my head pounding. I hoped I'd make it in time.

dolce

A sea of people waited in a cordoned-off area as the Navigators pulled around back of the arena. I wasn't in the mood, but I waved to the fans through the window and smiled. There were posters and streamers, and confetti flew through the air, some landing on the windshield of the limo. When we hit the end of the route and the driver threw the limo in Park, I jumped out and booked it to my truck.

With no time to waste, I peeled out of the lot and off to my destination. The guys knew what I was up to . . . I'd see them at the celebration parade. *Hopefully.*

Rounding the golf course toward to our house, I turned into the driveway, passed the garage, and drove down a newer gravel path. I stopped in front of a barn. We called it our castle mostly because of the cylinder-shaped chimney, and the lagoon that wrapped around the far edge looked like a moat. But this was also Orlando, and everything was make-believe here.

I'd surprised Cate with the barn when she returned from her first HBO interview. I'd had the whole thing framed while she was away, and then we watched it be built together. It was the most perfect place to celebrate with Cate, and I wanted to spend as much time as possible back there before we couldn't.

I jumped out of the truck and ran for the door, stopping short when I saw Cate standing there, round and plump and glowing in the doorway. Yep, I'd knocked my girl up pretty damn fast. It was an accident, I guessed you could say, but we didn't care. We were excited.

"Hey, baby." I closed the distance to run my hand over her distended belly. When she just smiled, I looked up and said, "Oh. Hey, Cate," and kissed my girl, prompting her to smack my arm while kissing me.

She was the first to pull away. "Nice game," she said with a wink.

"Did you watch?"

"I caught a few minutes," she said, squeezing my hip.

The doctors gave a firm no when she asked about traveling to the game. She was eight months pregnant and at just a tad over five feet tall, she pretty much looked like she was going to explode. The flight was too long and if she went into labor there, she would likely have the baby in another state without her own doctors.

After Mo had talked some sense into me, I tried to let it go. When I thought about what he went through with their baby, I realized it wasn't worth dragging Cate with us. But I was still a wreck over potentially missing my baby's birth as we sang the national anthem.

Our assistant coach—a female, by the way—came up to me right before the tip and said, "Shut it down, Steele. If she goes into labor, we'll win and you'll go straight there. But she wants you to win."

I'd nodded, realizing she was right, and then that's what I did.

"Come on." Cate tugged on my arm, dragged me inside, and pushed me onto the sofa. We didn't sit on the floor anymore.

An array of food was spread out on the coffee table. She nabbed a scone and sat down to snuggle into my side, and my hand went straight to her belly.

Rubbing figure eights, I asked, "Sarina take good care of you?"

"Yep, I think she was kind of hoping for me to have the baby. I think she misses that stage or something."

"Everything work out with her staying here? Her little guy sleep okay?"

I used my free hand to move Cate's hair behind her ear. When I bent to nibble on her lobe a bit, she leaned into my mouth.

"Yep, Sean had fun. He loved the guest room, and was super happy when Ri made pancakes in the morning. He likes his new school, and of course, thinks you're a god. Pretty sure he volunteered you to come speak to his class."

I laughed. "No problem."

Sarina had moved to Florida after Christmas when Cate told her she was pregnant. She'd still been making movies in Ohio, but Cate wanted her to have more choices. I'd anonymously provided two scholarships to the same college Cate was finishing up at, and made sure Sarina was offered one. Now she was studying business and tended bar in the evenings at the Capital Grille. She made good money there from the business travelers and all my NBA buddies who went in.

"Glad she was here for you," I told Cate, pressing a kiss to her cheek.

"She's my family now. Your mom too," Cate said matter-of-factly, and it was the truth.

Cate was still close with her dad. Anthony visited over Christmas, and I met him for the first time. Her mom and sisters were seething jealous over Cate's new celebrity status. They couldn't believe she'd landed a pro athlete, and were eaten up with jealousy. They mentioned it frequently in the beginning, but then we cut them off.

"By the way, your mom's planning to stay here for a week when we have the baby," she said.

"What about the dogs?" I clenched my jaw, thinking about the dogs she'd bring with her. We didn't need all those pets in the house with a new baby. "And my dad?"

"Apparently, her new boyfriend is going to stay with the animals, and your dad's going to come when the baby is a month old. I've got it all set. Plus, Ri is going to come with the baby and me on my first taping as an extra set of hands, and Sean's going to stay with your mom."

"Fucking A, my girl's good. But you don't need to do all that shit.

And the taping . . . I thought we were waiting three months before you went back to work."

She shook her head, biting her bottom lip.

I'd come to know that look. It was the same one she got when she was doing her "secret project." It was a cross between determination and stubbornness.

"Cate," I growled.

"Six weeks," she whispered into my neck. "It'll all be good. This is big. I already have most of the research done, and I want to get two segments taped before your season starts. Next year, I plan to be there when you win the finals."

Six weeks? Was that safe?

I knew better than to argue. I gave her belly a little tap, and she looked up at me.

"I'll be fine, Steele, don't you worry. Women have been doing this for centuries."

"I know, but not my woman."

"Please, don't go all caveman on me."

Her breath was warm on my face and spiked my already frazzled nerves. It was time I spoke my true feelings, and I wasn't sure how my little feminist would take it.

It's now or never.

I tilted her face so her gaze would meet mine. "Cate, listen, I know we said we'd be unconventional. You hated your parents' marriage, and I never wanted to be my dad, getting married for a baby. But, shit."

I roamed her cheek with my thumb, frustrated with myself. I was fucking this whole thing up.

"I want to marry you, Caterina. And right now, I don't care about all your feminist crap. You'll have your career and a baby and me and anything else you want. You can have your name or mine; it doesn't matter."

I slid to the floor and knelt at her feet. I kissed her belly and was rewarded with a kick in the face.

Looking up at her, I said, "I also hope we're not having a soccer player, because that shit's boring. So, what do you say, Cate? Make an honest man out of me?"

She didn't say anything.

"Cate? Are you going to leave me hanging?"

"No . . ."

"No, you won't marry me?"

I gulped air. We were having a baby, and as far as I was concerned, getting married was the best thing for all of us. Cate was mine and would be forever; there was no reason not to.

"No, I'm not going to leave you hanging. Yes, I'll marry you."

I reached up to wrap my hand around the back of her neck and brought her lips to mine.

"Good," I murmured.

Almost forgetting, I tugged the ring out of my pocket and put it on her finger. It looked damn good there.

"Matches my lucky underwear," I said, taking in the deep emerald in the center, framed by two emerald-cut diamonds.

She ran her finger over the gemstones, tracing each plane and sharp corner as she let out a little sigh. "It's gorgeous. Our son can give it to a special woman one day."

"Our what?"

"Oh shit."

Cate clapped a hand over her mouth, her eyes wide as she stared at me. She'd made it this long without telling me the sex of the baby.

"Oh my God. You had me so flustered, I just went and ruined the surprise for you, babe," she said, and I couldn't tell whether she was laughing or crying.

"It's a boy?"

"Yup, a boy. Maybe the soccer player you've dreamed of."

"Another Southern gentleman." I lifted her shirt and planted my lips on her smooth skin.

"I hope not right away, if what you mean is going south on a woman. In fact, I'm pretty sure he'll be a boob man to start."

"Now I know where your head was at, my little Cate with the dirty mind."

Not bothering to crawl back up the couch, I squeezed Cate's ass and she squirmed, giving me access to tug her leggings down.

"I'm hungry," I said, working my way down her neck with kisses.

"There's food," she teased.

"It can wait." I tugged her panties down, revealing a bare mound.

"Mmm." I lowered my tongue to the top of the triangle and breathed in her scent.

And then I ate.

Three days later, Cate and I became a Twitter sensation all over again.

We'd arrived at the Magic Kingdom early in the day for a private hour in the park just for the team and their families. The guys with older kids rushed off to Space Mountain and Thunder Mountain Railroad for unlimited rides with no wait. Sarina, Sean, and I walked—and Cate waddled—to It's A Small World, which was about all she could do.

After a boat ride through the little people, Sean begged me to take him on Space Mountain with all the other cool kids. Ri promised she'd stay with Cate by Cinderella's Castle, and I could send Sean over with one of the other wives after the ride.

I'd done just that and then went to the back of the park for the parade, where I was greeted by Mickey and his helper.

"Good morning, Mr. Steele, right this way." They led me to a float, and I hoisted myself up next to Chip and Dale. They were wearing sweatbands across their chipmunk heads and oversized replicas of my jersey over their furry bellies.

We started down Main Street USA as the park opened and the street flooded with people cheering and saluting us. Lance Johnstone, the center, rode behind me with Goofy, and they tossed beach balls styled to look like basketballs into the crowd.

Fans passed the balls up and down the sidewalk, and a few bounced back to me. I put on a show, pretending to dunk and sending them back out to the wave of fans until we made it up to the castle.

I spotted Sean sitting with Johnstone's wife and kids, but where was Cate . . . and Sarina? I kept my eyes focused on Sean and when he saw me, he ran toward the float, but a Disney employee promptly blocked his way.

"Hey," I yelled. "That's my relative . . . my, um, nephew!"

"I have to go see Blane," Sean yelled.

The Disney dude looked up at me, and I nodded. Sean took a running jump onto the float, and I bent down so he could whisper in my ear.

"Cate's having the baby."

I shook my head to make sure I wasn't dreaming, and for the second time in seconds, shouted, "Hey!"

Disney dude hurried back and walked alongside the float,

cupping his ear to hear what I had to say.

"I gotta get off this thing! I'm having a baby."

When he nodded and spoke into his walkie-talkie, I jumped off the moving float and gestured to Sean to jump into my arms. Carrying him, I ran through the tunnel in the middle of the castle. On the other side, a Disney employee was waiting with a golf cart, which shuttled us to the rear of the park and into a waiting taxi. Apparently, Cate had already gone to the hospital by ambulance.

Sean fidgeted next to me, and I tossed him my phone. "Here, download some games or apps."

He looked as thrilled as a pig in shit at the idea, and I grinned to myself. *I can do this parenting thing.*

At the hospital, I rushed the information counter to find where Cate was. Behind me, I could hear people murmuring, "Is that Blane Steele?" Phones clicked and people nudged each other, whispering, but I didn't care.

The receptionist said obstetrics was on the seventh floor, and I didn't wait for the elevator, just snagged Sean and tossed him over my shoulder as I rushed to the stairwell. I took the stairs two and three at a time, and he giggled as he bounced on my shoulder.

At the top of the stairs, I burst through the door to find Sarina pacing the hallway.

"Thank God you're here," she said, reaching out to take her son from me. "That girl of yours is ready to go. Seriously, fastest labor ever."

In less than twenty minutes, Logan Sean Steele was born as Cate squeezed the shit out of my hand, calling me some very creative names.

Two days later, when we took our baby boy home wearing a miniature Orlando Magic sweatband, Cate whispered in my ear.

dolce

"You better tell him to stay away from ball babies."

No way my boy was going to be a soccer player, but he would definitely be a card-carrying member of the feminist party.

the end

vérité

prologue

Last August

Although my back was pressed against the door, my entire body surged forward, seeking him. If I'd been in a dream or having an out-of-body experience, I would have seen my long limbs and lean torso straining to get closer to the man in front of me. My heart was beating to the most vibrant pace I'd ever experienced. I felt like I was practically coming out of my skin to get closer to the horny, hot-blooded man caging me against the door.

Mon dieu, he was like a god. His hands were splayed against the wall on either side of my head, and my legs were wrapped around his waist. I was in heaven, and it had only been a few hours since I'd last visited this paradise.

My pelvis rocked back and forth, searching for his erection and my salvation. They were one and the same, the only balm I needed for the yearning that centered between my legs, but burned everywhere else.

I wanted his hand down there, or maybe his mouth. Or both.

"Pierre." I moaned his name as I moved, trying to connect my sensitive spot with his cock. Desperate, I craved friction like I imagined a habitual smoker longs for a cigarette.

"*S'il vous plaît*," I begged, *please*, then sucked in a breath to indulge in a long inhale of his cologne into my lungs. It was something fancy and French, of course, and another in the long list of reasons why I was head over heels for my Frenchman. *My older Frenchman.*

He shifted his hips away, teasing me, and I whimpered with need, making a noise that unfortunately sounded like a dying guinea pig. I was so desperate for him. He was my world, my universe. I wanted to spend the rest of my life lost among the planets circling his orbit. He was the moon and I was a lowly stalk of wheat bowing to him in the middle of the night, and I didn't care what that said about me. I was that weak and pathetic when it came to him.

I'd never lived a moment until Pierre was buried inside me. We didn't need to profess our love for each other or send each other cute texts. When he claimed me with those slow, languid strokes in and out of me, I knew he was the one to make everything else go away. Far away. He was the man of my dreams, and I wanted him inside me right that second, that very millisecond. I was an extremely demanding girl.

Finally, he ran his hand inside my panties and separated my folds with his slim fingers. He dove in with one finger, then two, and my body bucked into his strong, yet well-manicured hand.

My head fell back against the wall with a soft thud. "Oh, baby, more," I managed to wrench out.

And then he lost control as I'd been hoping and praying he would. When I heard my panties tear and drop to the floor, I moved my hand to his zipper and opened his khakis, firmly grasping what I wanted. He was conveniently commando, hard and ready. I rubbed my hand up and down his length, pumping him. Before I knew it, my hand was pushed away and he was deep inside me, riding me fast and recklessly.

"Faster!" I demanded. "I love it when you're rough." I squeezed his ass, tilting my pelvis to allow him to slide in even deeper.

"Easy, Tigger," he panted, calling me by his nickname for me in that sexy French drawl, but not bothering to slow his pace. He was always in control, even if I thought I held the power.

I was kneading the shit out of his ass with my hands as he ran his tongue over my neck. He nipped and sucked before biting a bit harder, causing my orgasm to build in preparation to barrel through me. I didn't want it to start or end because it always finished the same—with me wanting more.

"*Monsieur*, I'm coming," I semi-yelled or gurgled, I wasn't even sure because I was unraveling, tightening my thighs around his waist like a vice.

"Tigger, *ma chérie*." He growled the sweet words, pumping faster, his release vibrating through my bones. A drop of sweat fell off his brow into my cleavage, and he leaned in to kiss me.

My entire body trembled; I was shaking with release and need all at the same time. I never wanted that feeling to end.

At that moment the door from the hallway into Pierre's office banged open, apparently not locked as securely as we'd thought. The fancy diploma hanging on the wall above my head—the one that read DR. PIERRE DUBOIS—rattled from the impact, nearly falling. It didn't really matter if it had because within a matter of days, the gilded frame was gone. And so was Pierre.

It all ended, and I felt like my life was over.

one

One year later

"Yes, sir. I'm older now. Wiser. Smarter, I promise. I swear I'm ready, Coach Wallace," I said as I nodded, yet I suspect it was more for me than him.

My coach knew what progress I'd made over the last year. My therapist and my guidance counselor had kept him up-to-date without revealing anything personal, but up-to-date, nonetheless.

"I know, hon—" He stopped and caught himself before he automatically called me *honey*. With me and my history, using any term of endearment was an extremely bad judgment call. Even though we both knew he didn't mean anything by it, it was in his best interest to be professional.

With a pained glance at me, he started again, keeping himself on the straight and narrow. "I know, Tingly. I just want to make sure you're ready to handle it all again. School, homework, the practices and upcoming meets." Obviously uncomfortable, he fidgeted with his hands before folding them on the desk in front of him.

Coach Wallace was wearing his dark-green-and-white university tracksuit as I sat across from him wearing jean cutoffs and a dark gray tank top. I hadn't worn my uniform in a year. My teammates told me it still hung in my locker, awaiting my return.

The others didn't get me, but they missed me, or so they said when they texted or called. Mostly it was Nadine who stayed in touch; we'd been recruited together. Like the other girls, she wondered why I couldn't love frat boys and jocks, or why I didn't think beer pong was just *the best*. Or, wait—wasn't skinny-dipping in the university pool even better than beer pong?

Getting in trouble for either of those minor infractions was nothing, nowhere near as severe as what I did. Maybe those girls who seemed so immature and silly were just inherently wiser than me, because banging my French professor in his office and getting caught by the head of the department was pretty damn bad.

Even better was when my professor's fiancée, Patricia, came bouncing into the room a few seconds later, babbling about wedding cake tastings and honeymoon destinations only to find me *in flagrante delicto* with the man she was going to marry. In just a few months, as a matter of fact.

For me, it had been the worst possible scenario. Pierre's semen had dripped down my leg while I stood there trying to cover myself up with a varsity track hoodie. It was the only thing close enough to grab as my underwear lay torn and tattered on the floor at my feet.

So there I was, Tingly Simmons—athlete, foreign language major, professor fucker, and obsessed idiot girl—definitely not a frat rat or beer-pong player extraordinaire. I was only at this school because of my athletic prowess, and I had no explanation for my embarrassing behavior other than I was utterly, totally in lust with Dr. Dubois.

And now, a year later, I was doing everything I could to pick up the pieces of my fucked-up life.

"I'm really good, Coach Wallace," I said with a fake smile plastered on my face. "My shrink signed off on my progress, and my counselor has me signed up for a full course load. And since I took three more credits over the summer, I won't be too far behind. Maybe just a semester." I laid it on thick; it was critical that he accept me back on the team. Being on the track team meant that I could keep my athletic scholarship, plus I needed something to focus on to keep myself out of trouble.

I sat there pulling at one of the frayed strings hanging from the hem of my jean shorts. My long blond hair hid my tanned face as I looked down, which was good because I preferred not to look Coach in the eye. He'd been immediately called to the scene and had been the only eyewitness other than those who'd found us—when I was caught with my hand in the proverbial cookie jar.

Except the cookie jar was a giant hunk of a French professor complete with wavy blond hair, heavy cologne, an aristocratic accent, and false promises.

"Great! That's all I needed to hear." The relief was obvious in the coach's voice. "Practice is still at six a.m. sharp. Be at the track at quarter till, so shoes are tied and drinks are drunk. I still don't wait for anyone. Oh, and Tingly, there's a mandatory nightly study hall for new athletes this year. It starts tonight over in Henderson Hall at seven o'clock. And before you argue, there's not much I can do about it. Since all your trouble started at the end of last summer, before your season got under way and we were lucky to redshirt you last year, you're considered a *new* athlete again this year. I know you're almost caught up credit wise but according to the rules, any student athlete coming off redshirting a season needs to adhere to the academic study session policy. So you're stuck attending study hour with the other newbies." Coach Wallace ran his hand along his forehead, clearly not entirely comfortable speaking about my *trouble* as he explained the rules from the academic handbook.

I nodded, finally lifting my eyes to meet his. "Okay. Thank you," was all I said before I stood to leave.

"And Tingly?"

I stopped in my tracks. "Yeah?"

"Welcome back. I look forward to you competing this season."

I managed another nod and a thank-you before I headed out, avoiding the locker room and anyone else who might want to see how I was doing.

Back in my dorm room, I stepped out of my jean shorts and tank, tossing them on my bed before changing into running shorts and a sports bra. I quickly pulled on socks and laced up my running shoes—extra tight, borderline painful, the way I liked them—and tied up my long hair in a ponytail. Snatching my iPod Shuffle and a water bottle from the counter, I was out the door and pressing START on my pacer watch before any of my roommates noticed me.

I started off fast, and my lungs quickly adjusted to the burn. As my feet hit the pavement, striking first with the ball of my foot, I glanced down at my watch. I was running a steady 7:20 pace, and I decided to keep it there for about five or six miles. Speed and endurance were my only true friends these days. They had kept me company through my darkest hours, and the days and months since Pierre left.

Pickles. Dr Pepper. Poisson. Petunias. Purple. Pimientos. Penelope. The artist formerly known as Prince.

Needing to dismiss Pierre from my mind as soon as he popped in it, I used one of the little coping tricks I learned in therapy. Anytime Pierre and his feathered blond hair and sea-foam green eyes appeared in my rattled excuse for a brain, I was supposed to think of anything else positive that began with the letter *P*. The concept was ridiculous, but it worked.

I played this game for about a mile or so, and then my mind was temporarily free of *him*.

Checking my watch, I kept pushing myself, making a second loop around campus before I headed up to the agriculture department. Clocking cows at ten o'clock and a barn at high noon, I continued barreling forward. As I ran back toward campus, College Avenue came into view, and my mind drifted to the weird contradiction that was my university.

Hafton State University, a Division One school, was situated in the middle of Ohio near the bustling cities of Cleveland, Cincinnati, and Columbus, but surrounded by miles and miles of pristine farmland. Hafton, the school's namesake, was the quintessential small town, ripe with big-city wannabes and earthy granola crunchers.

My friends—or my classmates, to be more accurate—were a strange mix of agriculture majors and business-minded people, nothing like me in their professional or personal pursuits. And none of them slept with their professor, or fell in lust with him. Not one of them was desperate or foolish like me, or had a nervous breakdown when her professor chose his fiancée over her.

Then again, none of my classmates came from a bullshit family and a fake place like me; they weren't needy and craving attention and acceptance like I was. They were more worried about finishing their exams and calling *next* in a game of beer pong because they were "normal" college students.

As for me, I was searching for someone, anyone who would love me as I was, for who I was, no matter what truths were revealed. I just didn't have a clue who that might be or if he even existed.

acknowledgments

This story came together quickly, and without the fast and furious help of Terilyn Smitsky and Robin Bateman, this book would never have materialized. Thank you, ladies, for all of your valuable feedback, texting, and commiserating (or at least listening to mine), and for both of you being wonderful readers, friends, and part of my original squad. There is a special place in heaven with unlimited cocktails for both of you after all you have dealt with, thanks to me.

I also need to say a huge THANK YOU to my assistant, Nicole Snyder. She's the friendly voice behind many of my e-mails and posts. Without Nicole, nothing would get done these days. *Nothing— absolutely nothing.* Thank you from the bottom of my heart.

Thank you to Pam Berehulke, my editor, for being the umbrella in my storm. My husband calls me the hurricane for a good reason—I set off monsoons everywhere I go. Without Pam, I would be nothing more than a drenched author in a puddle of my own words. Love you.

This book wouldn't have a gorgeous cover without Sarah Hansen. After six releases, I don't argue. I just do.

To my family, for putting up with my hormones and me. I love you hard.

HB, you're my guy; nobody else could fill those shoes. Love you more than eighteen years ago. Especially with the scruff.

To Queen Virginia Carey, there are no words. Your smiling face and kind words have been with me since *before* the beginning, and I love our daily check-ins.

To Sawyer Bennett, your face has been a welcoming beacon for me in the last few months. Thank you, fellow Pittsburgh lover, for all your warm thoughts and support.

To Susan Ward, without our convos and commiserations, I would be a general mess. You could be my mom and your daughters could be Judy's girls. XO

To Ilsa Madden-Mills, God, our clandestine talks are the best!

To Christy and Fab, I worry if we don't have our daily check-in or chat while I'm in the bath. #soapythighs

To my F-the Noise ladies, love ya!

To Neda Amini, for being the yin to my yang. We argue over every little thing. What would I do without you playing devil's advocate?

To Erin and *The Southern Belles*, thank you for all your welcoming kindness at signings and helping me share this stunning cover with the world. XOXO . . . see you soon!

To Milasy and Lisa at *The Rockstars of Romance*, for their wealth of knowledge and undying support to the indie author world.

To Maryse, there isn't enough room to thank you.

To Jennifer Wolfel, Becca Manuel, Miranda at *Red Cheeks Reads*, Fran and Greta at *Twin Sisters Rockin' Book Reviews*, Ellen at *The Book Belles*, *Stephanie's Book Reports*, Jesey at *Schmexy*, thank you for reading my books, loving me, and holding my hand all through the night.

For all the bloggers out there, your job is thankless and there are not enough bottles of wine, cups of coffee, or doughnuts to thank you. YOU make all this happen every day, posting, sharing, reading and reviewing, and pimping.

To Jennifer Dicenzo, reader extraordinaire. Thank you so much for letting me bend your ear . . . all the time.

This book wouldn't work properly without Emily and Stacey Tippetts. Thank you, dolls!

And to all my readers, friends, and fans. Without you, my books are a great, big, huge nothing.

Special thanks go to my Electric Readers. My day is not officially started until I say good morning to you, and it doesn't end until I say good night. You're the most amazing, incredible, lovable group. YOU ARE FAMILY!

If you liked *Dolce*, feel free to leave a review on Amazon or Goodreads (or any other retailer). Without reviews, books are lost in a sea of releases, and your review could make a difference in this book finding a new reader.

Send me e-mail when you do, and I will thank you personally!
rachelblaufeldauthor@gmail.com

Please connect with me in my private reading group, The Electric Readers, where I share insider information and casual conversation with my readers:
www.facebook.com/groups/TunnelVIPS

www.rachelblaufeld.com
Facebook: www.facebook.com/rachelblaufeldtheauthor
Twitter: twitter.com/rachelblaufeld

about the author

Rachel Blaufeld is a bestselling Coming of Age, Romantic Suspense, and Sports Romance author. A recent poll of her readers described her as insightful, generous, articulate, and spunky. Originally a social worker, Rachel creates broken yet redeeming characters. She's been known to turn up the angst like cranking up the heat in the dead of winter.

Turning her focus on her sometimes wild-and-crazy creative side, it only took Rachel two decades to do exactly what she wanted to do—write a fiction novel. Now she spends way too many hours in local coffee shops downing muffins while she plots her ideas. Her tales may all come with a side of angst and naughtiness, but end lusciously.

Blaufeld, also an entrepreneur/blogger, is fearless about sharing her opinion. She captured the ears of stay-at-home and working moms on her blog, *BacknGrooveMom*, chronicling her adventures in parenting tweens and inventing a product, often at the same time. She has also blogged for *The Huffington Post* and *Modern Mom*.

Most recently, her insights can be found in *USA TODAY,* where she shares conversations at "In Bed with a Romance Author" and reading recommendations over at "Happy Ever After."

Rachel lives around the corner from her childhood home in Pennsylvania with her family and two beagles. Her obsessions include running, coffee, basketball, icing-filled doughnuts, antiheroes, and mighty fine epilogues.